Forever Hidden

Book #2 in the
Forever Bluegrass Series

Kathleen Brooks

D1519028

Chapter One

Sydney Davies had never been so happy to be headed home. She pulled her long golden-blond hair into a sloppy bun and opened the tailgate to her small SUV. She tossed in her luggage and looked out from the Bluegrass Airport's long-term parking lot. The sight of the snow-covered horse farms surrounding the airport brought back so many great memories.

At twenty-eight, Sydney was a force in the international fashion industry. However, she was no longer gracing the covers of magazines or walking the shows like she had as a teenager or when in college. Modeling wasn't her lifelong dream; instead she used modeling to make a name for herself and for her company: Sydney International. Sydney was the founder, CEO, and chief designer of everyday clothing, haute couture, home, family, outdoors, and wedding fashion design.

She'd spent two weeks in Europe meeting with designers, investors, and businesses that wanted Sydney International in their stores, then ended her trip with a fashion show for her wedding dresses. But now she was home, and she couldn't wait to finally remember how to breathe again. Sydney enjoyed watching the light snow cover the rolling hills of Kentucky as she made her way out of Lexington toward her small hometown of Keeneston. Keeneston's population was smaller than her employee roster at Sydney International, and gossiping was the town's favorite pastime. But it was home, and she couldn't wait to see the people who knew her as just Syd.

Her friends and family couldn't care less that her company was a Forbes dream. They had known her since she was born and still gave her crap for modeling in wings and barely there underwear. The only trouble with Keeneston was that she was related to many of the available bachelors in town. Finding a single guy was like unearthing new gossip before the town's oldest gossiping pair, Miss Lily and her husband, John, did—basically impossible. But after two weeks as the face of her company, she was tired of men anyway, especially the way they sucked up to her and pretended to be chivalrous before tearing her down the second she turned her back on them. It was exhausting keeping a smile on her face and not punching theirs.

Sydney rounded the corner of the small country road and smiled as Main Street came into view. The sun was setting and the historic buildings painted dusty blues, neutral tans, pale yellows, and gentle greens warmed under the orange glow. American flags were on the light poles, Valentine's Day displays were in the large plate-glass windows, and the smell of her favorite café filled the crisp winter air.

First up was a stop at the Blossom Café for some good southern food and then bed. Sydney drove up the street toward the packed café, but the sounds of a siren behind her had her pulling over instead of getting that delicious bread pudding.

The sheriff's car turned off the siren as it parked behind her with its lights flashing. Sydney watched in the mirror as the door opened and a man in jeans and a heavy brown quilted jacket with an embroidered gold star on the breast pocket stepped out. Sydney rolled down her window and sighed.

"Hi, Dad." Sydney smiled tiredly at her father, Marshall Davies, the sheriff of Keeneston.

"You weren't answering your phone," he accused in a way that made Sydney roll her eyes. Her father liked to think he was still in Special Forces, barking out orders. She and her mother, Katelyn, always found it amusing. Sydney pulled out her cell phone and stared in surprise at the thirteen missed calls from her father, six from her mother, and three from her younger brother, Wyatt.

"It was on airplane mode, sorry. What's going on?" Sydney asked worriedly. Her family was close but not obsessive-phone-call close.

"It's your great-grandmother," her father said seriously.

"Is she . . .?" Sydney gulped. She couldn't say the word.

Her father shook his head and a couple snowflakes fell to the ground. "Not yet, but soon. Your mother sent me to get you. She and Wyatt are already out there, but your great-grandma is asking for you."

Sydney gulped down her sobs of grief as she nodded her head. "I'll meet you there."

"I'm sorry, Syd. I know how close you are to her. Can

you drive?" her father asked. The ironic thing was that her father looked even closer to breaking down.

"I can. It's only a couple minutes away."

Her father grimaced and turned to head to his car. "I'll follow. Take it easy; the roads are slick."

"Yes, Dad," Sydney muttered as the first tear fell.

Great-grandma was also known as Mrs. Ruth Wyatt. She and her husband, Beauford, had been married for over sixty-five years before he had passed away nine years earlier. But Great-grandma had declared herself a tough old broad and had managed to run a massive horse farm, continued investing the family's assets, and even found time to meddle in her granddaughter's and great-granddaughter's lives. Ruth Wyatt was of an undeterminable age. She had hidden it so well that Sydney didn't even know in which decade she had been born. But based on her long, flowing dresses, big hats, white face powder, and bright red lipstick, Sydney guessed her prime came during the Roaring Twenties.

Great-grandma was tough in the perfect southern genteel way of times gone by. Wyatt, Sydney's younger brother, bore those same manners, as did her mother. *Poor Mom.* Great-grandma had raised Sydney's mother, Katelyn, after her own mother had abandoned Katelyn at a young age. And when her father, Marshall, came into the picture, they mutually adopted each other. Great-grandma loved them as if they were her own children. Syd's father and mother adored her for it.

Sydney passed the hibernating crop fields and cows in pastures with steam coming from their noses, finally arriving at the tree-lined drive of Wyatt Farm. She pressed the opener in her car for the large, scrolled wrought iron gate. Inside, on top of a hill stood Wyatt Estate, which had been in the family since 1785 and was her great-grandfather's heritage. It had started as a small cabin but expanded in the beginning of the 1800s. The white Federal-style house came into view, and Sydney pulled to a stop next to her brother's truck. Her father pulled in behind her and, without saying anything, took her hand in his as they walked silently inside.

Three years before, Sydney's father and mother converted a downstairs sitting room into a bedroom for Great-grandma so she wouldn't have to climb stairs. Her father squeezed Syd's hand as they approached the room. Sydney heard her mother's trembling voice as they neared, followed by the elderly woman's frail voice.

"Dear, I'm so proud of you. Proud that you are more than your mother's sad legacy and proud of you for giving me the great honor of making up for my failure at raising her by raising you. I'm proud of you for making your own way in the world. For coming home and making sure every day of my life was filled with happiness as I watched you develop into a town leader, not to mention the best veterinarian and mom the town has ever seen. You married a fine young man, too, even if he couldn't keep his clothes on in the house." Her great-grandmother coughed as she laughed. Syd's father took his hand from hers to swipe at the tears in his eyes as Syd looked questioningly at him.

"I want you to do me a favor. I want to be buried in the dress I wore to your wedding. It was Beauford's favorite. And have Paige make me a new hat to go with it.

Something bright and happy for I'm going to see my love again."

Sydney put her fist to her mouth to stop the cry that was choking her throat for escape. Her father used the back of his hands to wipe his eyes before he slowly opened the partially ajar door.

Her great-grandmother looked so small on the bed, propped up with a mountain of pillows behind her. Sydney's mother was in tears as she gripped the dying woman's hand. Wyatt stood quietly behind his mother with his hand on her shoulder in a silent show of support.

"Ah, there's my boy now. And Sydney, dear." Mrs. Wyatt smiled weakly before coughing again. Sydney rushed forward and took the seat next to her mother.

"I'm glad you're all here. There are things I need to say to all of you. I've already told Katelyn what is to be hers. Marshall, I want you to have anything you'd like from Beauford's collections. He thought of you as his own son, as did I. We can never repay you for taking such good care of our most precious treasure." Mrs. Wyatt looked to Katelyn, and Sydney saw her mother smile back with fresh tears in her eyes.

"It's been my pleasure, Nana. But it should be me who is thanking you," Marshall said with a hitch in his voice as he came to stand next to his wife.

"Always such a kind young man. It's now up to you as head of the family to look out for them. And you, too, Wyatt. Come here, dear."

Sydney moved out of the way so her brother could sit on the bed and take their great-grandma's hand. Her brother was tall, strong, and masculine, but right now he looked like a little boy as his shoulders hunched in emotional pain and silent tears rolled down his cheeks.

"There, there, dear. All will be well," Mrs. Wyatt said softly as she patted Wyatt's hand. "To you, I leave the house and farm. I leave the legacy of the Wyatt family. I also leave to you three tubes of my favorite lipstick. Make sure to find a woman who will be good to my little dears."

Sydney smiled at the thought of Wyatt telling some future wife that she must put on this lipstick and kiss all the horses. It was something her great-grandma did every week. The horses expected it, and recently her mother had taken over that role when Great-grandma could no longer do it.

"You're a good man, Wyatt, and so much like your great-grandfather. When I see him I'll tell him all about how you became a veterinarian and how well you'll do as owner of Wyatt Farm. Now, everyone, come give me a kiss."

Wyatt leaned forward and pressed trembling lips to her frail cheek. "I love you," he whispered.

"I love you too, dear, so very much." She smiled up at him.

Sydney's father stepped forward and placed a gentle kiss on her great-grandmother's cheek. "I promise to take great care of everyone."

"I know you will, dear. A better son was never had. Please convey that to your mother. I shall miss her dearly."

Marshall nodded wordlessly and went to stand next to Wyatt.

"Go ahead, Syd. I'll stay here," her mother said gently.

"No. I need to speak with Sydney alone," her great-grandmother said kindly.

"Yes, Nana." Katelyn looked stricken as she stood and placed a kiss on her grandmother's forehead. "I couldn't have asked for a better grandmother."

"Oh, dear, you gave my life such meaning. And now it's up to you to remember all I taught you for someday soon you will be Nana. You are what I am most proud of. I love you, my dear granddaughter."

Katelyn sniffed as she fought her emotions. "I love you, too, always." With a gentle squeeze of her hand she got up and walked to her husband and son. "We'll be right outside."

"Come here, Sydney. I don't have much time," her great-grandmother said weakly.

Sydney hurried to sit on the bed and took her great-grandmother's hand in hers. "What can I do for you?"

"I need you to put my face on for me while I tell you. I can't leave this world looking a fright. Not when so many people will be seeing me." Sydney smiled at the frail woman in bed who, in her many years, had not once left the house without all her makeup on.

Sydney got up, opened the drawer to the nightstand, and pulled out the face powder, eye shadow, blush, and bright red lipstick.

"See this ring?" Mrs. Wyatt barely moved her right hand. "I want you to have it. Please take it off for me, dear."

Sydney put down the powder and gently removed the ring from her great-grandmother's arthritic hand.

"This is yours, along with the secrets it holds. You all know Beauford's family history, but now it's time you learned mine . . . and yours. This ring and so much more have been passed down from oldest woman to youngest woman for generations. It tells the story of bravery, adventure, independence, and love. And as the oldest woman prepares to leave this world, she tells the youngest of the Woodbury treasure. See, that's who we are. As women our names change, but our story really begins with Elizabeth Woodbury."

Sydney looked down at the ring. Two teardrop diamonds were angled together to form a heart among the intricate carvings. Sydney slid the ring onto the ring finger of her right hand and smiled down at it.

"Like my middle name?" Sydney asked.

"Yes, dear. I begged your mother to use my middle name as yours—Elizabeth. It's shared throughout our history." Her great-grandma struggled to speak. "Inside the family Bible in my room, you will find the location of the treasure. I want you to swear to me that you will go to Atlanta and find it. It's time for it all to be together. It's time for the story of the women of the Woodbury family to be told, and it's you I want to do it. But I don't want you to whisper a word of it until you've seen it all, because only then will you know the right thing to do. Promise me."

Sydney shook her head. "I don't understand. Treasure?"

Her great-grandmother smiled feebly. "A buried treasure, my dear. Find it and bring it home. Your brother gets the farm, but you get something much more important."

Sydney carefully applied the lipstick to her great-grandmother's lips and held up the mirror for her. "Is this good?"

"Perfect. But you must promise, Sydney. You're the one to carry on our family's legacy."

"Are you talking about the silver your great-grandmother buried in the backyard before Sherman ransacked Atlanta?"

Her great-grandmother just smiled weakly. Her eyes started to focus on something far away. "Promise . . ."

"I promise," Sydney swore before bending down and placing a kiss on her cheek.

Her great-grandmother focused on something beyond Sydney, and her hand shook as she tried to raise it. "Oh, Beauford, how handsome you look."

Sydney leapt from the bed and flung open the door as tears streaked down her cheeks. Her family hurried in. Surrounded by those who loved her most, Mrs. Ruth Wyatt left Keeneston to be reunited with her true love.

Chapter Two

Sydney stood staring at the lowered casket. Her great-grandparents were buried side by side in the family cemetery at the back of the farm. During the spring, it was the most beautiful place on the farm. Pink and white dogwoods shaded the area with their blooms while tulips and daisies lined the wrought iron fence. But not in February. In February it seemed as lonely as Sydney felt.

As the people quietly left the service and headed to the farmhouse for the celebration of life, Sydney continued to stare. Cold air whipped against her face. Gray clouds threatening a snowstorm held the sun hostage. Sydney felt as bleak as the weather. She wasn't ready to go back to the house and hear words of sympathy from her aunts and uncles on the Davies side of the family.

"Syd?"

Sydney didn't turn around as she heard the footfalls crunch against the frozen grass. He stopped next to her, her brother's shoulder bumping hers.

"What am I supposed to do with all this?" Wyatt drawled quietly as he looked out at the expanse of Wyatt Farm.

"Put on the lipstick and pucker up," Sydney managed

to tease as her brother put his arm over her shoulder and pulled her against his side.

"Don't tell anyone, but I did that this morning. The horses were so happy. I thought it was appropriate to have red noses as they drew her casket up here."

Sydney did laugh then. "That's why your lips were so red! And you said it was because it was cold out."

"I just don't understand why she didn't give you anything. I could use your help running this place. There's more than enough for the two of us."

Sydney looked down at the ring she hadn't taken off since her great-grandmother had given it to her. "No. She gave me something—something precious. I just have to go get it."

"Is that what she wanted to talk to you about?" Wyatt asked.

"Yes, but she made me promise not to talk about it until I had it all together. You know Great-grandma; everything is always done just so."

"Which is why Mom sent me to get you," Wyatt said apologetically. "It's time to do our duty at the house."

Sydney groaned. "I can't take much more of this. It's been exhausting. The whole town has stopped me at least once a day since she passed to express sympathies. And yesterday's wake almost did me in. Six hours of standing, hugging, and shaking hands."

"I know, Syd. But she'd have loved it."

Sydney smiled as she looked at the tombstone. "That she would. And because I love her, and you, I'll do my duty."

Sydney should have bolted. Her father was the second oldest of six children — five boys and one girl. And they'd all had kids. She had a slew of cousins ranging from thirty down to eighteen years old. That's not even counting family friends who were so close she called them aunts and uncles.

"Here," a voice whispered from behind her.

Sydney smiled. When she turned, she saw auburn hair and green eyes full of sympathy — Sienna Ashton, her best friend. Well, now she was Sienna Parker since she'd married Sydney's cousin, Ryan. Sydney took the teacup and sipped the hot liquid.

"Holy . . ." Sydney couldn't finish as the burning caused her to cough.

"Did I put too much bourbon in it?" Sienna asked sweetly.

"Is there any tea in it?"

"Nope." Sienna grinned. "I thought you could use it."

"Have I told you how much I love you?" Sydney asked as she took another sip of bourbon.

"Not nearly as much as I do."

Sydney rolled her eyes as her cousin Ryan slipped his arm around his new wife's waist. Since Ryan was about six-two, he made Sienna's five-feet-five inches seem tiny as he pulled her close to him. "How are you holding up, Syd?"

Sydney was stopped from answering when yet another person came to offer condolences. As soon as the person left, Sydney downed the cup. "I know Great-grandma touched so many people's lives. She was always first with a cake when tragedy struck. Food baskets mysteriously appeared in front of doors when she heard people were having a tough time. And don't get me started on the people in the horse racing industry. I am pretty sure she was an adopted grandmother to every jockey and trainer at Keeneland. I would give anything to be alone so I could mourn. Does that sound selfish?"

"I can help with that. Ryan, catch me," Sienna whispered a second before her hand was pressed to the front of her head as she collapsed. She would have fallen gracefully to the floor except Ryan caught her.

"Are you okay?" he asked, full of concern.

"Ooooh. I'm so weak. I felt like I might pass out. Maybe it was because I couldn't keep anything down this morning," Sienna said breathlessly as she pressed her hand to her very flat stomach.

"You need to lie down," Ryan ordered as he scooped her up into his arms.

"Yes. Sydney, be a dear and come with me."

"Of course," Sydney said at once, grasping the chance to escape. "Right this way."

They weren't even halfway up the stairs when the shouting started—ten dollars here, twenty there. Sienna and Ryan had started Keeneston betting pandemonium to rival the opening bell on Wall Street. Keeneston folks loved their betting, but the best bets were on babies. For a town as small as Keeneston, every new addition was celebrated.

"Wait, are you two actually pregnant?" Sydney asked a she stopped at the guest room door.

"What, and give you an unfair advantage in the betting pool?" Ryan asked as he sent her a wink.

"Ugh! You two are impossible together. It's really quite

sickening how in love you are," Sydney teased with only a hint of jealousy.

"Yes, but now you love us, too, since we got you up here and got everyone talking about something besides death. Mrs. Wyatt would love it. Honey, go put the rest of the bourbon in the punch. We're turning this into the party Mrs. Wyatt would want."

Ryan kissed his wife's forehead and set his "tea" on the nightstand. "Anything for someone in a delicate condition."

Sydney waited until he disappeared down the back staircase before rounding on her friend. "So, what gives?"

Sienna took the teacup and downed it.

"Ah. You're good." Sydney laughed and sat down on the bed next to Sienna. Sienna wrapped her arms around her and before Sydney knew it, the laughter had turned to tears. Sienna simply held her as she cried for the loss of someone as important and loved as Mrs. Wyatt.

Sydney didn't know how long she had been crying, but finally the tears were gone, and when she blinked her dry eyes she saw two teacups sitting on the nightstand. Ryan must have come back and dropped them off.

"Feel better?" Sienna asked.

"I do, thank you. I'm sorry I fell apart like that. And I'm even sorrier Ryan is having to handle the fallout from your fake pregnancy announcement."

Sienna gave a snort in reply. "Are you kidding? He's eating it up. There will be cakes and casseroles arriving at our house for days now. It's payback for getting stopped every day. *When are you going to have a baby? Wouldn't a baby be lovely? Is there a bun in that oven yet?"* Sienna mimicked. "And my favorite, *you're not getting any younger, you know."*

"I promise I won't ask ever again." Sydney laughed as they toasted with their teacups. In a quick gulp, Sydney took fortification in the stiff drink and stood up. "I better get down there. Thank you. You're the best friend I could ever have."

Sydney gave Sienna a hug, and then, arm in arm, the two friends headed downstairs. The crowd was still there, but the atmosphere had shifted. Gentle music played in the background as people laughed and told stories of the grand love Ruth and Beauford shared.

Her mother and father sat on a loveseat with their fingers entwined. Her mom laid her head on her father's shoulder, and Syd watched as he automatically put his arm around his wife and kissed the top of her head. Sydney's great-grandparents weren't the only couple in this room with a grand love affair. In fact, Sydney was starting to feel rather singled out. While most of her cousins weren't married – in fact, only Ryan was – the love she saw in her aunts and uncles, and now Ryan and Sienna, had her feeling like she was missing out.

"And then when Joe pulled that cannonball from the ground," her mother laughed, "Nana was so disappointed. She thought it was a treasure she'd buried long ago."

"Her good set of silver," Sydney's father finished as the group laughed.

The treasure! Sydney had been so busy writing the obituary, planning for the funeral, and meeting with lawyers that she'd completely forgotten to look for the family Bible. She had a little more than a week before she had to get back to work, and she was going to spend it on a treasure hunt.

Sydney had thought she wanted the party to end quickly before, but the next hour and a half seemed like a lifetime. As people slowly started saying their goodbyes, she found it harder and harder not to herd them out the door. Finally the door closed behind the last visitor. Her parents declared that they were exhausted and wanted to go home, while Wyatt collapsed on the couch.

"We have to clean up, though," her mother said with a sigh.

Sydney jumped at the chance to have the house to herself. "Don't worry, Mom. I'll get it. You *all* just go home, and I'll get everything taken care of here."

Her mother looked around at the plates and glasses littering the living room and the dining room table full of food. "Are you sure? You've done so much this week already."

"Absolutely. This will all go right into the trash. Poppy and Zinnia already covered and stored all the food people brought." The two cousins of the infamous Rose sisters had been a huge help earlier that afternoon. They had taken over running the bed and breakfast and the Blossom Café for their elderly cousins, Miss Lily, Miss Daisy, and Miss Violet. They had fit right into this small town.

Her mother wrapped her in a hug. "Thank you. I don't know how much longer I could stand it. I just want to climb into a hot bath and go to bed."

Sydney kissed her mother and then was pulled into a

big hug by her father. "Thanks a lot, kiddo."

Her father kissed the top of her head as if she were still six years old before gathering his wife's purse and helping her out to the car. Wyatt raided the refrigerator and came back with an armful of food.

"You still eat like you're a teenager," Sydney teased as her brother shrugged.

"I may be many things, but a cook isn't one of them. This will hold me over for a month." Wyatt looked at the food he was carrying and grinned. "Okay, a week. Are you sure you don't want me to stay and help you clean up?"

"No, I'd rather be alone. There's been so much talking this week; I just want to have some time to myself."

Wyatt leaned forward and placed a kiss on her cheek. With a sad smile, he headed out to his car, and finally Sydney found herself alone. She looked at the oil painting of a young Ruth and Beauford Wyatt hanging on the wall of the living room and smiled. They were together again, and that brought her a sense of comfort.

Sydney walked down the hall to the kitchen and passed the cannonball from the Civil War that Great-grandma had used as a doorstop and laughed as she pulled out a couple trash bags. Her great-grandmother had refused to let an Army munitions expert look at it after learning his last name was Sherman. She had declared there had only been one Sherman on her family's property, and there would never be another.

Smiling to herself, Sydney worked quietly as she cleaned the living room and dining room. She took the full trash bags out to the trashcan and stored all the leftovers in the second refrigerator in the garage. With relief, she headed upstairs to the master bedroom.

It hadn't been used in years, but when she opened the door it still smelled of a mix of her great-grandmother's perfume and her great-grandfather's pipe tobacco. Happy memories filled her with warmth and a little bit of sadness, too. She could picture herself as a young child, bouncing on the large four-poster bed while her great-grandmother put on her makeup and her great-grandfather smoked his pipe and read the paper.

The room was like walking straight into the history of the old South. Beautiful navy and white wallpaper covered with magnolia blossoms adorned the wall above the white chair rail. On one side of the room a brick fireplace had been painted white; an old oil painting of her great-grandmother's family's plantation outside of Atlanta hanging over it. Two upholstered chairs with matching ottomans and a coffee table sat in front of the fireplace. Lining the walls on either side of the fireplace were photos in gilded frames. Photos from when Ruth and Beauford Wyatt were children, first married, new parents, and then photos of Katelyn all through her life as well as Marshall, Sydney, and Wyatt.

The rest of the room contained a massive walk-in closet, master bath, makeup table, and pictures of Wyatt Farm over the centuries. Sydney headed for the nightstand and stared down at the items so familiar to her childhood. Her great-grandmother's hand-painted jewelry bowl that she put her earrings in each night, the book she'd been reading before getting sick and moving downstairs . . . it felt as if Sydney were invading her great-grandmother's privacy.

She shook her head. Ruth Wyatt wanted her to do this. Sydney opened the drawer and looked down at the old Bible she'd never been allowed to touch as a child. It was much larger and thicker than the newer versions. The book cover was rich, reddish-brown leather with an intricate design on the front cover. Most of the gold text had been worn off.

Inside were the secrets of the past. Secrets her great-grandmother had kept from her and her family for some reason. Sydney took her time running her fingers over the opulent cover, feeling its history. She took a deep breath and slid her finger under the cover to open it. It was time to learn about the secret treasure.

Chapter Three

The pages were yellowed with age, but the ornate printing was still legible. Sydney turned to the front of the thick tome and read the elegant script filling the page. *A gift for the birth of my granddaughter, Lady Elizabeth Margaret Woodbury, this third day of September in the year of our Lord 1703. Affectionately, Victoria Gander Woodbury, Dowager Countess of Sladen.*

Countess? 1703? Sydney let out a long breath. This Bible was hundreds of years old and contained the family history she had no knowledge of. They all knew about the Wyatts settling Keeneston in the 1700s, but seeing her great-grandmother's Bible was something completely new.

Sydney turned the page. *Family Record* was elegantly scrolled across the top of the next several pages. In the same handwriting that had written the dedication was a record of the family's births, marriages, and deaths going back five generations and ending with Lady Elizabeth's birth. After that, different handwritings took over, recording births, marriages, and deaths all the way up to Wyatt Davies written in by her great-grandmother.

Sydney ran her fingers over the pages in wonder. So many lives were touched by the people listed there. As she skimmed over the page with her and Wyatt's names on it, she felt something underneath. Sydney turned the pages and found several folded pieces of paper.

"The treasure . . ." Sydney whispered as she took the Bible and the pieces of paper to the seat by the fireplace. Nervously, she opened the first paper with a broken red wax seal on it. The handwriting was old and the date on the top read 1721; it was addressed to Lady Elizabeth.

> *You will return from finishing school and promptly marry the Duke of Eastmont. I will suffer no more of your delays. It is your duty to me as your father and to your family. If you fail to comply you will suffer at my hand.*

Sydney finished the short missive signed by Elizabeth's father, the Earl of Sladen. She felt terrible for this eighteen-year-old girl from long ago. It was obvious she had no wish to marry this duke. But as her father pointed out, she was his property and had no say in her own life. Sydney set the letter down and reached for the next.

It was addressed to Lady Elizabeth at Sladen House in London, in the familiar elegant hand of Elizabeth's grandmother. Sydney took care opening it at the crack in the wax and saw it was addressed three weeks after her father's letter. Sydney's heart beat hard as the words flowed from the page.

> *I must beg you to turn your back on your family and do what I was never strong enough to do. Run. The Season was full of talk of Eastmont's search for his sixth*

wife. All his previous wives have died suspiciously. Because of his rank in society, he has never been held accountable, nor will he ever be. He's as rich as Croesus and related to the king. I will not stand by and allow my only granddaughter to be his next victim. Look for me tonight at your engagement ball. If you are agreeable, you will leave tonight and never return to England. We can only pray that you can outrun Eastmont's reach.

Sydney folded the letter. What did Elizabeth do? She knew what she would have done — run. There were two more packets left. Sydney opened the next and started to read the first page. It was dated 1722 with Albany, New York, inscribed below the date. The handwriting was bolder, yet elegant. After Sydney scanned the first page, she saw that it was a diary of sorts from Elizabeth. It was the letter she wished she could send to her grandmother but knew she never could.

I have never been so frightened or so sure when I accepted the duke's ring that I would never marry him. I had thought my only recourse would be to kill myself, then I received your missive before the ball. It gave me strength to go through the whole charade of an evening. It gave me the strength to ignore Eastmont's vile threats of what he was going to do, to quote him, "to my young nimble body" once we were married as we danced our engagement waltz. I needed strength to ignore the pain in his grip and the violence in his eyes. Your note gave me the courage to tear my hem and politely kiss my mother and my brothers goodbye as I went to fix it. Such relief could never be described at finding you in the retiring room with my valise. You handed me five hundred pounds and passage under a pseudonym on a ship to America leaving that night. That generous gift was enough to last me a lifetime in a quaint cottage in America. But as I write this letter that I know I can never send, it is the second gift that is even more valuable to me: the diamond heart ring your true love gave you that you wore in defiance of the husband forced upon you. Your parting words encouraging me to find my true love gave me courage and hope that all men are not like Eastmont. I am now writing to tell you they are not.

I found him, Grandmère. We are to be married tomorrow in the small chapel in Albany, New York. John Abbott is a farmer and business owner. He owns a warehouse and a barge to transport goods between Albany and New York City. And he has no idea who I am.

After a harrowing journey across the Atlantic, I arrived in New York. I checked into an inn under the name Mrs. Winfield, a newly widowed woman from Inverness, Scotland. It's quite a shock to hear these Americans speak. But the openness of my new country was refreshing. I knew that Eastmont would be looking for me and after a few days recovering from the journey and exploring this fascinating city, I sold my engagement ring. I then inquired about smaller villages out in the wild from a hackney driver and the owner of a tavern I enjoyed. I learned that Albany, a town north of New York, was primarily a trading post, but was quickly growing. It sounded like a perfect place to start a new life.

I was shopping at a dressmaker's to gather necessities for my new life in the wild when I overheard the owner of the shop talking with a man. He mentioned working with the local natives in Albany to acquire more fur for her customers. I desired to learn more about my future home so, not so politely, I interrupted. To my surprise, the man was young, not more than eight years older than my nineteen years. Grandmère, he was so handsome, brave, and intelligent! He introduced himself and answered all my questions about Albany. He instructed me on what materials I should buy in New York and asked when my husband and I would be moving. When I informed him I was not married, he insisted on escorting me to Albany himself. He said it was his gentlemanly duty. He assumed I was a widow, and I did not correct him on that misguided thought. However, I do believe he will figure it out on our wedding night.

We took his boat up the Hudson River to Albany. By that time, I was already madly in love with John and he with Mrs. Elizabeth Honeywell from New York, the false name I used when we met. After we marry, I plan to tell him the truth. We arrived in Albany, and John took me by carriage to a boarding house for women. He asked if he could call on me the next day to show me around town. I said yes and every day for two weeks he drove his carriage into Albany and escorted me around the town and the countryside. He showed me his farm and told me how he supplies all the food for the traders in the area and how he rents out his warehouse and transports good for local suppliers.

After two weeks, he took me to a nearby waterfall

and asked me to be his wife. I happily consented and
now will only wear the small band he gives me during
the marriage ceremony instead of the large emerald of
Eastmont's I had sold. My heart has never been so full. I
will give the ring you gave me to my own
granddaughter and tell her of my brave Grandmère who
rescued me and gave me the gift of opportunity, love,
and freedom.

Sydney reverently refolded the letter and took a deep
breath. She looked down at her ring and now understood
what her great-grandmother had meant by her family
history really starting with Elizabeth Woodbury. How
brave she had been. Sydney picked up the Bible and
looked at the marriages. There, recorded in 1722, was
Elizabeth Woodbury to John Abbott. A year later, the first
of seven births were recorded.

Sydney hugged the letter to her chest. How alone
Elizabeth must have felt. She'd left her family and
everything she knew behind her but had found the kind of
love that Ruth and Beauford had shared. With a smile,
Sydney picked up the other letter and opened it.

An Evelyn Elizabeth Curtis had dated this letter over a
hundred years later, in 1864. The smile Sydney had on her
face vanished as she read the quickly scribbled note.

Sherman is on his way. The family treasure dating
back to Elizabeth Woodbury has been buried in order to
save it, as I fear the house will be burned and all our
possessions stolen. As much as I want to pick up arms
and shoot the soldiers for burning Atlanta, destroying
the crops, and stealing what little food we have, I

*cannot. Instead, I will smile and offer them the use of
our home in order to save it and us. I am hiding this
note and the ring my grandmother Sarah Elizabeth
Majory gave me on my person. I will sew it into my
corset in hopes that I survive. The treasure is buried five
paces from the old oak tree and ten paces from the well.
If I do not make it, keep it safe for the daughters of
Elizabeth yet to come, for it is our legacy.*

Sydney stared dumbfounded at the letter. There was
the location of the treasure. This is what she had sworn to
find and bring home. This week Sydney had learned
something else about her great-grandmother. At the
reading of the will, Sydney discovered that she had been
left a piece of property outside of Atlanta. The lawyer had
handed her the deed with the instruction to remember her
promise.

Her family wanted to know what that promise was,
but she had been sworn not to divulge it until all the
treasure was together. So she had told them she had
promised to visit the old family home, even though none
of them knew it even existed. The deed had gifted the
property from the Evelyn Elizabeth Seeley Trust by
Georgia Elizabeth Ellery as Trustee to Ruth Elizabeth
Ellery in 1937. Evelyn Curtis must have married to become
Evelyn Seeley. She looked at the Bible and saw that
Georgia Ellery was Ruth's mother. And there in the Bible
was great-grandmother's real age. Sydney smiled as she
closed the book. Ruth Wyatt was good at keeping secrets
and so was Sydney.

Now that Syd knew exactly where the property was

and exactly where the treasure was, all that was left was to drive to Atlanta, retrieve the treasure, and fulfill her promise. She'd leave tomorrow and be home a day later. Then she would fly to one of the private islands off the Bahamas and decompress before going back to work. With a game plan in place, Sydney Elizabeth stood up and closed the door to Wyatt Estate.

Sydney grumbled as she sat in the Atlanta rush hour traffic on I-75. She should have left sooner, but her mother had grilled her as to why she was leaving now and wanted to know where she was going and when she was coming home. Some things never changed. It didn't matter she was almost twenty-nine; when it came to travel, her mom still insisted she check in to make sure she arrived safely.

It had taken a while to convince her mom that she didn't need to accompany her and to finally get out of Keeneston. Sydney promised she would call when she checked into her hotel, and she would if she ever got there. With each mile Sydney inched toward downtown, the idea of going on a treasure hunt became less and less appealing while the thought of lying on a beach became more and more enticing.

Finally, the Ritz-Carlton came into view, and Sydney pulled into the hotel entryway. With a smile to the valet, she handed him the keys, grabbed her small bag, and checked in.

Sydney slid her keycard into the door and walked into her suite. She tossed her bag on the floor and fell back onto the bed. Maybe a beach house with a hammock between two palm trees as opposed to a resort. She knew just the person to call to borrow a private island. She didn't like to flaunt her money—if she ever did in Keeneston, they'd call her out for a disgusting lack of manners. Then they'd tell her parents, and she'd get in trouble.

"I can't believe I'm still scared of my mom," Sydney groaned as she picked up her phone and texted her friend with his own private island to find out if she could borrow it for a couple days. He and his family were rarely there, and when he texted back that it was all hers, it gave her motivation to get this treasure hunt over with.

Sydney texted her mom to let her know she'd arrived and then ordered room service before getting into the shower. The hot water rained over her, and she felt her muscles relax. She washed her long hair and wondered once again what this treasure could be that mattered so much. And why was it a secret?

She got out of the shower, toweled off, then pulled on an oversized sweatshirt and flannel pajama bottoms. Sydney was brushing her hair when her dinner arrived. She tipped the server and flipped on the television while she ate. And that was her mistake. She was warm, full, and her eyes began to close as she watched the movie. When the music of the credits woke her up, she groaned. It was almost midnight.

Sydney wrinkled her nose in distaste as she exchanged her flannel pajama bottoms for black jeans. She pulled out her black down jacket. It was the South, but it was also February. Atlanta had been plagued with barely-above-freezing temperatures and very damp air. This made her plans seem daunting, but she was determined to find this treasure and be on the beach by dinner.

The shovel was in the backseat of her SUV. She put the address into her GPS and left for her treasure hunt. Her mind wondered at all the possibilities of the treasure, but nothing prepared her for the vision of Twin Oaks. The manicured drive was lined with overarching oaks, which formed a tunnel that blocked out the dim rays of moonlight. Then suddenly out of the darkness, the house appeared.

No lights were on, but the white mansion seemed to glow. Six two-story columns stretched across the front of the square house. A veranda ran the length of the dwelling on both floors. As Sydney grew closer, she saw that the columns and the verandas wrapped all the way around the house. It was simply stunning.

She parked her car to the side of the house, pulled out her flashlight and a shovel, and looked around the property. "Shit," she whispered into the night. There was no well, but there was a big oak tree. In fact, there were about twenty of them. Letting out a sigh, Sydney decided to start with the first one. She approached the big oak, turned toward the house, and took five paces. She stabbed the ground with the shovel. It had to be here somewhere, and there was a one in twenty chance it was in this vicinity.

Chapter Four

Deacon McKnight's eyes popped open as he reached for the gun strapped to the side of his nightstand. A sound not natural to the chilly Georgian night had woken him from his sleep. He closed his eyes and focused on opening his ears to the sounds of the night. There it was again. He slipped all six-foot-three inches of his body silently from the bed and crept to the master bedroom window. He pulled back the curtain slowly and let his eyes scan the backyard.

"What the hell?" he whispered to himself as the glint of moonlight reflected off a shovel. A person in black was digging up his backyard. The person reached for the knit winter hat on her head and pulled it off. Golden blond hair cascaded from the hat and Deacon's eyes went wide in surprise.

As a private investigator, he had seen a lot of things that surprised him, but a beautiful woman with long, blond hair and a shapely athletic build was truly unexpected. Her face was all smooth angles. Even from where he stood, he could see that her generous lips looked perfect for kissing.

Deacon smiled as he watched her look at the row of

oak trees, move to the next tree in line, and count off five paces. When she dug the shovel back in the ground, Deacon decided to enjoy the show. After his last case, he kind of expected the intruder to be someone wanting to kill him before he could testify at the murder trial of the cold case he'd solved.

Deacon was a private investigator, but he wasn't your normal PI. He didn't handle cheating spouses or disability fraud cases. He didn't need to. He was "old money" to his utter disappointment growing up. He'd hated the debutante scene, the society functions, and definitely the country club crowd. He'd followed in six generations of McKnight men's shoes and attended Emory University. Unlike prior generations, it wasn't economics and business that caught his attention. Criminology was his passion.

His father owned and ran the family's investment firm and refused to hear of a major that had nothing to do with money, so Deacon had double majored in economics and criminology. Upon graduation, he had served his time at the family's firm, making lots of money. At night, he got lost in cold cases his buddy in the Atlanta PD secretly passed along to him. The morning of his twenty-fifth birthday, Deacon headed to the bank, transferred the trust from his grandfather's estate into his name, and quit his job. His father had barely spoken to him since that day.

That same day, Deacon filed for his PI license and opened his own company. Since he had plenty of money, he didn't take any case he wasn't invested in personally. He could take missing-persons cases from people unable to afford their own investigator, or the cold case murders that the police had long ago forgotten. He'd found missing siblings, missing heirs, murderers, and rapists. And he'd never been happier.

He'd had his car keyed and his tires sliced. He'd been shot at, egged, flour bombed, tased, kissed, and then stabbed after the kiss. But never had he found a beautiful woman digging holes in his backyard. His amusement heightened as she moved to the next tree, turned, walked five paces, and began digging again.

Deacon grabbed the jeans he'd flung over the back of the chair and stepped into them. He slid his feet into a pair of running shoes and quietly headed downstairs. He didn't want to spook his mysterious digger. He headed for the side door off the formal sitting room and slipped soundlessly into the night. He stopped behind the woman and smiled as she bent over and cursed at the shovel. He had been right; this woman was a knockout. Deacon just hoped she wasn't here to kill him.

His smiled widened as the woman drove the shovel into the ground and talked to herself about family obligations. She stabbed the ground again and jumped on the shovel to dig it deeper into the cold earth.

"Is there something I can help you with?" Deacon asked with an amused drawl in his deep, southern voice.

The woman let out a shriek, spun, and lashed out at him with the shovel. Deacon ducked his head and the shovel sliced through the air where his head had been just seconds ago. Okay, maybe she *was* here to kill him.

Deacon's amusement fell to the wayside as he rolled backward and sprang to his feet. Warm puffs of breath escaped his mouth as he raised his gun and pointed it at the most beautiful woman he'd ever seen. The odd part was she looked faintly familiar to him.

"Okay, we'll do this the hard way," Deacon said with steel to his voice.

The woman gasped, dropped the shovel, and put her hands on her hips. "Are you seriously pointing a gun at me right now? It's the middle of the night. You're trespassing, and I'm not having the best day."

Deacon's lips twitched in bemusement. The woman was pissed off. Her hazel eyes flashed with gold streaks. If she was scared, she wasn't showing it. Which, somewhat worried him. Assassin? The case he had just solved had put a very powerful music executive in jail for killing his second wife and causing the death of his first wife to be reopened. Could he have sent this woman as retaliation?

"I'm not trespassing, you are. What are you doing in my backyard, and who sent you?" Deacon demanded, his voice growing as cold as the night air.

"I'm not the one trespassing. I own this land."

Deacon gave her a hard smile. "Sorry, darlin'. Wanna try again before I call the cops?"

"How dare you threaten me? This is my property, and I can prove it. Go ahead and call the cops, but it won't be me they are arresting. It'll be you," the woman threatened as she pointed a finger at him.

Deacon grinned at her, and her mouth fell open in disbelief. Her hands went inside her jacket, and Deacon's grin flatted as he moved his finger to his trigger. "Hands up," he ordered.

"I'm getting proof that I own the property," she shot angrily back, but she raised her hands into the air anyway.

"Darlin', I've lived here for five years, and I can

guarantee you don't own this property. And if you did, why would you be dressed in black, digging around the backyard with a shovel in the middle of the night?"

Her eyes narrowed. "That's none of your business," she said haughtily. "And if you would let me get the paper in my inside pocket, I'd prove I own this land and have you kicked off it."

Deacon looked to the partially unzipped jacket and back up to her determined face. "Okay, hands laced behind your head. I'll get the paper, and you don't move."

"Like hell," she spat at him, her hands balling into fists.

"So, you *are* armed. Did Max send you?" Deacon questioned as he kept the gun trained on her heart.

"Max who?"

"Max Salem, the president of Salem Studios."

The woman shook her head. "Never heard of him. Look, my great-grandmother sent me. This really is my house. I don't know who you are, but will you please lower your gun. I'm tired, I'm cold, and I just want to fulfill my promise and get out of here."

"Then with one hand, slowly unzip your jacket and open it so I can grab this proof and make sure you aren't armed."

The woman rolled her eyes in annoyance. He was surprised she didn't stomp her foot, but she didn't seem the type to cry and throw a fit to get what she wanted. No, she seemed way too sure of herself for that, and that's what had him worried.

"Fine," she spat as she unzipped her coat and with one hand, held one side of it open. A piece of paper stuck out from the inside pocket, and for a minute Deacon wondered if she really did have proof. He slowly stepped forward.

"Would you hurry it up already?" she scolded.

He closed the distance and slipped his hand slowly along her waist where her shirt skimmed the top of her jeans. His fingers danced along the hem of her shirt and she sucked in a breath when his fingers touched flesh. Their eyes met and held at the feel of his fingers moving along her skin. She was soft, warm, and very feminine. His fingers felt the indention of her waist and the flare of the top of her hips as he reached behind her to check for a gun before reaching for the paper.

He put his gun in the back of his waistband as he opened the folded papers and scanned the paperwork. His eyes stopped on the two names listed. The previous owner was listed as Ruth Elizabeth Wyatt, and the copy of the last will and testament stated that the new owner was to be Sydney Elizabeth Davies. His eyes shot up to hers. He didn't just recognize her name; he recognized both names on the legal papers.

"You!" he gasped in surprise.

"Yeah, yeah, you used to have a picture of me in my bra in your dorm room," she said with annoyance.

"No. I mean, yes. But you're *the* great-granddaughter Mrs. Wyatt always wrote to me about," he said with astonishment.

Sydney had her mouth open ready to unleash a lecture on respecting women and knowing there's more to a woman besides some photoshopped figure in a magazine when her mouth snapped shut. "Wait, you knew my great-grandmother?"

The man smiled at her with a look of wonder in his eyes. In the dark, they looked brown like his hair, but she couldn't really tell. What she could tell was his jeans fit in a way that would make the male models she knew green with envy. The black fleece pullover he wore showed his shoulders were wide and his stomach flat. What got her the most was the way his lips quirked as if he knew something funny that she didn't. But that didn't mean she was just going to forgive and forget he had held a gun to her on her own property.

"Of course I know Mrs. Wyatt. She's my landlord. I've been renting this property from her for five years." He paused and Sydney saw him frown. "You said *knew*. Did something happen to her?"

Sydney wanted to curse the tears that burst forth and flowed down her cheeks. She took a deep breath and said the words she'd been denying for the past week. "She passed away a little less than a week ago."

The man moved so fast she didn't have time to jump back. His arms were around her, and his hand pushed her head to his chest. Sydney stood stiffly, not knowing what to do.

"I'm so sorry," he whispered against the top of her head. That was unexpected. Syd was five-feet-nine inches and most men were only an inch or so taller than she, but not this man. He was tall enough to look down at her with sympathetic eyes.

"I wish I had known so I could have paid my respects. She was a remarkable lady in the truest sense of the word," he said softly as he held her tight, not caring that her silent tears were soaking into his shoulder.

Sydney took a deep breath to collect herself. She was not going to fall apart in front of man with a gun she didn't even know. She pulled her head back to look up at him. Russet. His eyes were russet. They were a warm brown that matched his hair.

"Thank you. I'm sorry. I'm still kind of a mess. We were very close." Syd's breath caught as his hands came up to cup her cheeks. Ever so slowly he used his thumbs to wipe away her tears.

"I understand. I feel as if I know you from all of our letters." He smiled as if remembering them. "She didn't tell me your full name, though. You were always her very special great-granddaughter who paid your way through school and saved to start your own design business. She certainly never said you were a world-famous model and owner of Sydney International."

Sydney briefly gave into the warmth of his hands before stepping back. "I feel disadvantaged with you knowing so much about me and me standing here having never heard about you. I don't even know your name."

The man's amused smile was back. "Deacon McKnight. How about we head inside? I have a feeling the story of why you are digging around the backyard in the middle of the night isn't a short one. Besides, I think you'll want to see the house. The furnishings are all yours now anyway. I guess that's another reason I feel as if I know you. Mrs. Wyatt left most of her family heirlooms here. I'm pretty sure I can name every one of your ancestors back to the 1700s." He laughed and turned toward the house.

Sydney walked with him, shaking her head in

confusion. "I don't understand. How do you know so much about us, and she never told us about you? She didn't even tell me about the house. The estate lawyer did."

Deacon shrugged his muscled shoulders. "I don't know. But if I know Mrs. Wyatt, and after five years of exchanging letters I sure feel as if I do, there's a reason for it. Maybe it has to do with why you're digging up the yard?"

Sydney walked through the door he held open and stepped to the side. She was the stranger here. This was his home, no matter what the legal papers said. He walked forward and flipped on a light. A small hall to the right led to a sitting room and one to the left led to the kitchen. She followed Deacon into the sitting room with soft, white cushioned chairs and an exposed brick floor partially covered by a thick rug. Behind him, in the room with the light now on, was what looked to be a large living room. The floors were old hardwood with runners and large area rugs covering them. Dainty antique furniture was mixed with dark leather pieces. Oil paintings of people in clothes from another era hung on one wall. Small sketches and photographs in heavy frames were mixed along another wall. And all of it just felt like her great-grandmother.

"Make yourself comfortable. I'll put some tea on and be right back."

Sydney barely acknowledged him as she started to walk slowly around the room. The paintings were very reminiscent of the one of her great-grandparents over the fireplace at Wyatt Farm. Most were of couples and a few were of young children. There were sketches of Twin Oaks showing the changes over each generation, but even the last one had to have been done eighty years or so ago. There seemed to be nothing modern in the place except for some furniture and electronics she was sure belonged to Deacon.

Sydney came to an old photograph and stopped. It was of a young woman in a long, dark dress with a wide collar. She had a smile on her face and a baby on her hip. Her hair was pinned up and a ribbon with the word *VOTE* on it was worn as a sash from her shoulder to her waist. Behind her was a *Vote Here* sign at a polling precinct.

Sydney looked closer at the picture. That must be her great-grandmother as a baby. Her mother must have taken her to vote. By the style of clothes and the sash, it could very well have been the first time a woman in her family had the right to vote.

"That's Mrs. Wyatt as a baby, and her mother, Georgia. Georgia was head of the women's suffrage movement in Atlanta. It was taken after she cast her first vote."

Sydney could see the pride and triumph in the young woman's smile. "How do you know that?"

Deacon handed her a cup of hot tea. "Over the years, Mrs. Wyatt sent me the history of every picture and piece of furniture in the place. Some I remember, but I kept all the letters because they told so much history."

Sydney turned from the picture and took a seat on the chair facing the couch. "So, Deacon, what are you doing renting a place like this? It seems pretty big for just one person." She paused and looked to where he was sitting on the couch. "Or are your wife and children upstairs wondering if their lives are in danger?"

He chuckled and shook his head. "No wife. No kids. I run my business from here. I needed a place to stay since I didn't want to live with my father anymore. I saw an advertisement in the paper seeking a caretaker and renter for the property. My family has lived in Atlanta for generations so I knew of Twin Oaks. I responded to the ad. After an hour on the phone with Mrs. Wyatt, I moved in two days later. So, now are you going to tell me what you're doing digging in the backyard in the middle of the night?"

Sydney took a sip of the tea and felt exhaustion set in. "I made a promise to Great-grandma that I wouldn't say anything."

"Okay," he said slowly. "How about in very general hypothetical terms?"

Sydney smiled. "Hypothetically, someone close to me made me promise to find something."

"And what are you to do, hypothetically, once you find it?" Deacon casually asked.

"Bring it all together and then decide what needs to be done. Sadly, that's as specific as my directions got." Sydney was beginning to feel as crazy as this whole buried treasure story.

To his credit, Deacon didn't laugh. "And this something you're to find is in the backyard?"

"You guessed it!" Sydney teased.

"I knew there was a reason I'm a private investigator," Deacon teased back.

Sydney's eyebrow rose as she took him in along with the house he lived in. Catching cheaters must pay well. "You're a PI?"

"I can sense you don't have a high opinion of my job. Don't worry, I'm not *that* kind of PI."

Sydney just shook her head. "Sorry. You see, my dad's a sheriff, and he's had some problems with PIs before. It's nothing personal. I'm sure you're very good at your job."

"I am very good. I happen to be in between cases right now and will be happy to help you. But, it's almost one in the morning, so how about we call it a night and start fresh in the morning? I'll even bring my own shovel."

Sydney shook her head. "I'm going home tomorrow."

"Then you should have brought a bigger shovel if you're going to be digging up the whole back yard."

Sydney fell back against the back of the chair. She had thought it would be so easy. "Okay. I'll extend my reservation at the Ritz by a couple days." She was tired, she was mourning, and she was quickly seeing her trip to the beach disappear.

"Reservation? You don't need to do that. There are six bedrooms here. I can go tomorrow and pick up your bags. I have an appointment downtown anyway. I'll give you something to sleep in tonight. You're exhausted and shouldn't be driving all the way downtown."

Sydney wasn't amused. She hated being told what to do. "Have you met my father? Because you sound an awful lot like him."

"Well, then maybe I will like Marshall, even if he doesn't like PIs." Deacon grinned.

"How did you . . . ah, the letters," Sydney said, answering her own question.

Deacon just winked in response and stood up. "Come on. I'll take you to the blue room. It has a great view of the backyard."

Sydney followed him up the sweeping staircase and down the long hallway. He pushed open a door and flipped the light switch. Sydney had traveled all over the world and stayed in the most luxurious places, but this room took her by surprise. Three floor-to-ceiling windows and a pair of French doors that led out to the wrap-around veranda took up the whole left sidewall. Another set of doors and windows were against the opposite wall of the large corner room. A king-sized canopy bed and a sitting area filled the rest of the space. It looked just like her great-grandmother's room.

"This was Mrs. Wyatt's room. Would you like me to start a fire for you?" Deacon asked gently, as if reading her mind.

"No thanks, I can do it if I want one later." She took a slow turn of the room, seeing pictures of her great-grandmother as a teenager and even one with Great-grandpa when they must have been dating. Warmth, comfort, and love washed over her as she took it all in.

Deacon returned with a soft knock and stood by the door with his hands full. "I brought you a toothbrush, a hairbrush, and a shirt to sleep in. I'm not really a pajama type of guy, sorry," he said as he handed her the things.

Sydney looked at the shirt and smiled. "The Georgia Vultures, my second-favorite team. Thank you."

"I guess you have to like the Thoroughbreds, huh?" He smiled back at her.

"Of course. I know the owners of the Thoroughbreds and Trey Everett. Since Trey played for the Vultures, they're my second-favorite team."

"That's right, Everett coaches the Thoroughbreds running backs."

Sydney smiled as she thought of Trey. She'd known him her whole life. Plus he'd babysat some of the kids she grew up with. "And he's from Keeneston."

"Well, if you're around more, I guess I'll have to get a Thoroughbreds shirt. I'm down the hall on the right if you need anything. Oh, and what's your room number at the hotel?"

Sydney told him, but then stopped. "I'll get my stuff."

"Don't worry about it. Spend your time digging up the yard. I have a meeting at seven a block over from your hotel. I'll pick up your things and be back before you even have breakfast. And Sydney, it's great to finally meet you."

Deacon closed the door, and Sydney stood staring at it for a full minute. This whole thing was too weird. He seemed to know her as if they were old friends while he was a complete stranger—a complete stranger who was going to be in her hotel room. No, she would get up and go into Atlanta tomorrow to get her things. And just to be careful, she flipped the old lock in the door.

Chapter Five

Sydney looked up as the door to her room slowly opened. The room was still dark, cast only with the warm glow of the fire she had started the night before. She held her breath, fearful of who was sneaking into her room. Should she scream?

But then the person stepped from the darkness into the orange glow of the firelight. "Deacon," Sydney gasped. "What are you doing here?"

"Whatever you wish me to do, Sydney." His voice rumbled and Sydney felt it caress her body.

She gulped as she held the sheets to her chest. "How did you know I wanted you?"

Deacon's lips formed a cocky smile as he walked toward her. He pulled the fleece from his body and tossed it on the floor. Oh god, he was male perfection, and Sydney wanted him right now.

"The only question is, what do you want, Sydney?" Deacon asked quietly as he stopped beside her bed and looked down at her. "You're a woman who deserves to be worshiped from head to toe. What will make you scream in pleasure?"

Sydney let her eyes trail up the muscled ridges of his

stomach, across his defined pecs and corded neck to lips made for worshiping. "You," she whispered in response.

"Then come and get it," Deacon dared. Sydney's eyes shot to his. Slowly, she reached out a hand and fumbled with the button to his jeans.

"Don't be shy, Syd. I know all about you. You're not one to sit back and follow. You take what you want. So, take me," Deacon's voice challenged her.

He was right. She didn't sit by and let others make the hard calls. She made them herself. She went after what she wanted and got it. Sydney pushed up to her knees and slowly, tauntingly, raised the jersey he'd loaned her over her head. The appreciation in his eyes gave her the courage to unzip his jeans and shove them to the floor.

Sydney felt flushed as she took in a nude Deacon. And when he cupped her face and kissed her hard, she melted into him. He pushed her back onto the bed and covered her with his body. Sydney had never felt so alive, so hot, and so feminine all at once. And when Deacon started to move, she screamed out in the pleasure he promised. The headboard banged over and over again, beating loudly to the point of distraction as she raked her nails down his back. Then suddenly the vision of her and Deacon disappeared as Sydney's eyes opened on a gasp. Her shirt was around her waist and damp with sweat as she sat in the middle of the bed, tangled in the sheets. The sound that had been interrupting her dream wasn't hot headboard-banging sex but was, in fact, someone knocking on the front door. Sydney shot from the bed and raced downstairs when the knocking faded and a woman's sobbing scream replaced it.

Deacon had spent most of the night thanking his lucky stars for having *the* Sydney Davies just down the hall from him. The rest of the time he thought of all the things Mrs. Wyatt had told him about her. The fact that he was already half in love with the mysterious great-granddaughter he'd heard about the past five years was embarrassing in itself. But now he felt ridiculous. Sydney Davies was the closest thing to perfection there was. She had dated a prince, a pro quarterback, and a Hollywood actor. She sure as hell wouldn't be dating a private investigator who wore old jeans and helped solve cold cases.

He had left the house that morning slowly. He didn't want to leave her but when he'd knocked on her door, she had only groaned in response. So he had headed to his meeting in Atlanta alone. And as Deacon rode the old elevator up to his meeting, he found himself lost in the disbelief of the memory of finding Sydney — supermodel, entrepreneur — digging in his backyard.

"Deacon, good of you to come in."

"No problem, detective. What can I do for the Atlanta PD today?"

The old detective shook his hand and led him through the locked doors into their bullpen. Desk after desk was lined up with dry erase boards covering the walls. Most of the detectives knew him, and after his pitch of swearing he wouldn't do anything to hurt their cases, had grown to trust him.

"I just need you to sign your statement on the Salem case. The DA and I are meeting with his attorney this morning. The DA is pushing for a plea deal. They're afraid of retaliation from Salem's gang if there's a long public trial. We're hoping your statement, along with the sister's statement, will show his attorney we have enough for the death penalty. If he pleads guilty to life without parole, the DA won't bring any charges against him for the probable murder of his first wife."

Deacon ground his teeth in frustration. "But we know he killed his first wife, too."

"I know," Detective Gentry said as he handed Deacon his statement to sign. "But we both know there's a lack of physical evidence. It's a loose, circumstantial case and he would walk. But he doesn't know that yet. He knows you're a bulldog when you get a case so we'll let him worry about it. This way, he's off the street and won't have to fear the death penalty. The DA is hoping he'll take it."

Deacon signed his statement, and a secretary notarized it before handing it back to the detective. "He should. Two murders for the price of one. And with his history, there're bound to be more skeletons in the closet."

"At least this will get him off the streets."

Deacon nodded. He'd just hoped the family of Salem's first wife would have closure. "True. Good luck, detective."

They shook hands and Gentry escorted him back to the elevators. The Ritz was right around the corner. Deacon would stop there next, pick up Sydney's bag, and check her out. His mind was already organizing the facts she'd told him about what she was looking for. He knew it had to be five paces from the tree line and buried. It could have been buried five years ago or two hundred years ago. He filed that away as a piece of the puzzle he needed to investigate further.

He felt the familiar excitement from a new case as he walked into her hotel room. Syd had left the key on the counter the night before, intending to go with him this morning. After hearing how deeply asleep she was, he took it and hoped she wouldn't care. He found her bag and tossed her pajamas into it. He walked around the room and into the bathroom, picking up things and putting them in her bag as his mind searched for clues from the letters Mrs. Wyatt had written him. He would have to reread them, but there had been a story from the night Sherman had started his march toward the sea that he thought might be helpful.

Certainly the idea of working closely to Sydney was also causing his heart to beat a little faster this morning. As he closed the hotel room door, he remembered Mrs. Wyatt's last letter.

My poor great-granddaughter. She's been working so hard I fear her heart has been filed away with last season's designs.

Letter after letter, Mrs. Wyatt had told him of Sydney's hopes, dreams, and achievements. He felt as if he were cheering her on when Mrs. Wyatt would write of meetings with "boutiques," which he now knew were major deals for her clothing lines. He had even thought of driving to Keeneston before the Salem case took off to meet Mrs. Wyatt in person and, he hoped, the great-granddaughter and great-grandson he had read all about. Over the years, Mrs. Wyatt and her family had become closer to him than his own.

Without thinking, Sydney flung open the door to find a woman crumpled on the doormat. Her thin shoulders heaved with body-wracking sobs. Having heard the door open, the stricken woman looked up.

"Oh, thank God. Is Mr. McKnight here?" the woman asked as she reached out and clung to Sydney's hand.

Sydney didn't know what to do. The woman was desperate, but was she a crazy stalker or someone who needed help? And where was Deacon? Oh, his meeting. How had she not woken up for that?

"I'm sorry, he's not here right now. Are you injured? Do you need an ambulance?" Sydney asked and looked the woman over for blood. She wore tan slacks, a blouse, and blazer and looked to be in her mid-forties. She didn't look dangerous — she looked distraught.

"No, I need Mr. McKnight. It's my baby . . . she's gone!" The woman let go of Sydney's hand and covered her face as a fresh round of sobs took hold of her.

The sound of tires on the drive made both Sydney and the woman look up. Please let it be Deacon. The truck pulled into the garage, and a moment later Deacon appeared, carrying her bag.

The woman saw him and scrambled to her feet. She raced across the yard and collapsed into his arms. Sydney hurried out to help. Deacon looked gently down at the blubbering woman and silently handed Sydney her bag so he could wrap his arm around the woman's waist and use his other to support her arm as he silently led her inside.

"They took her." *Sob.* "The police said she's eighteen

and has the right to leave under her own volition." *Sob.* "But they're not good people. I just know she's in danger." *Sob.* "But we had a fight about her sneaking out to go to a party, and the next morning I go to talk to her and she's gone."

Sydney tried to piece it all together as she held the door open for them. Deacon escorted the woman to a front sitting room and Sydney followed, not knowing what was going on.

"Syd, can you please get Ms. . . ." Deacon looked questioningly at the woman he was helping to the couch.

"Vander. Eloise Vander."

". . . Ms. Vander a glass of water?" Deacon asked calmly.

Sydney turned and walked to the kitchen. Deacon wasn't surprised at finding a woman in hysterics on his porch. In fact, he was so calm that Sydney was starting to think this was no big deal. Except, it sounded like the woman's daughter had run away.

A minute later she handed Ms. Vander a glass of water and gave the jersey a tug to hide the fact she just realized she didn't have pants on. Looking around, she grabbed a throw, curled her legs under her, and took a seat across from Deacon who was sitting next to Ms. Vander on the couch.

"Now, Ms. Vander, I'm Deacon McKnight and this is my friend, Sydney. How do you think I can help you?"

Ms. Vander took a deep breath to steady herself. "I read about you in the newspaper, solving that missing-child case when the police had all but given up. I called the police first, but they said they couldn't help me. So I thought of you."

Deacon gave her a gentle smile. "What happened? Start from the beginning."

"My daughter, Bailey, is a senior in high school. She turned eighteen three days ago, but she's been talking to these older men on the Internet. I caught her talking to them two weeks ago and told her how dangerous that is and grounded her from using the computer for a week. We had a horrible fight, so two days later when she stopped complaining, I knew something was up. While she was asleep, I looked at her phone. She had been texting a number I didn't know. On top of that, she had been sending pictures of herself in her underwear and bikinis, along with her measurements, to this number."

Ms. Vander took a small sip of water and set it down again. "You can imagine what the morning was like when I confronted her about it. I took away her phone and grounded her until a couple days before her birthday. She complained and said I didn't understand. She said she was texting them for a job and they cared about her success, unlike me. She said they were some kind of modeling agency she met at the mall. I asked for the name of the modeling agency. It was Tristan something or other. I asked if they'd given her a card, and she said no. His name was Vic, and she just gave him her phone number. I tried to tell her that's not how these things worked, but he promised her fame and fortune, and I was just the dumpy mother who didn't understand. I can't say for sure, but I think he's the one she was talking to on the Internet."

Sydney felt her breath catch as she listened to the story. When Ms. Vander paused, Deacon raised his eyes and met

Sydney's. She had been around the industry her whole life. This was starting to sound like some of the nightmares other models told her about when they were traveling for shows.

"So," Ms. Vander picked up, "I thought I had gotten through to her. We had a great birthday and then the next morning I got a call from the school telling me she never arrived that morning. I used the app on her phone to locate her and found her having lunch with a man in his mid-thirties — Vic. He was holding her hand and doing a hard sell for her to come with him to New York to audition for some agencies. Bailey lost it when she saw me. The man looked amused. He sat back and watched our argument almost gleefully. And when I demanded she come home with me, the man finally spoke and informed me that Bailey was eighteen and had the legal right to do whatever she wanted."

"And she chose to stay with him," Deacon finished.

Ms. Vander nodded. "I stormed out to the car and called the police. They said she wasn't in danger and was an adult. There was no crime being committed. I knew Bailey didn't have the money to go to New York. We're not a rich family. I work two jobs just to get by. My ex-husband, her father, left us five years ago with nothing — just disappeared with his secretary. He said he was tired of being a husband and a father. So, I headed home and waited for Bailey. Finally she arrived and stormed up to her room. There was some yelling, some threatening from both of us, but finally she promised to open the door and talk to me in the morning. Well, morning came and I knocked on her door. Nothing. I ended up breaking down the door. Her window was open and her cheerleading duffle bag and backpack where gone, along with some of her clothes and toiletries."

"Did you try the police again?" Deacon asked.

Ms. Vander nodded. "The police found a note partially hidden on her bed saying she was eighteen and going to pursue a modeling career. She didn't want me to come after her. She was voluntarily taking her future in her own hands. So the police shrugged and again said there was nothing they could do."

"That's a strange way to word it," Deacon said. "Did she normally talk like that?"

Ms. Vander shook her head. "Never. You didn't see that man's face, Mr. McKnight. A mother knows when things aren't right, and that man was pure evil."

"Did she leave any of her electronics behind? The computer, phone, anything?" Deacon asked.

"I still have the laptop in my room. I hadn't given it back to her yet. Will you help me?" Ms. Vander looked like she was putting all her effort into holding herself together.

Sydney looked between Deacon and Ms. Vander and knew in that second if Deacon didn't, she would personally hire an investigator.

"Of course. I'll meet you at your house and look over her room. If I have your permission, I will bring the computer back here. Now, it may take time to find her. Are you prepared for that?" Deacon asked seriously.

"Yes, I just need to know someone is looking for my baby. But," Ms. Vander stopped and bit her trembling lip, "as I said, we don't have much money."

"Then it's a good thing I do," Deacon said matter-offactly. Ms. Vander collapsed against Deacon in tears, and even Sydney felt a lone tear trickle down her cheek. And in that one second, the vision of the PI hiding in bushes trying to catch cheaters or bust insurance disability cases disappeared. In its place, Deacon McKnight became a white knight.

Chapter Six

Deacon opened his lower desk drawer and pulled out the box containing the letters from Mrs. Wyatt. He had wanted to spend more time with Sydney, but he needed to meet Ms. Vander at her house to go through her daughter's room.

He looked up from the antique desk when he heard a soft knock at the door. Sydney smiled sadly at him as she stood in jeans and a tight V-neck sweater. It was white and caused the bright red lipstick to draw all of his attention. Thoughts of smearing her lipstick with heavy kissing kept him from standing to greet her.

"You were great with Ms. Vander," Sydney said softly as she walked into the room and sat in the whiskey-colored leather chair across from him.

"It's what I do. I help those who are out of options."

He watched as Sydney gave a slow nod of her head. She flipped back a long strand of her hair and then raised her eyes to his. "I want to pay you for finding Bailey."

"What?" Deacon asked, insulted.

"You need to make money. Since Ms. Vander can't pay you, I will. I want all available resources used to find Bailey. This hits close to home for me, Deacon. I have heard rumors of this happening in the industry. It's common to hear about people preying on young girls and boys who want to become models."

Deacon understood now. She saw herself as Bailey. And if it hadn't been for an already famous mother, it could have been her ill-fated introduction to the modeling world.

"Sydney, I understand your motive. However, it's not needed. I will always take a missing-child case, whether payment can be made or not. I have the money. It's actually a point of contention with my father. He thinks I should use my money to make more money . . . and I do. I just use some of that money to solve cases for people that can't afford any other option."

Sydney let out a slow breath. "That's very kind of you. Are you heading over to see Ms. Vander now? If so, I'd like to come, too."

"If you want to come, you can. However, I had thought you might want to see these." Deacon pushed the box across the desk. "They're all the letters from Mrs. Wyatt. I'm not the only one investigating something, am I?"

Sydney looked torn as she took the box slowly off the table and held it in her lap. She looked down at it, but only a second later looked at him with resolution in her eyes. "Bailey is a more immediate need than some family treasure. It's been buried for over 150 years. Another couple of days won't hurt it."

Deacon's respect for the woman sitting across from him rose even more. It was easy to forget that someone who was so famous could actually be a good, caring person.

"Then let's go." Deacon stood up and walked around the desk. He took the box from Sydney and placed it on the desk before holding out his hand to her. He waited to see if she would take it. When she did, he felt invincible. Deacon helped her from her chair and, with a hand resting gently at the small of her back, guided her to the car.

Sydney looked around the bedroom of the small home. Ms. Vander had done the best she could to make the small row house a warm and inviting place. Pictures of her and Bailey lined the walls. Deacon looked around and studied every inch of the house. It wasn't as if Sydney knew what she was looking for, but she had a feeling it wouldn't be in the living room. It would be in Bailey's room.

They followed Ms. Vander up the narrow staircase to the second floor where the two bedrooms shared a bathroom. The first door was covered with cutouts from magazines and Bailey's name. Ms. Vander stood back and allowed Deacon and Sydney to go into the small, square room first.

"I'll go get the computer and meet you downstairs. Call if you need anything," Ms. Vander said before walking to her room and then disappearing down the stairs.

Sydney didn't say anything as Deacon walked to the window Bailey must have climbed out. "It's only an eight-foot drop or so. The plants are smashed down, so the man probably stood there and caught her as she dangled from the window."

"What am I looking for?" Sydney asked as she took in all the teenage girl things — clothes on the floor, hair bands piled on top of a chest, and way too much makeup.

"A journal, notes from class to her friends, receipts . . . anything to give us a clue who Vic and Tristan are," Deacon said as he lifted the mattress.

Sydney pulled out her cell phone and Googled Tristan Models. There was a webpage with a model she'd heard of on the front of it. There were also several social media accounts. She copied the links and sent an email to her contacts in the modeling world to see if they had heard of either Tristan Models or a recruiter named Vic. Syd let them know she was in Atlanta at her family's home for the next day or so and to get back to her as soon as possible. Then she took a slow turn around the room. Where would she hide something?

She searched the drawers but found nothing. When she went to the closet, she immediately went to the darkest, farthermost place she could find. She reached blindly into the back corner and felt something. She pulled it out and looked at the ordinary shoebox. Sitting on the floor, she looked onto Bailey Vander's keepsake box.

"I found something," Sydney said excitedly as she stood up and placed the box on the bed.

"Good job," Deacon called out and came to stand next to her. "Now, let's see if there's anything worthwhile in there."

Sydney let Deacon open the box. Inside was a broken cell phone, an old letter from her father, and a variety of sentimental things.

"This is why they couldn't ping her location. She

smashed the phone and hid it." Deacon turned the phone over and smiled. "The memory card is still intact. I can get this up and running in no time by putting the card into a new phone."

"Why would she break her phone?" Sydney asked with confusion.

"Vic probably told her to destroy it. She didn't know it was only the memory card that needed to be destroyed. By only breaking the screen, you don't affect the stored data."

"Will we be able to see the text messages Ms. Vander was telling us about?"

Deacon nodded as he slid the phone into a plastic evidence bag. "I hope so. And also Vic's number. Let's go get the computer and see what else we can find."

Sydney stood back as Deacon explained the significance of finding the cell phone and what he hoped to find on the old, beaten-up laptop Ms. Vander handed over. Deacon promised to keep in touch. Sydney felt her phone vibrate in her pocket, pulled it out, and smiled her goodbye to Ms. Vander. As she walked down the sidewalk toward the car, she read the email from her former agent.

"Deacon!" she gasped as she finished reading the email.

"What?" he asked as he opened the door for her.

She sat in the passenger seat and looked up at him. "I got us a clue!"

Deacon grinned and closed the door. He hurried around to the driver's side and got in. "Tell me."

"My former agent says she reps a girl who had been with Tristan. She left them when her roommate disappeared one night. She went to a modeling gig and never came back. When the girl asked about it, she was told her roommate decided to go full-time with one client. It made her nervous, so she left the apartment that housed all of the Tristan models and found my agent the next day. My agent bought out her contract and has made her a very popular model since then."

Deacon's hands tightened on the wheel until Sydney saw his knuckles go white. "What else did your agent say?"

"She said they're a small firm with many contacts abroad, especially in Italy where the owner, Durante Ingemi, is from. They have some popular models out there right now, but rumor has it they're not completely on the up-and-up. About twenty years ago — that's before any of these models were even born — the owner of Tristan was investigated for statutory rape of one of his clients when he worked at a different modeling agency as a recruiter."

"Recruiter?" Deacon asked.

"Yeah, they travel all over the world looking for models to sign with the agency. They bring all these young girls and boys, usually fourteen to eighteen years old, to the agency and get a bonus for each model the agency signs. Since these young kids will do almost anything to become a model . . . well, you get the idea." Sydney closed her email and watched as they turned down the oak-lined drive.

"And now this former recruiter owns his own modeling agency?" Deacon shook his head. "Unbelievable. I'm going to wait to see what I can get from Bailey's phone and computer, but I fear we're dealing with something far worse than a rebellious teen."

Sydney felt sick to her stomach. She didn't need Deacon to say it. She knew what was hiding on the underbelly of the fashion world—and it was truly ugly.

Sydney sat with her legs curled under her as she read the first note from her great-grandmother to Deacon. She could hear Ruth speaking as she read the history of the property and what she wished Deacon would do to keep the property up.

Deacon sat on the couch across from her with the laptop on the coffee table. Sydney looked at him over the letter she was reading. His face was knitted with concern as he focused on the computer.

Sydney picked up another letter and fell into the history lesson that was her great-grandmother's life. She found the portrait her great-grandmother was talking about in this letter and studied it. Her great-great-great-grandfather had painted the skyline of Atlanta.

"I got it!" Deacon shouted in excitement as his fingers flew over the keys.

Sydney leapt up and hurried around the coffee table to sit beside him. "What did you find?"

"The online chat session Ms. Vander was talking about. The men are clearly soliciting her."

Sydney leaned forward and read some of the chat. "Oh, that's horrible. They're manipulating her."

"Look here, they tell her at eighteen she can leave her mother's house voluntarily and her mom and the police can't do anything about it. Then they tell her about being a model and traveling the world. They put it all in her head, and then someone a couple days later just happens to bump into her at the mall. The same mall she tells them she's going to be at."

"That's the same language Bailey used in her note," Sydney said with wonder.

"What about you, have you found anything?" Deacon asked her. He shifted toward her and suddenly his leg was pressing against hers, and she realized the feel of having him close was addictive. She'd wanted him to touch her again ever since that morning when he helped her from her chair.

"Not really. But I'm only a couple of letters in. I was thinking of going back outside to see if I can find the old well." Sydney didn't dare move. She didn't want him to move his leg from against hers.

"Just don't fall in," Deacon smirked, and Sydney involuntarily leaned toward him.

Deacon stood up suddenly and Sydney tumbled forward onto the couch. "Oh, sorry," Deacon said as he jumped farther back. "I'm going to run to the mall and see if they still have security footage from that day."

Sydney sat up, feeling foolish and very embarrassed. "Um, I'll be out back digging up the yard. Let me know what you find."

And Deacon was out the door faster than two shakes of a lamb's tail.

Deacon slammed the door to his car and laid his head on the steering wheel. He was such an idiot. Sydney Freaking Davies had her leg against his and was leaning toward him, and what had he done? He'd freaked out. He didn't want to brag, but he didn't have problems where women were concerned. Well, until now.

Her breast had brushed against his arm, and he knew if he didn't put some distance between them he would do something he would regret—like try to have sex with her on the couch right then and there. Well, he wouldn't necessarily regret that. What he would regret was being like all the other men in her life. He'd seen the tabloids and the way men talked about Sydney. They only cared about her body. The football player had paraded her around like a championship trophy, and the Hollywood actor dumped her when she got more press than he did.

As much as it killed him, he wasn't going to get physical with her. Deacon had fallen in love with Sydney before he'd even seen this great-granddaughter Mrs. Wyatt had written about. He wanted to take the time to get to know Sydney and date her the way she deserved before they, he hoped, made love. She deserved it, and if they ever did make love, it was going to be for more reasons than just how beautiful she was.

Chapter Seven

Sydney wiped the sweat from her face and looked down at the sixth hole she'd dug in the backyard. Nothing. She couldn't find an old well and now she had about fourteen more oak trees to go. It had been hours since Deacon fled. It irritated her that he knew so much about her, and she really hadn't learned that much about him. Okay, she was really more irritated by the fact that she wanted to know him better . . . in more ways than one. That darn dream had messed with her all day. When he was sitting next to her, she could think of nothing but the dream. But to have him run away like that? She'd never had a man run from her before.

Sydney let the shovel fall to the ground and sat cross-legged on the cold grass, pulling out her cell phone. She was going to do the one thing she'd sworn off years ago. She was going to look Deacon McKnight up online.

She typed in his name and waited as the screen filled with articles and pictures. *Atlanta PI solves cold case. Atlanta PI finds missing boy. Atlanta playboy attends debutante ball.* What? Sydney pulled up that article to find a picture of a devastatingly sexy younger Deacon in a tux, dancing with a woman in a massive white gown. She scanned the article and froze. *New Vice President of McKnight Investments Deacon McKnight dances with heiress Isabella Grafton.*

He wasn't kidding when he said he had enough money to cover the case. She knew his father, Walter McKnight. He had met her when she was in Atlanta for a charity event a couple years ago. Funny, he never mentioned having a son. He did mention wanting to invest her money, though.

It appeared from the articles that Deacon left his father's firm on his twenty-fifth birthday and started his own private investigation firm the same day. Since then, there were no more pictures of debutantes or mentions of him with his father. Well, at least Sydney knew he wasn't here to try to invest her money.

He seemed charitable. His name and picture were always in the society section for the Drake Charles and Elle Simpson-Charles Charity Ball funding the children's hospital each year. It seemed Deacon was as genuine as he appeared to be in person. Damn. That made Sydney want him even more.

She heard a car coming up the drive, stood up, and walked around to the front of the house in time to see Deacon pull into the garage. She wanted Deacon McKnight, and Sydney wasn't one to give up. She was going to get to know him better to find out if her feelings were lust or something more.

Deacon strode into the kitchen and looked out the windows into the backyard. He set the copies of the mall's security DVDs onto the granite island and stared in appreciation as Sydney bent over and scooped dirt out of another hole. The sky had turned gray and now a gentle sprinkle started to fall. Deacon put on water for a cup of tea for Sydney, but when the back door didn't open, he looked back outside.

Deacon's fingers tightened on the edge of the counter as his erection pressed painfully against his jeans. Sydney's damp, long-sleeved, white thermal shirt clung to every curve of her rounded breasts. She stuck the shovel in the ground and raised her hands above her head to stretch. Deacon felt his mouth go dry as her breasts thrust forward.

He didn't even notice when the clouds darkened further and the rain began in earnest. He was glued to the window as Sydney wiped her hands across her flat stomach before picking up the shovel again. Pieces of her wet hair clung to her cheeks as she turned to dig again. On a baser level, Deacon knew he should tell her to come inside. He could tell she was freezing out there. But another instinct riveted his eyes to the pebbled nipples begging to be warmed by his mouth.

When a clap of thunder shook the house, Sydney jumped. She dropped the shovel as rain pelted down. She wiped her hair from her forehead and looked surprised at seeing Deacon in the window. Damn. He'd been caught staring. At least she couldn't see anything below the kitchen counter. She started to head to the kitchen when suddenly her foot slid out from under her. Her arms pinwheeled, and before Deacon could move, Sydney fell forward on the wet ground.

Deacon darted for the door but froze as he came sliding to a halt in the yard. Sydney's face and upper body had fallen into the mud from her sixth hole. As she peeled herself up, Deacon bit the inside of his cheek to keep from smiling. Her face, her hair, and her shirt were caked in mud.

"Let me help you!" Deacon yelled over the rain.

Sydney didn't say a word; she just shook her head as she slowly stood up.

"You'd make a great mud wrestler," Deacon teased as he held out his hand to her.

"You're laughing?" Sydney questioned. "I'm covered in mud!"

Deacon laughed again but then grunted as she yanked his arm. His foot couldn't gain traction on the wet ground, and in a flash, he was on the ground. Sydney stood over him, her white teeth flashing through the mud. He looked to see what she was smiling about when the clump of mud landed on top of his head.

"Don't start something you can't finish," Deacon warned. In answer, Sydney tossed a mudball at his face. He used his hands to wipe his cheek. "I warned you."

Sydney squealed as he reached forward and grabbed her around the waist. He turned, falling back toward the mud and taking her with him. Mud flew, his deep laugh mixed with her higher-pitched shrieks, and one of American's most powerful businesswomen smeared mud all down his chest before trying to leap away.

"Oh no, you don't!" Deacon taunted as he dodged another mudball. They were both covered in gunk from head to toe. Only their eyes and wide smiles were visible. Sydney wiped a muddy sleeve against her mouth and stuck out her tongue.

Deacon similarly wiped his mouth and grinned. He

pretended to look away, and when Sydney bent to scoop up some more ammunition, Deacon dove at her. Sydney only had time to let out a surprised squeak before Deacon dragged her down into the mud with him. They laughed as he rolled her into the mud. She was the most beautiful sight he'd ever seen. He stopped laughing as he realized he was very intimately lying on top of her. She seemed to notice at the same time.

Deacon used one hand to cup her cheek. He couldn't tear his eyes from her lips. He felt her breathing hitch as he bent his head toward hers. One of her hands ran down his back while the other grasped the bicep of the arm he was propping himself up with. And when his lips met hers, the earth shook. The cold disappeared as heat flooded his body. Her fingers tightened on his arm as her mouth opened to his. His tongue plunged in and Sydney moaned as she arched against his shaft. They were electric together. Light burst around them, and Deacon was brought crashing back to reality.

"Shit. We have to get inside. That was lightning." Deacon leapt up and helped Sydney from the ground. As they ran hand in hand toward the house, Deacon cursed himself. He'd done exactly what he swore he wouldn't do. He wasn't any better than any of the others, and if there was one thing he wanted, it was to make her feel like the most cherished woman in the world. He couldn't do that while he was grinding against her like a teenager.

He pushed open the door to the mudroom, and they tumbled inside. Mud and water pooled on the tile as they stood dripping. Deacon opened the washing machine and slid out of his shoes.

"We can toss our clothes directly into the wash. There are towels right over there."

Sydney turned to grab the towels. Her mind was in shock. Never had a kiss been so powerful. It was supernatural the way the heat had flooded her body. She was astonished by her desire for a man she'd just met. The thought of them in a shower washing the mud off so they could pick up where they left off made her blush.

But when she turned to hand Deacon a towel, he was standing with his back to her. His shirt and pants were off, and she admired the view of him in his boxer briefs. Everything about Deacon McKnight screamed male.

"Here you go," she smiled as she held out the towel. Deacon only turned at his shoulders and grabbed the towel. In a flash, he had it around his waist. He slid off his boxer briefs and tossed them in the wash without giving her so much as a peek at what was underneath.

"I'm going to take my shower and order dinner. I'll let you change in privacy."

And then he was gone . . . again.

"What the hell?" Sydney mumbled to herself as she stripped out of her muddy clothes and turned on the wash. Baffled, Syd headed upstairs. She stopped in front of Deacon's room and stared at the closed door. Behind it, she could hear the shower running.

"You've never taken a chance, Syd. Come on," she told herself as she reached for the doorknob. She turned it, but then couldn't move it anymore. It was locked.

She stood staring at the locked door. No man had ever locked her out. She hung her head and walked to her room, grateful he didn't see the knob turn. It appeared

Deacon was ultimately uninterested.

Sydney turned on her shower and stepped inside. No. She knew he was interested. She felt Deacon's interest pushing eagerly against her not ten minutes ago. He'd said there was no wife, but he didn't say there wasn't a girlfriend. Maybe that was it. Well, one way or another, she was going to find out more about Deacon. She wouldn't make a move until she was sure he was the loyal, kind, and totally available man she thought he was.

Deacon's cold shower didn't do the trick. He'd even taken himself in hand and that didn't do it either. It was the fault of the woman who'd been dancing around the kitchen in her flannel pajamas. The feel of Sydney lying under him was something he wasn't going to forget easily.

When he'd made it downstairs fifteen minutes earlier, he'd found Sydney bent over and wiggling her curvy bottom as she plucked things from his fridge. He'd had to hide behind the counter again.

Then, for the next five minutes, she'd quizzed him on all the foods he liked and didn't like. She'd promised to make him a dinner he'd love. When he'd told her he could just order a pizza, she'd laughed.

"It's my way of saying thank you for letting me stay here. And for the letters." She'd tossed him her million-watt smile and started rummaging for pots and pans.

And that was how he wound up sitting on the nearby couch listening to her sing — badly, as she cooked — and falling more in love with her by the second. He was supposed to be looking at the mall surveillance tapes.

Instead, all he wanted was to be closer to Sydney. He shook his head to refocus on the tapes.

His world narrowed to his computer screen as Bailey Vander came into view. She was with friends. They stopped in front of a store and her friends went in while Bailey went to a nearby ice cream cart. Then Vic came into view. Deacon watched as Vic stood near her. He had her do a spin for him and smiled at her. Bailey glowed as Vic talked to her. He reached out and ran a hand down her arm. Bailey nodded and entered her number into the phone he handed her. Bailey's friends started to come out of the shop, and Vic looked at his watch and left.

Deacon paused the image on Vic's smug face as he walked away from Bailey. He hit print and heard the printer in his office turn on.

"Is that the man?" Deacon looked up and found Sydney standing behind the couch looking over his shoulder.

"I think this is Vic. I'm emailing it to Ms. Vander to see if this is the same guy she saw having lunch with Bailey."

"Send me a copy of the picture as well. I can send it to my fashion contacts right now. After my shower, I checked my email again. I heard from a few more friends. Tristan Models is in the strange position of having a couple top models out there right now, which allows them certain leeway in the industry's mind. Those who are younger think Tristan is the next hip place to be. Those who are older remember numerous rumors of rape and some models who disappeared."

"So, it's either you love them or you hate them?" Deacon asked as he flipped in a different DVD. He had to push aside his anger and focus on the case. Emotions got in the way of seeing the small clues.

"That's right. What are you looking for now?" Sydney asked as she leaned over his shoulder to look at the image of a side exit.

"I'm looking for where Vic goes. I want to see if I can get a license plate. How did Durante Ingemi get away with raping women, allegedly?" Deacon added sarcastically. No matter how hard he tried to think of them as pieces to the mystery he had to solve, he couldn't.

"Well, the one that my friend told me about was when Durante had offices in New York, L.A., and Milan. It's real easy through coercion. 'If you want to be represented by me, then you'll do this.' Or it's easy for things to get overlooked when they are constantly on the move between different locations around the world. Who is going to believe some poor girl from some farm in the middle of nowhere Poland who can't even speak English or Italian when Durante is sitting next to a high-ranking politician at Milan fashion week? Most women would just keep quiet and go back to their home countries or try another agency."

Deacon looked up from the laptop. His mouth was dry as he looked at the vibrant woman standing behind him. "Did anyone ever hurt you?" he asked quietly. He would kill anyone who had hurt her.

Sydney obviously saw that in his eyes for she stepped back quickly and shook her head. "No. My mom was always with me. She managed me until I was eighteen and attended every meeting and photo shoot I ever had. Even after I was eighteen and had my own agent. Plus my dad . . . well, it's hard to explain Keeneston and my family."

"Your father was the sheriff. I'm sure he taught you self-defense. That's good. If I have a daughter, I'm going to teach her how to protect herself." A daughter with blond hair and hazel eyes popped into his mind. Deacon took a deep breath to slow down his runaway mind.

"Well, yes and no. See, my family is a little . . . how do I say this? Different. My whole hometown is a little different. So, yes, my father taught me self-defense. And so did Aunt Annie, who was DEA. And then Aunt Paige taught me how to shoot. And well, you don't need to know what Ahmed taught me."

"Ahmed?" Deacon asked.

Sydney nodded. "I had a fashion show in Europe. There was some unrest nearby and my mom wanted to make sure I knew how to handle myself. Ahmed is the retired head of security for the royal family of Rahmi. The rumors I've heard from the aunts were that Ahmed was something of a legend. A superb soldier who never failed in a mission, no matter what the circumstances. And judging from what he's taught me, I would say those rumors are definitely true."

"I knew I liked your mother." Deacon grinned before returning to the tapes.

"Dinner will be ready in thirty minutes. I'm going to read some more letters. Since it's raining out, I don't think I'll be able to go digging in the backyard anymore tonight. Maybe I can find a clue," Sydney told him as she grabbed the box of letters from Mrs. Wyatt and took the seat next to him on the couch.

He tried to ignore the sweet smell of her shampoo as he kept his eyes on the screen. People came and went from the mall, and then he finally saw Vic. He watched as the man sauntered onto the sidewalk. He stood smoking a cigarette, and a minute later a car pulled up. He opened the passenger side and got in. As the car drove off, he froze the image on the license plate.

"He's not working alone," Sydney whispered in shock from beside him.

"No, he's not."

Chapter Eight

Sydney jumped up from the couch as the buzzer on the oven went off. She couldn't shake the image of two men taking Bailey from her house and delivering her to Durante.

She shivered as she pulled the baked pasta from the oven. She had finished a couple of her great-grandmother's letters when she had looked over at the screen and had seen Vic walk outside as if no one could touch him. Well, Deacon would find him. She had seen the determination in his eyes. By the way he silently clenched his jaw as he watched Vic get into that car, she knew he would do whatever it took.

"Dinner's ready, Deacon. Or if you're working, I can keep it warm in the oven."

Deacon shook out his shoulders and stood up. "No, that's all right. I'm starving, and this will be a nice break for me. It's hard to keep your distance from a case. But if you let yourself get sucked into the darkness, it'll stick in your mind long after the case is over. And the last thing you want to do is allow evil to turn you evil."

Sydney scooped the pasta onto plates as Deacon filled glasses with wine. They opted for comfort and took their dinner to the couch. Deacon closed the laptop and cleared off the table.

"Did you find anything in Mrs. Wyatt's letters?" Deacon asked.

"I'm learning a lot about the family. It's so strange that she never really talked about them before. I know all about the Wyatts, but the women in her family really were quite extraordinary. I read the letter about the women's suffrage movement. That was really fascinating." Sydney wished her great-grandmother were still here to tell her these things herself.

"I'm sure she wished she could tell you all the stories herself. Maybe you'll find the reason she didn't in the mysterious treasure box," Deacon joked.

"I'm thinking about going to the store tomorrow and getting a metal detector," Sydney smiled back. Then all thoughts of darkness receded as they laughed about their mud fight and whether this box even exists.

"Tell me about yourself," Sydney said as she dried the dishes Deacon had washed.

Deacon shrugged. "I'm not that interesting. I like to help people. I really like football. And I've always wanted a dog. But to tell you the truth, I was afraid my landlady wouldn't like a puppy chewing on an antique chair."

"I have a puppy at home. My parents are watching her while I'm away. I'm going to start taking her with me on business trips when she's a little older. And I like football, too, but not nearly as much as my best friend does. Sienna is Will Ashton's daughter. You know, the former QB for Washington? She could have played college ball except that it would've have thrown the team for a loop. She has a bullet of an arm."

"I think I'm in love. You know both Will Ashton and Trey Everett?"

Sydney laughed. So that's what it took to get his love — football. "Did you ever play?"

Deacon shook his head. "I played rugby, much to my father's distaste. He thought I should play golf. However, I'll let you in on a secret."

"What's that?" Sydney asked as Deacon leaned close.

"I'm horrible at golf. I can't hit the ball straight to save my life."

Sydney dissolved into giggles. "I can't either! I'm hopeless at it. Now, riding — that I can do."

As they cleaned the kitchen, Sydney found herself telling Deacon all about her life. To her surprise, Deacon told her all about his. He even told her about the fight with his father and the fact that they hadn't talked in six years. In return, she cheered him up with stories from Keeneston. The Rose sisters, the three women in their late nineties who practically ran the town's gossip tree, had Deacon laughing the most.

"I can't believe it's already midnight," Sydney said with a sigh. They were sitting next to each other on the couch. Sydney had turned some time ago and swung her legs onto his lap. As they told stories, he had absently rubbed them. The heat from his hand was as much a comfort to her as his voice. And she had been right. Deacon McKnight was a white knight — loyal, loving, and protective.

"I'm going to head upstairs and work on Bailey's

phone. Tomorrow I want to trace this license plate. I have a buddy in the Atlanta PD who will do it for me."

"Sounds good. Tomorrow I'm buying a metal detector. Tonight I'm going to pass out. All that digging has worn me out." Sydney struggled to her feet and yawned.

Deacon picked up his laptop and various cables along with Bailey's phone. He slid his other arm around her waist and together they quietly headed upstairs. Sydney rested her head against his shoulder as they walked up the last few steps. Tonight had been wonderful. And while Deacon didn't kiss her goodnight, she went to bed knowing she wasn't the only one who was interested.

Deacon sat in the darkness of his room reading the texts between Bailey and the unknown number he presumed to be Vic. The heavy drapes were closed and blocked out the flashes of lightning as the storm raged on outside. It was nothing, however, to the storm his emotions were experiencing.

The texts read straight from the sexual predator handbook. Vic had manipulated Bailey into believing he had fallen in love with her. He told her over and over that it was her mother who was the enemy, keeping them apart. The messages stopped when Ms. Vander took the phone away. As soon as she gave it back to Bailey, the texts started again. They were counting down the days until she was eighteen and they could be allowed to love each other. He wanted her to move in with him and together they would build her modeling career.

The one time Bailey had questioned him about the fact

she had cheerleading, the man had berated her. He had embarrassed her by sending back her pictures in lingerie with them marked up, showing how fat and ugly she was. He told her the cheerleaders probably made fun of her for being so disgusting. Only he saw the beauty inside. And only he could shape her into a famous model so she could then rub it in the cheerleaders' faces.

She had immediately written back that she would do whatever he told her to do. She trusted him. She loved him. The man had texted back to Bailey that only he saw the beauty within, but that someday others would, too. That was when Bailey agreed to leave with him. But it was the date that made Deacon close the laptop in excitement. He had a lead. The man told Bailey if she did everything he said, then she would have a big gig in a week. Now he knew she wasn't dead. He just had to figure out where that gig was going to be, and he could rescue Bailey. He knew she was never going to be a model. Sadly, he'd seen it before. She had been sucked into the underground sex trade.

Something was wrong. Sydney had been so tired she'd crawled into bed wearing only her bra and panties and had immediately fallen asleep. But something was pulling her from her sleep. Thunder boomed, lightning crashed, and her skin prickled.

"You're beautiful. But you know that, don't you?"

Sydney tried to keep calm as she sat up in bed. The terrace window was open, rain was blowing in, and a man was sitting at the end of her bed. He was cloaked in the shadows until the lightning flashed, and Sydney got a quick glance at the devil himself.

"I hear you've been looking for me." His menacing voice reached out to her in the night.

The lightning struck again, and this time it wasn't the face of the man she had seen earlier on the surveillance footage that caught her attention, but the glint of light that flashed off the knife resting in his lap.

"Should I call you Vic?" Sydney asked as she slowly moved the sheets away from her body.

Vic looked her over with appreciation. "You can call me whatever you'd like, Sydney. I've had a lot of women, but never one as famous as you."

"And you're not going to have me," Sydney said sweetly as she pushed the sheets off her legs. She wasn't trying to seduce the bastard; she was getting ready to fight for her life.

"Sure I will. Just like I had this sweet young thing the other day. She was a virgin. You should have heard the screams. But after the eighth, or was it the ninth, man that had her? Either way, after that she stopped screaming and hasn't screamed since. I think you'll be a little harder to break, though. Somehow I don't think you're a virgin, either. Pity that. They're always easier to break," he told her evenly as he got up and walked toward her, tossing the knife from hand to hand.

Sydney had to work hard to stop from throwing up. Her stomach clenched and rolled at his words. But she had to focus on the knife. She had to disarm him or else.

"Where is Bailey?" Sydney asked instead of throwing up.

"Wouldn't you like to know," he crowed.

"Duh, that's why I asked."

The man's jaw hardened. He didn't like to be laughed at. "I'll teach you, you slut. How you were ever famous I don't know. You're old and a good thirty pounds too heavy. But when it comes down to it, you're just a woman who's going to be fucked like all the rest of them. You're nothing special. You asked about me, and now you're going to get all you asked for and more."

Sydney stood up quickly. "One, I'm not so easily manipulated. I'm not an innocent teenage girl you weave stories to and manipulate. And two, you're not so hot yourself. I may be thirty glorious pounds heavier than I was when I retired, but eww, your bone structure is horrible. And while I can lose weight if I ever decide to, you can't change ugly. Oh, and one more thing . . ."

Sydney sucked in a deep breath and screamed for all she had. The man leapt at her, and she darted around the bed. She heard Deacon running down the hall shouting her name, but right now she had to concentrate. The man feigned one direction, and she fell for it. The knife slid along the outside of her upper arm, but it also brought Vic close enough for her to get her hands on him. She grabbed at Vic's knife hand. Sydney wrapped her fingers around his wrist in a move Ahmed had taught her and pushed down on the tendons. The knife clattered to the ground, and with a quick kick, the knife went skidding under her bed and out of Vic's reach.

Sydney made a dive for the door, but Vic leapt and grabbed her as they smashed onto the floor. Pain radiated up her arm, but she didn't care. Sydney fought with all she had. She heard the door rattle, but it didn't budge. The thick door was bolted shut. Vic tore at her bra, and Sydney lashed out with an elbow. She connected to his nose and felt the warm blood dripping onto her bare skin.

Vic cursed and went to punch her, but she blocked it with her arms. In a swift move, she bucked her hips and then twisted. He fell to the side, and Sydney pulled back her leg and kicked for all she was worth. He grunted and grabbed for her. She scrambled backward until she was free from his grasp and jumped up. Sydney didn't think twice as she picked up the small antique stool and smashed it over Vic's head. Vic sprawled to the floor with a curse.

"Where is Bailey?" Sydney screamed as she moved to his side and delivered a hard kick to his stomach.

"Where you will never get her," Vic growled as he grabbed the back of her knees and pulled her down hard to the floor. Her knees cracked against the hardwood floor and jarred her body. He used her off-balance momentum to push her down and climb on top of her.

"Now it's time for you to take your punishment. You will learn to keep your mouth shut, or I will come for you again and again. And next time I won't be alone."

Sydney had never felt panic like she felt with Vic pinning her hands above her head as he fumbled with his pants.

"I don't think so," she snarled.

She shot her head up and felt her forehead connect with his. He loosened his grip on her hands, and Sydney went for his eyes. She was screaming so loud she hardly registered the sound of glass shattering. Vic rolled off her and jumped up with a curse.

"I'll be back for you!" he yelled before running through the open window and out onto the terrace.

"Sydney! Are you okay? Are you hurt? Damn, you're bleeding!" Deacon fell to the floor next to her and ran his hands over her, looking for injuries.

"I'm okay. Get him!" Sydney panted. Deacon looked torn, but after a second raced through the large open window.

Sydney lay on her back with her eyes closed as she tried to remember to breathe. Her heart raced, her body throbbed in pain, and she felt as though she were going to be sick.

"He's gone. What the hell happened?" Deacon asked a second before Sydney shot to her knees and crawled to the trashcan to throw up.

Sydney emptied her stomach over and over again. She felt a soft blanket being put over her back. A water glass was set down next to her and then there was Deacon. He was on the phone with the police, but his hand never stopped lightly rubbing her back as she continued to vomit. Finally, she was spent. She pulled the warm throw around her shoulders and collapsed against him.

Deacon had been working in bed when he heard Sydney's scream. The sound of it had sent a shiver through his body, and he had bolted from his bed in the same second. The hallway had never seemed so long as he raced down it. He had slammed his shoulder against the door over and over, but the damn thing hadn't budged.

The muffled sounds of a fight had come through the thick door. After giving it one last kick, he had run back down the hall until he'd come to the empty guest room closest to Sydney's room. Deacon had unlocked those French doors and raced down to the terrace outside Sydney's room. And then he'd heard her scream again. Nothing had mattered. Not him, not the glass doors, nothing. He had flung himself through the first window he came to.

The man on top of her had rolled off and slipped out through the open window. It had been his first instinct to chase after him, but he'd seen Sydney lying on the floor. Part of her bra had been torn off, exposing red marks down her chest. She was smeared all over with blood, and the sight of her looking ready to throw up had brought him to his knees beside her.

"Thank you for coming to my rescue," Sydney said as he held her tight against his chest while waiting for the police to arrive.

Sydney had spent five minutes throwing up and was shaking so uncontrollably he hadn't known what to do but wrap her up and hold her tightly to him.

"It looked like you didn't need me. You weren't kidding about knowing self-defense. I'm just sorry I couldn't have gotten to you sooner."

"He must have locked the door. I didn't lock it," Sydney told him as another shiver went through her body. They were still coming, but not as frequently. The adrenaline was wearing off and the shock was turning to realization.

Deacon saw the lights flashing in the distant night and his urge to protect Sydney grew. "Do you want me to help you get dressed?" he asked quietly.

Sydney choked back a cry and slowly nodded. "He . . . he tried. I didn't let him. But he did it to Bailey. Oh God!" Sydney buried her head into his bare chest and sobbed.

Having all the police and other emergency responders find her wearing only half a bra and her panties would just further affect her. So, as she clung to him, he scooped her up in his arms and carried her to his room. He dug out a pair of sweatpants and a sweatshirt. The pants covered her feet and had to be rolled at her waist, but as Sydney sat there quietly crying, he dressed her as if she were a child, knowing the thick, big clothes would make her feel safe.

"Do you want to stay here or come with me?" Deacon asked as he ran his hand over her hair.

"I need to stay with you, please," Sydney begged as she reached for him.

"I won't leave you. I promise," Deacon swore, and he knew without a doubt he never wanted to leave this woman again for the rest of his life.

He put his arm around her waist and pulled her up. Slowly, they headed downstairs. By the time they opened the front door, police were pouring out of their cars and racing forward. An ambulance was right behind them, as was the detective he'd worked with on the Salem case.

"McKnight! What the hell happened here? Is everyone all right?" he asked more gently this time as Sydney came into view.

"We will be. She has a cut on her arm the EMTs need to look at, and a knife the intruder had was kicked under the bed. There're also some photographs that need to be taken, but it might be better if there was a woman to do that."

Sydney shook her head. "No, the detective can do it. You trust him. That's what matters. Can Deacon stay with me?"

Deacon felt a lump in his throat. He just wanted to protect her, but her shivers had stopped. While she held onto him, she was no longer leaning on him. She was strong, and she wanted to see this through on her own terms.

"Of course. I'm Detective Gentry, ma'am. Let's go into a private room and I'll take the pictures, then Deacon can make us both a nice pot of hot tea or coffee, and we'll talk if you're up for it."

Deacon sent the detective a thankful smile over Sydney's head. The old, tough lawman turned into a doting father around Sydney, and that alone was worth all of Deacon's thanks.

The next two hours seemed to go on forever. Pictures were taken. Blood evidence was collected, and Deacon had escorted Sydney upstairs to his bathroom to take a hot shower while Gentry talked with the crew collecting evidence from Sydney's bedroom. Sydney emerged from the shower looking much better than she had after the incident.

"Thank you, Deacon. You've been so kind to me. I'm sorry I fell apart there," Sydney said quietly as they walked downstairs to meet with Gentry in the living room.

Deacon stopped her on the stairs and made her turn to look at him. "Sydney, you didn't fall apart. You did what needed to be done. You're a strong woman who didn't give up. I . . . ." Deacon caught himself. He was going to tell her he loved her, but this wasn't the time. "I'm proud of you."

Sydney gave him a tentative smile. "Thank you." She rose up on her bare toes and placed a soft kiss on his cheek.

The sound of a throat clearing pulled her away, but it wasn't quickly as if embarrassed. Sydney looked up at him and smiled tenderly before entwining her fingers with his. "I'm ready, Detective."

Chapter Nine

How, out of something so dark, could there be light? Sydney stood next to Deacon as they said goodbye to the kindly detective. After a hellish night, feeling anything romantic was far from her mind. But Deacon proved himself to her over and over again through the night. Proved that he cared for her; proved that he was a good, kind, and honorable man. And through the night, her heart wanted more with Deacon McKnight.

"Are you ready for bed, Syd?" Deacon asked as he closed and locked the door.

Sydney felt a shiver run down her back. "I don't think I can go back into that room."

"You can stay in one of the other guest rooms," Deacon suggested.

Sydney looked up into Deacon's face. She took the time to see his chestnut eyes turn dark with emotion. She looked to his lips, full and soft, and his jaw, hard and clenched as if he were having trouble controlling his emotions. She shook her head.

"I don't want to be alone. May I sleep in your room?"

Deacon took a slow gulp and nodded. "Of course. I'll sleep on the couch."

Sydney shook her head again. Deacon's eye pulsed as if fighting for control, but he didn't question her. Instead, he quietly led her upstairs. Sydney just hoped whatever internal battle he was fighting would end with him having some kind of feelings for her. So far, he had been a confusing read. All the signs would be there, but then he'd pull back. No, running away at full speed was more like it.

It was a first, though, that someone wanted to get to know her before doing anything physical. It was very chivalrous. The side effect of that was she had wanted desperately for something physical to happen. There was no bigger turn-on than a gentleman. However, tonight she just wanted to be held safely as she thought about the new feelings she had developed for Deacon.

Deacon pulled back the covers to the bed and waited for Sydney to crawl in. She was still wearing his sweats, and she gave him a sweet smile and climbed into his bed. How many fantasies had he had about the unknown, unseen great-granddaughter doing just this? Then he couldn't keep up the fantasies he'd had when he found out the girl he'd fallen in love with through letters was as beautiful, kind, and strong as Sydney.

He ground his jaw tightly together as he turned off the lamp and went to lie stiffly on the other side of the bed. She'd just suffered a trauma, and he wasn't about to do anything tonight except think of ways to comfort her. He was a nobody compared to the men she'd dated. He wanted to settle down with someone he loved and start a family, have a home, and she . . . well, she was jet-setting around the globe, running one of the fastest-growing companies in the world.

"Deacon," Sydney whispered quietly into the dark.

"Yes?"

"Will you hold me?"

Deacon swallowed hard, but if she had asked for the moon he would have gotten it for her. And if she needed a warm body next to her to feel safe, then he would do that, too.

He rolled over onto his side, and she snuggled against him. Her head lay on his arm and her back was to his chest. Her bottom was pressed against him and no matter what he thought about, he couldn't stop from going hard. He was afraid it would scare her, but she just wiggled her bottom against him and sighed. Deacon held his breath and didn't move a muscle. With his other arm wrapped around her stomach, Sydney's breathing slowed and soon she was asleep. How—after having this for one night— would he ever be able to sleep alone again?

"I found it!" Sydney screamed as she jumped up from the kitchen table. Deacon was making breakfast and, still dressed in his sweats, she had picked up some more of her great-grandmother's letters.

Deacon slid some scrambled eggs onto her plate and smiled. She had woken first to find his hand cupping her breast and his erection against her bottom. This was heaven. The warmth and comfort of being next to him left her heart doing funny things.

"What does it say?" Deacon asked as she went to the oven for the biscuits.

"It's talking about an old oak tree in the backyard. Great-grandma writes that they named the tree Michael, as in the archangel. The tree had stood for hundreds of years protecting those who lived here. It's the tree in the middle of the yard, set slightly back from all the others."

"And you think that's the tree your ancestors buried the treasure under?" Deacon asked.

Sydney nodded her head. "It has to be. After breakfast, I'm going on a treasure hunt."

Sydney marked off five strides and stood still as Deacon marked the spot. She stepped back and, with excitement strumming through her body, watched as Deacon started digging.

"What will you do if it's not here?" Deacon asked.

"I guess go home," Sydney said, the excitement suddenly dying. "I have to be back after Valentine's Day to meet with the board of directors."

"Oh," Deacon said simply as he dug farther into the ground.

Oh was right. No more nights waking up with Deacon's arms around her. No more teasing. No more dinners where they talked about their lives and their dreams. Suddenly, her life didn't seem as interesting if Deacon wasn't there to share it.

"I heard the phone ring while I was changing," Sydney stated to change the subject. She didn't want to think about leaving just yet.

Deacon grunted as he dug the shovel into the cold earth. "Yeah, it was Detective Gentry. They've put out an APB on Vic's description. They've called Tristan Models, but no one is admitting they know him, and Durante is unavailable at this time."

"But it's what we fear it is, isn't it?" Sydney asked, not really wanting to hear the answer.

Deacon's jaw tightened in a move she came to realize was a way he used to control his emotions. "Yes. From what we saw on the video, the text messages, and what Vic told you, it appears Bailey is lost in the underworld of sex trafficking. They target girls with emotional problems at home and Bailey had those. She felt abandoned by her father and took it out on her mother. From the texts, it looked like Vic had no problem making her fall in love with him. Then traffickers break their victims, just as Vic told you."

"What do we do now?" Sydney asked.

"We?"

Sydney shot him a determined smile. "I'm not going anywhere until we find Bailey. I can't just leave her out there."

"I won't let that happen. I'll find her or what's left of the Bailey her mother knew."

"I'll get her help. I'll immediately get her into a recovery center and even pay for Ms. Vander to move nearby while Bailey's in therapy. There's too much bad in the world and if I can stop it, even just a little, then good wins. The only thing necessary for the triumph of evil is for good men to do nothing."

"Edmund Burke," Deacon said with surprise. "That quote is one of the main reasons I do what I do."

Sydney and Deacon fell quiet instantly as the sound of the shovel connecting with something solid reverberated in the cold winter morning. Their eyes shot to each other as Sydney scrambled to her feet and hurried to look into the hole Deacon had dug.

"Is it really there?" Sydney asked with excitement.

Deacon shoveled out some more dirt and smiled. "It's a trunk!"

Sydney dropped to her knees and started pushing the dirt from the top of the trunk. It was covered in some kind of leather with large, black leather straps around it. Deacon continued to dig out the dirt all around it, and soon the trunk was unearthed.

"I can't believe it," Sydney said with awe as she jumped to give Deacon a hug. Her breasts pressed against his chest, her breathing quickened, and she didn't care. She wanted to run her hand down the ridges of his abdomen; she wanted their tongues to dance and to feel the euphoria of finally coming together.

His jaw tightened again, and he stepped back. "Well, what are we waiting for? Let's get this thing inside."

He bent over and pulled, but the trunk wouldn't budge. "Here, I'll get this end."

Sydney moved to grab one end and Deacon grabbed the other. Together they lifted with all their strength. The box dislodged from the dirt and they heaved it up onto the grass.

"That thing weighs a ton," Deacon said as he breathed heavily.

"It's probably the family silver," Sydney panted.

"I have a dolly; let me get that, and we'll wheel it inside," Deacon told her as he took off, jogging for the garage. That was fine by her. She didn't want that trunk dropping on her toes.

"Okay, I'll lift this end and you wedge the dolly underneath it," Deacon instructed as he walked back with it behind him.

Sydney stood and took control of the dolly. Deacon bent and hissed out his breath as he lifted the edge of the trunk. Sydney moved fast and slid the metal lip of the dolly underneath. They worked together to move it into the mudroom and set it on some old towels.

"Look," Sydney gasped. There in faded gold lettering were the initials *E.M.W.* "This was Elizabeth Woodbury's trunk."

Deacon looked at the dirt-caked lock holding it closed. He reached down and gave it a tug. The lock held. He used his thumb to clear off some of the dirt, and Sydney leaned forward to give it a good look.

"That lock doesn't look like it's a couple hundred years old," she said as she stared at it.

"Any idea if you have the key or should I just bust it open?" Deacon asked.

Sydney thought about it for a second. "Let me look in the family Bible. It's so large that I could have missed something."

She hurried through the living room and up the stairs. Deacon had moved all of her things into the room next to his while repairmen replaced the broken glass window in her great-grandmother's old room. Sydney jumped onto the bed, pulled the heavy book from the nightstand, and placed it on the bed, careful not to damage the relic.

Sydney looked inside the front cover and then quickly thumbed through the pages making sure nothing was hidden inside. She carefully turned to the back cover and nearly jumped when she saw it. Two small keys were taped to the inside back cover.

"I found it!" Sydney screamed as she peeled away the tape and palmed the keys. She raced down the stairs, hurtled an ottoman in the living room, and slid to a stop next to Deacon.

"Here," she said, shoving the keys into his hand.

"Two keys?" Deacon asked as he looked at them closely.

"I don't know. They're about the same size, but that one seems newer and the head is very narrow on it," Sydney said, pointing to the shiny key.

"There's no way it fits this trunk, but it does fit something." He held up the black key. "This, however, has to be it."

Deacon had cleaned off the lock while she was upstairs. It looked old, but not dating back to the 1700s. He slid the key in, and after a little jiggling, the thick lock clicked open. Sydney held her breath as Deacon worked to pry the heavy lid open. With a groan and a creak, it gave way and finally lifted. She had done it. Sydney had found the family treasure.

Chapter Ten

Sydney breathed in and coughed. Her family treasure stunk! When Deacon lifted the lid, all she could see were layers of tan canvases overlapping. The trunk looked to be constructed of wood and then covered both on the inside and outside with leather. Then large sheets of canvas enclosed all the items.

"What is that? And why does it smell?" Sydney gasped as Deacon got up and opened the outside door. He tried not to turn green from the stench. The fresh air blew into the room as he also reached up to turn on the ceiling fan.

"It's waterproof canvas. The old-fashioned way to waterproof was with wax and oil. I know you want to jump right in, but let's let it air out with the fan for a bit. You never know if anything toxic has built up over time." Deacon guided a disappointed Sydney into the kitchen and closed the door between the two rooms. "I'll make you lunch, and then we can go in and check it out."

"I hate sitting here doing nothing," Sydney told him as she took a seat on the bar top.

Deacon reached for some bread and started making sandwiches. The night before, as he held Sydney in his arms, his mind had turned to losing her. He ran over every word the attacker had said to her and one thing had stuck out.

"We won't be doing *nothing*. We're going to work on finding Bailey. Something bothered me. He knew you had been looking for him. One of the people you emailed must have told him."

Deacon saw Sydney recoil in shock. "You're right. I can't believe one of my friends would be caught up in this. It's too horrible to even contemplate. The only people I emailed were people I've worked with for many years."

"Tell me about them. Who did you email and how do you know them?" Deacon asked as he pulled lettuce and tomato from the stainless steel refrigerator.

"I emailed my mom. I think we can cross her off the list," Sydney said dryly. "Then I emailed my old agent. I worked with her for six years. She's the one who told me about their shady reputation."

Deacon nodded as he cataloged the probability of the leak. "Most likely not. Who else?"

"I emailed some of my fellow models. None of them has ever been with Tristan, and they're women I traveled all across the world with. They're like sisters to me." Sydney took a deep breath and Deacon could see the thought cross her face that one of them had sold her out.

"Which one don't you trust?" he asked quietly.

"Emily Tamlin. We were close, but not as close as the others. She was always more concerned about being friends with us so she could use us than being a true friend. However, she was never mean about it. Just opportunistic."

"Anyone else?"

"Patrick Mawler. He's a famous photographer. Then there was Teddy Brown, the designer. That's everyone I emailed."

"What do you think of Patrick and Teddy?" Deacon asked as he sliced the sandwich in half and put it on a plate for her.

"They're geniuses. They've worked with everyone. They said they knew Durante, but they didn't go into much detail and said they never heard of one of his agents named Vic or a girl named Bailey."

"I think we have to put Emily, Patrick, and Teddy on the suspect list. I'll do some research into them and see if I can find a connection to Tristan." Deacon pushed the plate across the island to Sydney. She took it and didn't say much as she ate. That was fine with Deacon. He was too busy thinking of Bailey.

The night she left, she would have been taken somewhere private. Human traffickers worked by making their victims fall in love with them. They manipulated the young girls into relying on them for everything. Sometimes that took weeks. But, judging by the looks of the emails and texts Deacon found, Vic had already started brainwashing Bailey.

After Vic had her eating out of his hand, he would start the sob story. That he needed money to save his mother, sister, or grandmother. That he needed money to finance her career or any other excuse he could make her believe. After casually bringing up how beautiful she was and how anyone would pay a fortune to be her boyfriend, he would break her. Sometimes it was by force. Sometimes the girls willingly believed it would just be once to help the man they love. But it was never just once.

Vic would have to be sure he had completely broken her will and convinced her she would be abandoned if she called home or tried to escape. He would tell her that her mother would call her a whore and turn her back on her. Or possibly that if she went home he'd kill her mother. He would tell her he'd release the video of her with all the men. He'd remind her of the money she'd turned over to him for his sick relative or whatever tale he had spun. Then Vic would convince her she was a criminal for taking money for sex. If she went to the police, she would be arrested and sent to jail.

Vic would do or say anything to keep Bailey dependent on him. Drugs were most likely involved as well as a means to blur reality for Bailey. It was when she felt as if she had no options but to stay that Vic would sell her or turn her into a prostitute. And that's when she would be moved. That's when her trail would turn into dark whispers in the shadows of the night upon the lips of men so evil even the devil would shudder.

Tonight he would go out into that world and find her. He only hoped she had held on. If Bailey remained defiant, then she might still be in town. If not, he only hoped he could go deep enough into the shadows to find her.

Sydney ate quietly. Her mind had drifted from what was in her family's trunk to finding Bailey. What Vic had told her had given her nightmares. Only the feel of Deacon's strong arms holding her to the present prevented her from losing herself in the horror of Vic's words.

Could one of her friends really be in league with Vic?

There was no other way for him to find out about her connection to Bailey. It had to be Emily, Patrick, or Teddy. She pulled out her phone and sent a text to each of them as Deacon worked on his computer across from her. She thanked each for their help and then told them she'd like to pay them back. She asked if they were going to be anywhere nearby so she could take them out to dinner. And then she waited.

Emily was the first to get back to her. She has a photo shoot in Spain and wouldn't be back in the United States for another two weeks. Teddy was next. He wasn't going to be in Kentucky, but he would be at the football championship game in Indianapolis the next week. There was a party he'd been invited to. Sadly, he didn't think he'd have the time to come to Keeneston for a visit. Finally Patrick replied. He too was going to be at the football game in Indianapolis as he shot some of the campaigns to promote the game.

"Too bad I only got one ticket or you could join me. I've heard the game is completely sold out. Unfortunately, the next morning I'll be flying to St. Barts for a photo shoot." Sydney read to Deacon.

She put down her phone and looked at Deacon. He had stopped doing research as soon as she had started to read the texts to him. She could see his mind working as he dissected every word.

"Do you find it strange they're both going to the football game?" Deacon finally asked.

Sydney shrugged. "It is one of the biggest events of the year. It's the place to be seen. A lot of models are married to football stars, and I have no doubt Teddy designed half of the wives' blinged-out jerseys. They'll be there for all the cameras and all the attention. It's the same with the Derby."

Deacon pursed his lips in thought. "And big sporting events like those are when human trafficking is at the highest. Do you think they could both be involved?"

Sydney felt her stomach plummet and then bounce up to her throat. She swallowed hard at the idea. "I hope not. I just don't know anymore."

"I need to talk to some of my contacts and then meet with Detective Gentry. I'll try to find out as much as I can about trafficking and see if Gentry has been able to get a lead on Vic or Bailey."

Deacon reached across the island and covered her hand with his. "I'm sorry you were attacked, but the good news is now the police are looking for Bailey. So, want to see what's in the trunk before I make my calls?"

Sydney let out the breath she was holding. It was too much horror to think about. Focusing on the trunk gave her a break from thinking of what was happening to Bailey. "You don't have to do that."

"I want to. I'll grab a bunch of clean sheets and lay them out here in the living room. I'll help you carry all the items out and spread them out for you to look over." Deacon squeezed her hand and turned to the mudroom. "Ready to see your family treasure?"

As she stared at the door, Sydney fingered the ring her great-grandmother had given her. Whatever secrets her family had been holding onto were about to come to light. "Yes, let's see what my family has been hiding."

Sydney followed Deacon into the mudroom. The smell

had decreased significantly, thank goodness. Deacon opened a cabinet and pulled out what looked like a tissue box, but instead of pulling out tissues, he pulled out latex gloves and handed her a pair before slipping on his own.

"To help preserve anything delicate and also you probably don't want to be touching some of this directly," he explained as he moved to open the layers of canvas tied tightly closed.

Deacon used a knife to slice open the twine and pull apart the canvas. Sydney held her breath and then rolled her eyes. There were multiple layers. Once again she was left waiting as Deacon reached to the far right and sliced open the canvas, pulled it open, and then sliced a third layer on the far left.

"It appears to be dry. It's a pain to open, but setting down so many layers seems to have kept the water out. Here we go," Deacon said finally as he pushed aside the canvas.

Sydney leaned forward and looked into the trunk. More fabric. Everything was wrapped in unbleached muslin and tied with ribbon. "It looks like someone really made sure to pack these with long-term care in mind. This may take a while," she said as she tried to make out how many items were in the trunk.

"I'll help you take them out, then let you at them," Deacon told her, and he reached into the trunk and pulled out the first big wrapped item. He carried it to the far side of the living room and set it down.

Sydney reached into the trunk and pulled out the next bundle. Strange. It seemed there were multiple items in the bundle. She carefully carried the awkward bundle into the living room and lowered it onto a separate sheet.

She stood and watched Deacon carry in the last bundle. She watched him silently as he bent over and placed the bundle ever so carefully onto the floor. Sydney didn't know what to think of him. Deacon was unlike any man she'd known outside of Keeneston. He didn't seem to care about her wealth or her job. He didn't ask to go in her plane or for her to buy him a sports car. He didn't even bring up finances, where she had houses, or what VIP rooms she liked to party in. He didn't try to impress her, and he certainly didn't try to get into her pants. In fact, it was the complete opposite. Deacon talked to her about Keeneston, her friends, and her family. He asked her what her interests were, talked to her about her puppy, and told her things her great-grandmother had told him. He wanted to hear some of the funny stories from growing up and asked about the Rose sisters and the Blossom Café.

Deacon's arms flexed as he gently set her family history onto the ground, and Sydney thought about having woken with those arms wrapped around her. She had felt their warmth, their strength, and had instinctively curled closer to Deacon. Then she had felt it. It had been as soft and fleeting as the beat of a butterfly's wings, but she had felt Deacon's lips against her neck before he slid from the bed. It hadn't been the action of a man who wanted to use her. It had been the action of a man who cared about her. In fact, all of his actions pointed to that. Deacon McKnight was tough, smart, and sexy as hell. He was also secure enough with himself to be gentle, supportive, and caring in a way that tumbled her heart into love.

"Oh shit," Sydney gasped as her brain processed the

feeling. She had wanted to kiss him simply because he hadn't reacted to her the way other men had in the past. Instead, he had proved he cared for *her* as a person, not as a model, not as a businesswoman, but for Sydney Davies. And she loved him for it.

"What is it? Are you okay?" Deacon asked as he hurried to her side with worry filling his eyes.

Sydney looked up at him. Oh no. She had it bad. Love couldn't happen this fast. Ryan and Sienna had hated each other for years . . . well, that wasn't exactly true. They had always loved each other; they just had to get out of their own way. But her parents proved time mattered. They told her they had started off not liking each other. Her father thought her mother was a spoiled brat, and her mother thought her father liked to intimidate people. Sydney cringed as she remembered them telling her their love story. But they had shared a love that was undeniable, even if they fought it. And when they had stopped fighting and had gotten out of their own way — well, they couldn't be more in love, even after thirty-one years of marriage. Story after story from her family all proved that once a Davies fell in love, they were in love. Forever.

"Sydney? You've gone white. Are you ill? Here, sit down." Deacon guided her to the couch and sat next to her. He looked worried.

"Sydney, breathe," Deacon ordered. Sydney finally reacted and sucked in air. Her head was spinning, her heart was pounding, and southern manners told her not to mention what was happening to other parts of her body.

"I'll call a doctor," Deacon told her as he reached for his phone.

Sydney shook her head and grabbed his hand. "No! No, it's okay. I'm okay. I was just overwhelmed for a minute."

Damn. A look of concern softened his hard jawline, and his eyes turned so tender she thought she would swoon just so he would catch her. Sydney closed her eyes to collect herself. A couple days in her ancestral home and she had reverted two hundred years.

She smiled at her own joke and opened her eyes. "Really, I'm fine. Thank you, Deacon." Then she decided to toss out the old ways of swooning at a man's feet. Now southern girls were taught to shoot a gun, throw a football, and down a shot of bourbon. And certainly how to kiss a man the way he deserves.

Deacon was worried. Something had happened to Sydney. She had been standing there looking down at the bundle she had just placed on the floor before glancing up to see him place the last of the trunk near her in the living room. Those sexy hazel eyes had gone glassy, her delicious lips had opened on a gasp, and all the color had drained from her face. She looked like she was ready to faint. She just stared blankly at him as if she were in another world.

It didn't get any better until he'd ordered her to breathe. He heard her suck in air as some of the color returned to her face. It wasn't until he told her he was going to call the doctor that Sydney finally blinked. But now, now she wasn't looking through him like she had been. No, now she looked determined. Color rushed to her cheeks, her eyes hooded with passion, and suddenly her voice wasn't distant. It was husky, as he'd dreamed of her sounding in the bedroom.

"I'm glad you're all right. You had me worried . . ." Deacon didn't get to finish his sentence. Sydney fisted both hands into the front of his shirt and pulled.

His mouth opened with surprise, and Sydney took advantage. Her warm tongue slid into his mouth and caressed his. Her lips were soft but sure as they moved over his. Deacon pulled back and looked into eyes dark green with desire. Flecks of golden brown streaked through them like lightning.

She wanted him. And not just to pass the time. She really wanted him. And he wanted her. Deacon kissed her back. He leaned back against the couch, and she followed without breaking the kiss. The room melted away. The whole world melted away until it was just the two of them. He placed his hands on her hips and picked her up. Sydney gave a squeak of surprise until he put her down on his lap. Her legs straddled his hips, her hands were still locked on his shirt, and her squeak turned into a moan as he moved his hands slowly up from her hips, over her ribs, and to her breasts.

He listened to her breathing change as he circled her nipple slowly. Deacon was overtaken by a desire to learn what caused every throaty moan, every unconscious tilt of her hips, every gasp, and every cry of desire.

Deacon rolled her nipple between his fingers, and she gasped. He trailed his fingertips teasingly down her spine, and she moaned softly. Deacon wanted to spend a lifetime getting to know every reaction she had to him. Nothing had ever turned him on more than knowing he was pleasing Sydney.

"Deacon, please," she gasped and rocked her hips against him. He wanted nothing more than to take her hard and fast right here, but he wasn't going to. He wanted to go slowly. To worship every inch of her body and to have her moaning his name long before they finally made love.

She rocked her hips again, and he moved both hands to her breasts. He was about to unhook her bra when the phone interrupted them. He was going to ignore it. Her breasts would take precedence over any phone call, but Sydney pulled back.

"You better get that. It may have to do with Bailey," she said as she adjusted her shirt.

Deacon groaned as he realized she was right. He dug into his pocket and pulled out his phone. "McKnight," he said, a little more harshly than he intended.

"It's Gentry. I have something on Bailey Vander. How fast can you be here?"

"Syd and I can be there—" Deacon didn't have time to finish the sentence before Gentry cut him off.

"She can't come. You'll understand."

"I can't leave her alone," Deacon told the detective. "Not a chance. Not after Vic came here."

"I figured that. I have two patrol officers en route."

"Give me twenty minutes," Deacon told him as he was already turning off the phone and looking up at Sydney. "I'm sorry, darlin', but it's about Bailey. Some officers will be here shortly to keep an eye on the place."

As if it were the most natural thing in the world, Deacon kissed her as he walked out the door. "I'll call you when I know something. Lock the doors."

He smiled as he slid into the car. He loved the idea of coming home to Sydney every day. The only trouble was, he knew when this was over she wouldn't be there to greet him.

Chapter Eleven

S ydney stood at the door and watched Deacon until he disappeared from sight. She couldn't stop thinking about him. And her. And them. She didn't know how long she stood staring at the empty driveway, but her phone vibrating in her pocket finally pulled her back into the now.

"Hi, Mom." Sydney smiled into the phone.

"John Wolfe said you were attacked while staying at Grandma Wyatt's house in Atlanta. Are you okay? What happened? When are you coming home? Do you want your father to come pick you up?" Her mom peppered one question after another.

Sydney just shook her head but let out the long breath she'd been holding. It felt good to hear from her mom. And she didn't even want to know how John, who was approaching 100 years old, had heard about the attack. It was Keeneston's biggest mystery. Some say he had the whole town bugged, but that wouldn't explain how he figured out when things happened outside their small town. Others thought he was a mystic. And then a growing contingent of people believed aliens told him.

"Mom, slow down and let me answer," Sydney rolled

her eyes.

"Don't roll your eyes at me. It's my job as your mother to worry."

"Mom! I'm a grown woman," Sydney said for the millionth time, not even asking how her mom knew she'd rolled her eyes. Maybe the aliens were talking to her, too.

"Does she want me to come get her?" she heard her dad ask in the background.

"I don't know, she won't answer."

"Mom, I don't need Dad to pick me up," Sydney insisted.

"She says she doesn't, but go ahead and pack a bag in case you have to go down there," her mom told her father as she tried, and failed, to cover the phone.

"Marshall Davies, don't you dare pack that bag," an old voice said somewhere in the background of her parents' house.

"Is that Grandma Davies?" Sydney asked her mom. Marcy Davies was her father's mother, and that sharp order spoke of rearing six children.

"Yes, she and your grandpa are here to watch the UK basketball game," her mother said absently as Grandma Davies and Sydney's father argued over whether he should pack a bag and drive to Atlanta.

Sydney dropped onto the couch and closed her eyes. She loved her family, and there had never been one day in her whole life she hadn't felt loved in return. But right now she was feeling a little too loved.

"She is a grown woman, Marshall Davies," her grandmother lectured. "If she needs help, she'll ask for it. My goodness, I thought I was done raising y'all. And you thought I interfered in your lives. Hello, pot, meet kettle."

Sydney snickered and drew her mother's attention back to her. "Fine, I won't send your father. But what are you still doing in Atlanta? What happened? Are you . . .?"

"Mom," Sydney cut off her litany of questions. "I am fine. That Vic guy broke into the house to tell me to stop asking questions about Tristan Models. That's suspicious, right? It also means someone told him I was asking. I'm assuming it's not you," Sydney teased.

"Of course it's not me! I knew you were in trouble when you asked about them. They're no good. There have always been people like that. People who prey on those weaker than themselves."

"I know. That's why I'm still here. I'm not weak, and I'll be damned if I let them get away with this."

"But are you safe?" her mother asked worriedly.

"Yes. I broke his nose. And Deacon busted in a window to protect me. In fact, he just had to leave to follow a lead and made sure a police cruiser would check on me."

"Deacon? Who's Deacon?" her mother asked suddenly.

"Deacon? Who the hell is that?" She heard the hard edge in her father's voice.

"If you want grandbabies, you'll hang up that phone right now!" her grandmother ordered.

"I don't want grandbabies. Do you know how grandbabies are made?" her father yelled.

"Well, I want grandbabies," her mother yelled back and suddenly the phone went dead. A second later, her phone pinged and Sydney pulled up the new text message.

We love you. Call us if you need anything. Can't wait
to meet Deacon. – Mom

Sydney groaned again and tossed the phone onto the other end of the couch. She had more important things to worry about than her mom's grandbaby schemes and her dad's grandbaby fears. In front of her were three wrapped bundles from the past. She was ready to fulfill her promise to her great-grandmother to find the treasure and bring it home.

She stopped at the last bundle to be set down. It must be the oldest since it was at the bottom of the trunk. It was held together by a yellow ribbon, which had faded and frayed over time. Her hands shook as she tried to untie a ribbon that could be hundreds of years old. And sure enough, when she tried to pull it, the ribbon frayed and started to fall apart. Not wanting to destroy the whole thing, Sydney went to the kitchen for a pair of scissors and carefully cut the base of the knot.

She pulled back the fabric, and almost cursed. She sat back on her heels and stared at the multiple bundles in front of her now, each separately wrapped. On top of them was a small, flat wrapped package with a large ribbon. She laid it out first and then the large heavy rectangular object and finally a soft clumsy bundle that she left lying where it was. Syd almost started to open the bundles when she saw a pale yellow ribbon sticking out from underneath the soft bundle she had thought was the bottom of the pile. She lifted the edge of the material and pulled out a small pouch of a bundle that clinked as it was moved.

Deciding that would be as good a place as any to start,

Syd neatly cut off the ribbon and opened the unbleached material. A dark tan leather pouch was inside, and it jangled as Sydney moved her hand. She took her time untying the thin leather straps holding it closed and slowly emptied the contents onto the ground.

"Holy . . ." Sydney couldn't even finish her surprised gasp as she stared at gleaming gold and silver coins. Her fingers shook as she picked them up and looked at them. Some appeared to be British, while she thought others might be French and Italian. There were over thirty of them in the pouch. Sydney didn't know how long she stared at them until the shock wore off.

She then went for the large soft package that had been sitting on top of the coins. Carefully opening it, she looked down at a beautiful cream-colored silk dress. A vine and flower pattern covered the dress as lace edging trimmed the low square neck and V-shaped stomacher. The dress was carefully folded and preserved. "I can't believe it," Syd whispered in shock as she jumped up and ran for the mudroom.

She pulled out a pair of latex gloves and wished she had a pair of all-natural cotton gloves to handle the delicate material. She didn't want to risk getting any of her body oils on such an old and beautiful dress.

Sydney took her time and unfolded the dress while piling the wrappings up in the corner of the room. The dress had elbow-length sleeves with lace flowing from the edges. The back of the dress had room for petticoats and any extra undergarments they wore at the time. It was simply stunning. Like a child at Christmas, Syd turned to the heavy bundle and opened it. An oil painting was tacked onto a wooden board. In the painting a young man and woman stared back at Sydney with the barest quirk of their lips. The woman in the portrait was wearing the dress Syd had just unpacked.

"Who are you?" Sydney whispered as she stared at the portrait. The small package caught her eye, and Sydney hurried to open it. Inside was a folded parchment, and Sydney read the shaky handwriting.

20th day of this October in the year of our Lord 1770.

I have lived a full life. I am dying, and I am lucky enough to know it for it gives me time to reflect on my life. I was born into privilege. I traveled the continent in preparation for my first Season. After all, as a future duchess, I should be well travelled, well spoken, and intelligent without necessarily being so. But after meeting my intended, I knew I had no choice but to flee my family, my friends, and my homeland.

I married my true love, Mr. John Abbott, and in our marriage I found a treasure grander than the duke's Mayfair House and worth more than all his money. I found love and happiness.

I gave birth to three boys and one girl we named Agatha. John and I worked hard to show our children a marriage of happiness and love. In return, our children looked for and found their own happiness and success in life.

My dear Agatha married a wonderful man, Stephan, and gave birth to a beautiful girl, Sarah. Harder than leaving all I had known to travel to a new country was welcoming a granddaughter an hour before losing my daughter. Stephan moved onto our farm so

*that I might help with little Sarah, and it's because of
her I'm writing this letter from my deathbed. For I
never want any daughter of mine to be in a position to
be forced to wed for money or property. Therefore, I have
given little ten-year-old Sarah my trunk I used to cross
the mighty Atlantic, my wedding dress, and the portrait
of my dear John and me on our wedding day so she will
know to always look for love and never settle for
anything less. I've also included all the money from my
trip on the continent for her to live on in case love
cannot be found. I now know I can leave this place and
see my dear John again in Heaven knowing that Sarah,
and all my daughters after her, are cared for.*

~ Elizabeth Woodbury Abbott

Sydney wiped the tears from her eye. Sarah must have
found love for she didn't touch the contents of the trunk.
But did that mean she added to it? Sydney scrambled on
her hands and knees for the second bundle. She hurried to
open the pale blue ribbon tied around it and was somehow
not surprised to pull out four wrapped packages. A small
one that clanked, a small one that looked to hold a letter, a
soft bundle, and a large hard one.

In a matter of minutes Sydney had the bundles open.
She looked down at a pouch full of British pounds sterling,
Spanish dollars, and what had to be new-at-the-time
American paper money issued by New York, New Jersey,
and Massachusetts, followed by American gold and silver
coins. A peach-colored, iridescent silk gown with lace-
edged elbow-length sleeves, rounded hem, ruched bodice,
and square neckline covered with a neck kerchief and

finished with a blue sash lay on the floor next to a painting
of a man and woman smiling close-lipped, the woman
wearing the peach gown. And finally Sydney opened the
letter.

7ᵗʰ day of March, 1839

*I am a grandmother to another little girl. Laura was
born last night. My second granddaughter and my
tenth grandchild. She came out screaming, and I had
never heard such a sound. It was demanding, persistent,
and utterly reminded me of myself. With Laura's birth,
I know when I depart this world I will leave to her the
security my grandmother left me. A security I luckily
never needed that I can now pass on to little Laura.*

*I have lived what some may say is a harrowing life.
But it was that independence and bravery Grandmama
Elizabeth taught me that led me to my own treasure,
Thad Majory. I will never forget that 7ᵗʰ day of October,
1777. The Revolutionary War was in full battle, and
our little farm near Saratoga became part of it. Father
was fighting for the colonies and had been called north
to fight with our local militia. At seventeen, I was put
in charge of my little brothers, and in the early morning
mist, I headed out to hunt. That morning I was
determined to get us some game, for the Crown had
taken our family's cows and pigs, and we had not eaten
meat in a month.*

*What I got instead was trapped in a tree as some
British soldiers came marching through the woods. They
were headed to Mr. Barber's wheat field, and I
overheard the command to divide their forces to try to
surprise General Gates. My father was on the other side*

of that farm in Bemis Heights with General Gates. The
fear of losing my father prompted me to climb slowly
from the tree and dart through the woods behind and
then around the British. It took me hours, but as the sun
was close to ten o'clock in the morning and I slowed
from being out of breath, I was captured as I neared
Gates's army.

A hard band of steel wrapped around my waist,
lifting me from the ground. A dirty hand clamped over
my mouth and pulled me tight against a hard, tall wall
of a man. I kicked, bit, and fought with all I had until I
heard the man chuckle, "It's all right, girl. I won't hurt
you. I just can't have you screaming." I stilled and the
man whispered into my ear, "I'll let go if you promise
not to scream. Nod your head if you agree." I nodded
and the hand was dropped from my mouth. I was spun
around to face a man about ten years my senior in a
blue Continental uniform. I let out a visible sigh of
relief, and the man quietly chuckled again.

I told him I had to see Stephan Wells right away,
but my heart dropped when he shook his head and told
me he didn't know anyone by that name. He then told
me that there were almost ten thousand people in the
camp and asked who if I knew his commanding officer. I
froze temporarily but practically shouted that my father
was with Morgan's Riflemen as I remembered the name.
I pleaded with the stranger to let me find him. The man
nodded, showing that he knew who Morgan was, but his
brow was still knitted in concern. He asked why it was
so important to find my husband. I explained how
Stephan was my father and that he was in danger.
When the handsome stranger asked how I knew my

father was in danger, I had to decide if I should trust this man. "How do I know I can trust you?" I asked. The man smiled at me with a look of respect — something that was hard to come by for a woman — and my heart sped up even more.

"I'm Captain Thad Majory, Miss Wells. If you would but tell me why your father is in danger, I can take you to Morgan himself who will help us find your father," he told me.

It was a hard decision, but the man looked to be trusted. He was respectful and patient, which wasn't the case with the British soldiers who had stormed our home a month prior. I decided to tell Captain Majory what I overheard and saw while hunting. His smiling lips faded to a frown. He ordered me to stay where I was and disappeared into the woods, only to return minutes later riding a horse.

He reached over and I grabbed his hand. I didn't hesitate. I saw the urgency in his eyes. I swung my leg astride, grabbed the horse's mane, and didn't flinch as the captain's arm wrapped around me tight before urging his horse to race out of the woods toward the encampment of soldiers. We leaned as one, low over the beast's neck. My bonnet flew from my head, but we didn't slow. Captain Majory only held me tighter and urged his horse faster. He called out to the guards who didn't stop us as we thundered past tents and small fires with men sitting around them. Finally we stopped at a large tent. A man rushed forward to help me down, but Captain Majory jumped from the horse and wrapped his hands around my waist, hauling me off the horse and dragging me into the tent.

I told the officers in the tent what I had seen and they sent Captain Majory to ride in haste to General Gates to inform him of this development. I wasn't allowed to return home to my brothers until after the battle.

The battle raged on all afternoon and into the darkness of evening. Suddenly there was silence, followed by the cheers of thousands of colonial soldiers. They had defeated the British.

The army thanked me for my service and Captain Majory was assigned to look after me and return me to our farm in the morning. I turned around and there he was. The man I hadn't been able to stop thinking about. He was bleeding, but alive. That night I bandaged his wounded arm and helped the doctors with the injured. I had never been so scared, but I didn't lose my stomach when bones were sawed or men died. The whole while, Captain Majory stayed by my side, silently assisting and supporting me. With every new man who came to the field medics, I prayed he wasn't my father.

As dawn broke the night sky, another soldier was brought in for help. It was Father. I clung to the captain as the doctor dug a ball from my father's arm. He was unconscious and raging with fever. At lunch, I was graced by a visit from General Gates himself, who thanked me for my bravery and sent Captain Majory and a small contingent of soldiers to lead my unconscious father and me home. Father had received an honorable discharge and was allowed to die at home in peace. Only I had other ideas. I wouldn't allow Father to die.

Captain Majory was unfailingly kind, and as he

helped me care for my father I lost my heart to him. He asked if he could write to me, and I said yes. After helping me settle my father in, hunting some meat for us, and chopping some wood, Captain Majory said his goodbyes. But it wasn't goodbye forever. For three years we wrote to each other. I've enclosed the letters here as they are my treasure. Soon after the war ended, Father passed away. Before I could fear what the future held, there was a knock at my door. My captain had returned to me. We married right away and had forty happy years together. I never had to touch Grandmama's trunk. So tonight I add to it and pass it to my dear little Laura Elizabeth for all the future daughters of Elizabeth.

~ Sarah Elizabeth Majory

Sydney looked at the happy couple in the painting and smiled. With excitement, she turned to the third and largest bundle.

Chapter Twelve

Deacon drove to the police station in downtown Atlanta and parked in the visitors spot. Detective Gentry was leaning against a cruiser, waiting for him to turn off his car. Deacon hated leaving Sydney, but Gentry promised to have her watched. It was the only reason he hadn't brought her with him.

Deacon got out of his car, and Gentry pushed off the hood of his car and opened his passenger door. "Get in."

Deacon raised an eyebrow in curiosity but got in anyway. He and Gentry had worked out a long time ago that he wouldn't step on the police detective's feet during an investigation. Having proven himself, Gentry tended to give him more leeway than other PIs. "Where are we going?"

"We got a tip from a confidential informant that there were some girls being held at a shipping yard. Put this on," Gentry reached to the floorboard at Deacon's feet and tossed a bulletproof vest with POLICE written across it into his lap.

"Is SWAT there?" Deacon asked as they sped through the seedier parts of town. Here people wouldn't care if they heard screams. It was a sad reality that Gentry had been working to fix.

"They will be in ten minutes. We'll go in, and once it's clear I'll signal for you to help me look for Bailey. You know the drill. Don't touch anything. And be ready; this could be a bad one."

Deacon nodded as they drove in silence to the abandoned shipping yard. Old shipping containers for the railroad were stacked in piles. Derelict business offices were gray and rusting. Windows were broken, and it was obvious people had been vandalizing and trespassing on the property for years. Shipping containers were great for everything from free housing and meth labs to hiding things you didn't want found.

"We're going in. You stay here," Gentry ordered as he and the SWAT team moved in. Locks were cut with bolt cutters and doors were flung open. Sometimes they were clear and the team went on to the next. But sometimes a small group stayed behind as the rest moved to a new container.

Deacon watched with anticipation as ambulances and EMTs lined up behind him waiting to be called in. At the fourth container, the door opened and SWAT disappeared inside. A moment later, four more officers came out and started scanning the rest of the storage containers. Gentry walked out of the container issuing orders before grabbing the side of the container, bending at the waist, and throwing up. When he stood, he motioned for Deacon to join him.

Any hopes of finding Bailey alive fled when Gentry reacted so violently. It had to be bad for a seasoned lawman like him to be so affected and he wasn't the only one. Other officers were similarly afflicted. Deacon passed the first container the officers cleared and found it empty except for some tables, chairs, and cabinets. It looked like an office of some kind. The second container held nothing but a stained mattress and a video camera. The third container was full of girls.

Deacon stopped and stared as they huddled in the corner, fear overtaking their dirty faces. There had to be twenty of them ranging in age from twelve to twenty. The smell of human filth had him coughing into his hand and breathing in through his mouth. The police were ushering the EMTs to that container, but no one was being ushered to the fourth container.

"What is it?" Deacon asked, but the smell in the air alerted him to what it was.

Gentry shook his head. "You don't have to go in there." But Deacon didn't listen. He steadied himself and walked to the open container door. He thought he had prepared himself, but nothing could have prepared him for this.

Deacon felt his stomach revolt as all his blood drained from his face. Bodies . . . there were so many bodies. Young girls stared at him with unseeing eyes, young ladies forever frozen in fear . . . all tossed in the container as if they were garbage.

Deacon turned away. He couldn't look anymore. "We're calling in the state coroner's office to help handle this. I don't know if it means anything, but the bodies closest to the door are the newest, and I didn't see Bailey," Gentry said as they walked to the container with the surviving women and girls in it.

"I didn't either. Maybe she's in this one," Deacon mumbled as his stomach knotted in fear and disgust. He didn't want to know what these girls were going to say. He didn't want to know what happened to them. But he had to ask. Someone had to bring these women justice. If it took the rest of his life, then he would find the bastards responsible.

"What do you have?" Gentry asked the SWAT leader as EMTs rushed to hook up IVs and evaluate the women and girls.

"Nineteen females in total. That one, Naomi, is the designated leader of the group. They all turn to her to answer for them. Most are still so scared they can't or won't tell us their names," the SWAT officer told them as he pointed out a girl with matted black hair that appeared to once have been in braids. She stood like a dark angel of war in the middle of the women, instructing the officers and EMTs who needed help the most.

Deacon followed Gentry toward the woman now covered in a blanket. She couldn't be more than sixteen, but her back was straight, her voice clear, and her eyes haunted.

"Miss Naomi, I'm Detective Gentry and this is Deacon McKnight. He's a private investigator hired to find a missing girl."

"Which one?" Naomi asked in a strong voice as if she were behind a desk, helping a customer and not a victim.

"Bailey Vander," Deacon answered.

Naomi nodded. "She was recent. Real pretty. Eighteen. Long hair. They took her to Indiana. She was educated enough and seasoned enough to take out in public."

Deacon's relief was short-lived. "What do you mean by that? What happened to her and to you?"

Naomi tightened her jaw, and like a queen, walked from the container with her head held high. Deacon and Gentry followed as they walked the short distance to the second container. "They picked me up off the streets a month ago. I dropped out of school three months ago. I thought it wouldn't help with my life. I didn't like being told what to do. I was high on drugs, and they offered me more. Told me they'd hook me up if I did something for them. I was too high to know better. They brought me here to season me, or to break me." She gestured to the mattress. She didn't have to say what they wanted; Deacon already knew.

"Once a week some fancy guy with an accent would come in, pull us all out of the container, and pick a few to sample. The ones he could control through abuse and torture were whisked away. Some were sold overseas and some are probably prostitutes on the street two blocks over. And then others . . ." she looked to the last container and her eyes went dead.

"I wasn't broken. After that first night, I fought. Some men like that and pay for that. But I hurt a good many of them. I found my strength in helping the others survive. We were planning to overpower Mr. Fancy Pants the next time he came. There are nineteen of us and only four of them. I had everyone ready to go, but then Bailey and Jules were brought here. The screams. We could hear the screams even locked in our container. No men came for us that night. We all knew what that meant and where they were. The other girls balked at an attack. Jules didn't make it. She's the girl with black hair in the last container. But when Bailey was thrown in with us after her 'introduction,' she would do anything they wanted just to escape the container. Turns out she was a claustrophobic virgin who had just been through mental and physical hell. We couldn't trust her with our plot. She would have sold us out. Not that I blame her. She left yesterday for Indiana. Mr. Fancy Pants doted on her, and she was acting like none of this happened. It was like they were a couple. He bought her some fancy dresses and told her he loved her." Naomi shook her head sadly.

"You're a brave woman, Naomi. Thank you for answering my questions." Deacon held out his hand and waited as she looked at it. Then she raised her chin, took his hand, and shook it.

"Would you mind if I stayed with the girls until their parents come for them? Many of them are too scared to speak and afraid their parents won't take them back."

"What about your parents?" Deacon asked.

Naomi shrugged. "I don't think they've even noticed I was gone."

"What's your last name, Naomi?" Detective Gentry asked gently.

"Patterson."

Gentry typed something into his phone and then quietly held it up for her to see. It was a news report showing Naomi's family, friends, and neighbors searching for her. The hard shell Naomi used to protect herself crumbled. She fell to her knees as sobs wracked her body. Gentry and Deacon crouched next to her as she cried.

"You're loved, Naomi. They noticed, and they have

been searching for you." Gentry handed her his phone, and with shaking fingers Naomi entered a phone number.

"Mom!" Naomi cried when the phone was answered on the first ring.

Gentry and Deacon shared a tight smile as Naomi sobbed into the phone.

"Bailey's no longer here. Try to find her. I'll call the Indiana State Police to alert them," Gentry said quietly as he wrapped his arm around Naomi and pulled her to his chest. Gentry spoke into the phone with Naomi's parents as she clung to him with tears wetting his bulletproof vest.

Deacon drove home without seeing the road, the cars, or the world around him. He had seen a lot of evil in his life, but nothing could compare to this. He drove up the driveway to the house and looked at the glow of warm lights coming from inside. It was like a balm to the horror of the day. Sydney was all that was good and, at least for today, he got to come home to her.

He parked the car and unlocked the front door of the house. Crying. The sound of soft tears reached him as he slammed the door and raced to the living room.

"Sydney!" Deacon yelled. She had to be all right.

He stopped as he looked down at her sitting on the floor with a letter in her hands. Two very old dresses, four large oil paintings, and a large silver tea service covered the floor.

"What happened? Are you hurt?" Deacon asked as he dropped to the floor next to Sydney.

She shook her head. "No, listen to this. It's from

Evelyn Curtis and dated 1864."

"Wasn't Evelyn the name of the person who gifted this property to Mrs. Wyatt?"

Sydney nodded. "This is she." Then she read from the letter in her hand.

"Mother didn't make it. After father was killed by the northern regiment last year, Mother whittled away to nothing. Tonight we received word that Sherman was beginning his march to the sea and vowed to take and destroy anything and everyone in his path. It was more than Mother could handle. Tonight I buried her next to the empty grave of my father. I engraved her name, Laura Curtis, onto the wooden cross just five minutes past. I am but sixteen and saddled with the protection of my younger brother and all of Twin Oaks.

I have ordered Tom to hide the livestock deep in the woods behind us as I clear the house of our most prized possessions, including what I have just learned this morning is the family treasure. I vow to keep it safe for my daughter and all future daughters. I am placing as many of the valuables as possible into it.

I smell the fire in the air. I don't have much time. This is for you, the daughters of Elizabeth."

Deacon stared wide-eyed at Sydney as she refolded the paper and looked up to him. "What happened to her?"

Sydney shook her head. "I don't know. But the house is still standing, and Evelyn went on to marry a man named Seeley, so she didn't die that night. But look at what she placed in the trunk. The names on the paintings read Whistler and Cassett. These are priceless. And the jewelry!

Oh, and look, every daughter of Elizabeth put her wedding dress and a picture of her on her wedding day in here, but Evelyn didn't get the chance to. And look at this!"

Deacon took the leather pouches from her and looked inside. "Are these real? These must be worth millions."

"But Evelyn didn't add to the trunk. She filled it the night Sherman marched through. It appears that the trunk was only then buried for the first time and hasn't been touched since. So, where is the rest?" Sydney asked with excitement.

"The rest?"

"Yes! Evelyn left the property to my great-grandmother, who left it to me. There's no way she didn't leave behind another letter, her wedding dress, and maybe something else."

Deacon's mouth grew dry. "Why would she do that?"

"The whole point of the trunk was to give each woman freedom. At the time of these letters, a woman didn't have her own money. She was essentially property and could be sold if her father wanted. Elizabeth gave them freedom, options, and choices. But Evelyn knew what the trunk held and didn't come back to get it. And my great-grandmother said I was to bring the treasure together. That means there's more, and I know where it is." Sydney grinned, and Deacon couldn't stop returning a smile of his own. Her excitement was contagious.

"Where is it?" Deacon asked.

"In Keeneston. It's time to leave."

Chapter Thirteen

"No," Deacon said quickly. "You can't leave. You're still in danger. What if Vic comes after you again?"

Sydney looked at him, and for the first time saw the shadowed look in his eyes. "Oh, no. Bailey . . . is she dead?"

Deacon swallowed hard. "No, but it's bad—real bad. It's the worst trafficking ring I've ever seen. We rescued nineteen girls from a shipping container tonight. There were twenty-seven we didn't get to in time."

Sydney gasped as she squeezed his hand. She was so excited over love and a treasure she had nearly blocked out the harsh reality of the world. "I'm so sorry. I shouldn't have been so wrapped up in this."

Deacon shook his head. "No, this brings me back from the darkness. You're my light, Sydney. And this treasure."

"What about Bailey?" Sydney asked, even though she wasn't sure she wanted to know.

"She's under their power. The girls call this one man Mr. Fancy Pants. It has to be Vic. He came and got her the other day. Told her he loved her, brought her pretty dresses, and took her to Indiana. I don't understand it, though. Why Indiana and is it the job that he texted her about?"

"I know," Sydney said as she leapt up. She grabbed her phone and sent a quick text. A second later her phone pinged, and she grinned. "The football championship is in Indianapolis this week."

"And major sporting events have the highest level of prostitution and trafficking," Deacon said as he stood up, too.

"Plus, Patrick and Teddy are going to be there. That seems like a pretty strong coincidence, doesn't it?" Sydney asked as she started to scroll through her phone again.

"But how can we to get into the parties where Bailey would be?"

"I told you, it's time to go to Keeneston. But first, I have a phone call I need to make." Sydney pushed the call button and held the phone to her ear. "Miss Sydney Davies for Allegra Simpson-Williams. It's urgent."

Ten minutes later, Sydney had Allegra's promise that her fashion house located in Atlanta would send over experts to preserve and wrap the wedding dresses in one hour. Further, Allegra promised to have her own transportation team drive them to Wyatt Farm in Keeneston for delivery tomorrow.

"Now that the dresses are taken care of, what about all the rest?" Deacon asked.

"We take it with us," Sydney said as she began to pack up the rest of the treasure.

"I'll start packing our things upstairs. We'll leave as soon as the dresses do. I'll also call Gentry and let him know what we suspect," Deacon told her as he started to head upstairs.

"Oh, Deacon?" Sydney called out after him.

"Yes?"

"Do you still have a tux somewhere in your closest?"

"Yeah, why?"

"You better pack it. You won't get into some of these parties without one." Sydney went back to packing with gusto. She finally felt as if she could do something to find Bailey. Plus it kept Deacon with her for a couple more days, and right now she would do just about anything to stay with him.

Deacon followed the GPS directions from Atlanta to Keeneston. Sydney had fallen asleep when they had crossed into Tennessee. He looked at the clock. It was almost four in the morning as he drove down the narrow, twisting country road in Sydney's car. Shadows of cows and horses standing still in the dark pastures gave way to a small main street.

It was eerie. In Atlanta there were clubs and things to do late at night and into the early morning hours. Apparently not in Keeneston. There wasn't one person on Main Street, and the windows of all the stores were dark except for red, pink, and white twinkle lights and hearts lit up for Valentine's Day. The stores were cute. Antiques, art studio, The Blossom Café, handmade items, insurance office, law office, bank, Southern Charms, and a feed store lined the short street.

And just like that, he was through Keeneston. He followed the road another couple of miles and turned off onto a private road but was stopped by a gate.

"Syd, I think we're here," Deacon said gently as he rubbed her shoulder to wake her.

"Hmm?" Sydney mumbled as sleep tempted her again.

"I said, we're here. I need your gate code," Deacon said a little louder this time.

Sydney struggled to sit up, reached to the rearview mirror, and pressed one of the buttons. The gate swung open, and Sydney fell back asleep. Deacon drove down the driveway lined with bare trees. He bet it would be just like the Twin Oaks drive in the spring. Then out of the darkness came a two-story plantation-style house. The only difference was this one was new and slightly more modern in design.

Deacon pressed the other button on the rearview mirror and the garage door opened. He pulled the car in and turned it off. He headed to the door and wondered if there was an alarm. He tried it, and the door silently opened. He shook his head. He'd have to make her start setting the alarm she had. Instead of lecturing her on safety, he went back to the car and scooped Sydney into his arms.

"Where's your bedroom, darlin'?" he asked quietly as she snuggled her head against his chest.

"Upstairs. Far end," Sydney mumbled against his shirt.

Deacon carried her up the stairs and to the bedroom at the end of the hall. He stepped inside and walked to the bed. Slowly, he lowered Sydney. Her arms let go of him and grabbed her pillow instead.

"Stay," Sydney sighed.

Deacon's heart pounded along with something farther

140

south on his body. "Stay? The night with you?"

"Mmm-hmm."

"I'll grab our bags and be right back." Deacon leaned over and placed a kiss on Sydney's temple. She sighed happily, her lips curved up into a smile, and Deacon felt like a hero.

He bounded down the stairs and out into the garage. It took a bit of work, but he got the trunk into the house and went back for their bags. Closing the door, he set the alarm to sleep mode and felt better about having all that treasure in the house. He could enjoy the night with Sydney without fear of someone catching them by surprise.

By the time he got upstairs, Sydney had stripped out of her clothing and was asleep in a lace-edged white bra and — he hoped — no panties. Deacon stripped to his boxer briefs and pulled down the covers to slide into bed. Sydney rolled over and flung her arm over his chest, a leg over his, and moved her head to the crook of his shoulder. Deacon leaned down and kissed her forehead. He was the luckiest man in the entire universe tonight.

Deacon awoke to the feel of feather-light kisses to his jaw. There was a warm weight on his chest, and he moved to wrap it in his arms. Sydney was chest to chest with him, tracing kisses along his face. He groaned when she shifted, her thigh close to a very active part of his anatomy.

"Good morning, Deacon," she whispered seductively.

Deacon opened his eyes then and looked into Sydney's smiling face. "Good morning, darlin'."

He didn't know what to say, but sometimes words

were overrated. He wanted to tell her he hoped to spend every morning like this, that he didn't want to go back to Atlanta without her, that she was even more wonderful than Mrs. Wyatt's letters had said.

Sydney bent down and placed a kiss on the tip of his nose. Her long hair fell like a curtain around them. Right now there were only the two of them — him and her — and that was the way he liked it.

Deacon moved his hand down her back to give her ass a squeeze. Sydney moaned and moved her lips to his. When she had wakened that morning, encircled in his embrace, she knew she was done with this little game they had been playing. It had moved past fun and into serious the other night on his couch.

The electricity from the lightning storm that night was nothing compared to what happened when they came together. His hand moved up her back, and with a flick of his fingers he unhooked her bra. Sydney moaned her approval, but Deacon broke the kiss.

"What . . .?" Sydney didn't finish the question as he flipped her onto her back.

"You know it, too, don't you?" Deacon asked breathlessly as he slowly lowered one of her bra straps.

She didn't bother denying it. She knew exactly what he was talking about. "Yes."

"When I make love to you, it isn't for today. It isn't for this week or even this month. It's forever. I'm done hiding my feelings for you, Sydney," Deacon said with a voice rough with emotion and restraint. Sydney could tell he was controlling himself, giving her an out if she wanted it.

"You were perfect, Deacon. I would never have given you a chance if you hadn't let me come to you. I love you. I know it's wrong to fall in love so quickly, but I did. I love you."

"Love is never wrong, darlin'. And this isn't fast. This has been coming for five years. For five years I've heard about you. I fell in love with the woman in the letters, but she's nothing compared to the real thing. I love you, Sydney." Deacon grinned as he peeled her bra from her. "Now, enough talking. I'm more a man of action."

As Sydney's nipple disappeared into Deacon's hot, wet mouth, she agreed. No more talking. Screaming, groaning, and gasping — yes. And that's exactly what she did when Deacon stripped her panties from her and slid into her.

Deacon smiled as he dried off. This was the best day of his life. The woman he loved returned his feelings. He'd made love to Sydney and had scratches on his back to remind him of it. Sydney stepped out of the shower he had just vacated and licked her lips. Twice had been nice, but three times was a distinct possibility. The first time had been in bed, the second in the shower, and the third was shaping up to be in the kitchen after he cooked her breakfast.

"I'll head downstairs and start on breakfast," Deacon said as he stepped into a pair of athletic shorts and nothing else.

"Sounds good. I'll be just a second."

Deacon laughed when she swatted his bottom with her towel. Happiness, contentment, and love . . . all the things he'd been looking for. It filled his spirit as he went down the stairs and headed for the kitchen. As he whipped up some scrambled eggs, sausage, and toast, he tried not to think of what was next. He was from Atlanta, and she was from here. How were they going to make it work?

"This is perfect," he heard Sydney say. He looked up from the stove and decided the *how* wasn't important. What was important was that they were together, and he would do anything to make that happen.

Sydney sat on a barstool at the countertop in her royal blue silk robe. Deacon stepped up to her and kissed her. His hand slipped inside her robe, and he smiled against her lips. No bra.

"Are you hungry?" Deacon asked as he stepped away to put breakfast on the two plates.

"In many ways." Syd winked.

Sydney and Deacon ate breakfast while they laughed and talked. It was one of her favorite things to do with him. He had a sharp sense of humor and an intelligence that she enjoyed. He would listen too. She could be talking about fabric types, and he would listen just as much as if she were talking about what she wanted to do with him after breakfast.

"That was delicious. Thank you," Sydney said as she pushed the empty plate away.

Deacon turned in his chair, his eyes molten with desire. "Ready for the best part of breakfast?"

His hands were at the tie of the robe, his lips working magic as they trailed down her collarbone, but the sound of the alarm going off made them jump apart.

"Get back," Deacon ordered as his hand reached for a

knife in the block on the counter. He shoved her behind him as Sydney peered around him to see the muzzle of a gun come around the corner. Deacon shoved her behind him again, and then all she could see were his shoulders.

"Drop the knife!" a man yelled above the alarm.

"No. You'll have to kill me to get to her," Deacon said with ice dripping from his words.

"Happily. What have you done to her? I'll kill you slowly if you harmed one hair . . ."

Sydney rolled her eyes and went to turn off the alarm. The two men were still threatening each other when she walked back into the room.

"Deacon, put the knife down," she said as she walked toward the other man in the room.

"What are you doing?" Deacon lunged and grabbed her, pulling her to him.

The other man snarled, and Sydney let out a frustrated breath. "Dad, does it look like Deacon's trying to hurt me?"

"Dad?"

"Deacon?"

The men spoke at the same time. They looked at each other again, and Deacon let go of her arm and placed the knife on the table.

"Dad." Sydney crossed her arms and waited for her father to put his gun away. "Thank you. Deacon, this is my father, Marshall Davies. Dad, this is my boyfriend, Deacon McKnight."

Her father's eyes narrowed, and Sydney thought maybe she should have confiscated the gun instead.

"Boyfriend?" her father said with no small amount of hostility.

Sydney had to give Deacon credit. He walked over to her father and held out his hand. "It's nice to meet you, sir. I've heard a lot about you from Syd and Mrs. Wyatt."

Her father looked at her and took in their state of undress. His lips tilted into a snarl.

"Dad," Sydney warned.

"Marshall, what is it? Is Sydney okay?"

Oh great. Sydney shut her eyes as her mom raced into the room.

"I told you to stay in the car until I knew it was safe," her father ground out. Her mother only rolled her eyes — eyes that quickly went from Deacon to her and back to Deacon.

"And who is your friend, dear?" Her mother practically cooed as the rust-colored Vizsla puppy bounded across the room and leapt into Sydney's outstretched arms. Sydney and her father both groaned at her mother as Syd picked up the wiggly puppy.

"Deacon McKnight. Nice to meet you, ma'am," Deacon said with a smile and a respectful bow of his head.

"Katelyn Davies, Sydney's mother. It's such a pleasure to meet a friend of my daughter's." Katelyn smiled a smile that had once made her a supermodel but now made her look like a scheming mother in search of grandbabies.

"Hi, Mom. What are you two doing here so early?" Sydney asked.

"Everyone was saying you were back in town, and we thought we'd find out how you were doing. And I thought I'd deliver Robyn to you. She's only destroyed three pillows and a pair of Prada heels," her mother said so sweetly that Sydney fought the urge to roll her eyes . . .

again.

"At least she has good taste in shoes," Sydney cooed at the puppy licking her cheek.

"We got in at four this morning. There wasn't anyone to see us drive through town," Deacon said with amazement.

"Freeze, asshole!" a woman yelled from the archway leading into the kitchen from the front door.

"Aunt Annie, it's just us." Sydney groaned yet again in embarrassment. Her aunt came through the door with her gun still pointed at Deacon. At least she was wearing her sheriff's uniform. Her father was in plainclothes and had given Deacon no clue as to why a strange man was in her house with a gun.

"Who's he?" Annie asked with zero subtlety.

"This is my boyfriend, Deacon McKnight. Deacon, this is my aunt, Annie Davies. She works with my father at the sheriff's department and is about to tell us why she's here, too." Sydney stared at her aunt and couldn't stop the eye roll when Annie just smirked at them. A smirk that got bigger as she looked at Deacon's bare chest.

"I was responding to your alarm. Boyfriend, huh? How long have you two been dating?" Annie asked as she holstered her gun.

Deacon held out his hand and shook Annie's. "It's nice to meet you, ma'am. We've been dating, what, one day?"

Her mother and aunt smiled at each other. Her father had steam coming out of his ears.

"Deacon has been taking care of Great-grandma's Atlanta estate," Sydney told them.

"Oh, that's nice. Do you do the landscaping and all

that, too?" her mother asked.

Deacon grinned with amusement. "Yes, when I have time. I run my own business so that occupies most of my day."

"How interesting. What kind of business?" her mother asked as she shot a winning smile to her husband as if to prove their daughter was dating someone who didn't just sit in a mansion, playing video games all day.

"I'm a private investigator."

"Well, shit," her mother whispered under her breath as her father's face turned five shades of red.

"Not that kind of PI," Deacon said with an amazing amount of calm. "I only take cases I really want. I don't muck up active police cases. In fact, I work very closely with police on missing person cases. Like now, I'm working with Detective Gentry of the Atlanta PD on a case to find a girl we believe was coerced into sex trafficking."

Sydney looked to her father whose face had gone down a shade to bright red apple. "One day," he muttered.

"Yes, but hopefully many more to come," Deacon said as he put his arm around her shoulders. Robyn leaned over to sniff him, and Syd put her on the ground. The roly-poly puppy sauntered over to Deacon and gave him the once-over. It was as if she were deciding if his shoes were good enough to chew on.

Her mother clasped her hands happily together while Aunt Annie casually took her father's sidearm. His face was back up to nuclear red.

"That's wonderful, Deacon. We're happy to have you visiting. You know, Sydney's Grandma Davies is having a family dinner tomorrow night. It would be lovely if you joined us."

"No!" Sydney said a little too loudly.

"I think that's a great idea," her father said with a feral smile on his face. Aunt Annie bent down and removed the gun strapped to Marshall's ankle.

"I'd love to." Deacon smiled like an idiot. The poor man didn't know the hell he had just walked into.

Chapter Fourteen

Sydney looked up at the house she had spent so much time in. A house that held warm memories, the smell of fresh-baked cookies mixed with pipe tobacco and secrets — Evelyn Seeley's secrets. Sydney was determined to find them and complete the quest her great-grandmother had tasked her with.

"So, this is Mrs. Wyatt's home. It looks just like she described it. And wow, what a farm," Deacon said with wonder as he took in the rolling hills dotted with horses and lined with black fences.

"It's beautiful here. It's why I moved nearby. I don't have the time to take care of this much property, though. That's why she left it to my younger brother, Wyatt. He's a large-animal veterinarian and spent the last couple of years helping Great-grandma take care of the farm," Sydney told him as she put her key in the lock and opened the old front door.

The inside of the house seemed frozen in time. Wyatt hadn't wanted to move in yet. He said it still caused him too much pain to think about living in the big house alone. Sydney walked into the entranceway and set her keys on the side table. On her immediate right was a formal sitting room. Up ahead on her right was a large wood-paneled office that had belonged to her great-grandfather. On her left was the living room that led to the dining room, which was next to the kitchen. All the bedrooms were upstairs.

"I think we should start in her master bedroom. Look for anything this key could fit," Sydney told Deacon as he followed her upstairs. "I've called some friends to help with Bailey's case. We've agreed to meet for lunch, so we only have a couple hours."

Deacon followed her into the master bedroom and took his time looking around. "Sounds good. I still don't know how your friends in this small town, while very nice, would be able to help locate Bailey."

Sydney just shook her head as she opened the nightstand by the bed. "We may be small in number, but trust me. They'll be able to help."

Deacon and Sydney worked in silence. He opened every drawer, knocked on every section of the wall, and practically cleared out the large walk-in closet. Still there was no hidden compartment, no large trunks, or anything that seemed out of place. He was about to give up with he heard a floorboard squeak in the old house.

Sydney was searching under the bed and was luckily out of sight. The sound came again, this time from out in the hall. Deacon quietly slipped behind the bedroom door and waited for the intruder to enter the room. It seemed like an eternity before he did. His instinct to protect Sydney at all costs prepared him to confront the intruder without hesitation.

The man finally stepped past the door, and Deacon

could tell from his hair, height, and build that he wasn't Marshall. This man was younger, had slightly lighter brown hair, and was strong. Not that Marshall wasn't, but from behind this man seemed to have even larger shoulders than the sheriff. He was tall, about Deacon's height, and would be an equal opponent.

Deacon made his move when the man cocked his head and began to bend down to look under the bed. Deacon leapt from behind the door and wrenched the man's arm behind his back. Normally this caused people to freeze, but the man promptly lowered his shoulder and tried to fling Deacon over it. This man was trained in combat.

The intruder stomped his heel onto Deacon's foot and flung his head backward in an attempt to smash Deacon's nose. Deacon darted out of the way, but the man took advantage and spun around so the two men were facing each other.

"Where's Sydney?" he growled.

"Someplace you'll never find her," Deacon snarled back as he threw a hard right cross.

The man blocked it and returned with a jab that glanced off the forearm Deacon had used to protect his face. The battle continued — cross, block, hook, block. Back and forth they challenged each other. Deacon never took his eyes off the man as they traded blows.

"Stop!" Sydney yelled.

Deacon let his eyes move from the man to Sydney, and that was all the guy needed to land a solid punch to the stomach. Deacon's breath whooshed from him as he reflexively bent over. Sydney screamed, but Deacon ignored her as he tackled the man by ramming his lowered shoulder into the man's gut. The men crashed to the ground as Sydney raced over to them.

"Wyatt! Stop! This is my boyfriend, Deacon. Stop," Sydney screamed as she tried to pull Deacon off this man named Wyatt.

"Deacon, this is my brother!" Sydney yelled as the two finally stopped swinging at each other.

Deacon looked from Sydney to the man on the ground. They both had hazel eyes, only Sydney's were more golden and Wyatt's were greener. "Damn. How many men are in your family anyway, and why do they all come sneaking into your house?" Deacon asked as he stood up and held out his hand to Sydney's brother.

"Her house? I'll have you know this is my house. It's you two who are sneaking around. And I've heard plenty about how you were sneaking around this morning at my sister's house, too," Wyatt shot back.

Deacon stopped himself from saying anything about this morning. This was Sydney's brother, and he could tell by the look on her face that she was mortified. "I'm sorry about this. I just wanted to protect her. I'm sure you can appreciate that. Mrs. Wyatt told me how close you two are."

Wyatt raised an eyebrow as he saw Sydney's hand gripping his. Deacon watched as Wyatt took them in and then gave him a quick nod as if saying he got that they were together. By the way Wyatt's jaw was still clenched, Deacon didn't think Wyatt liked it, though.

"You knew my great-grandmother?"

"Yes. We wrote for five years. She left something for Sydney, and I was just helping her look for it," Deacon explained.

"I thought you were here on some case." Wyatt folded his arms over his chest and stared him down.

"I am. We have a meeting at the Blossom Café soon, and I was helping her look while we had some spare time," Deacon explained.

Wyatt turned from him and looked at his sister. "What are you looking for?"

"That's just it. I don't know. She left me this key." Sydney handed the key to her brother who examined it.

"I don't know what this could be for," Wyatt said as he looked at the key. "But there's all sorts of hiding places in this old house. Now, why don't you tell me about this case that got my sister assaulted."

Sydney sighed. "Did Mom also tell you Deacon was the one who protected me?"

"Yes, but we'll discuss your *boyfriend* later. What's the case?" Wyatt ignored Deacon, who could see why Sydney tended to roll her eyes.

"Look, it's almost time to meet the group at the café. Just meet us there and then we only have to explain it once." Sydney was frustrated, and Deacon wanted to comfort her. Mrs. Wyatt had told him how close the family was. He didn't understand why Wyatt was giving her such a hard time.

"Darlin', why don't you head downstairs and get the car? I need to apologize to your brother here for getting the jump on him." Deacon purposefully needled Wyatt and as he expected, Wyatt immediately ushered Sydney out.

"What the hell was that about?" Wyatt demanded as soon as Sydney was downstairs. "You didn't get the jump on me."

Deacon held up his hands. "Look, you held your own. I'd rather have you on my side than against me. However, Sydney has just been attacked by two of the most important men in her life for dating me. I think it's time to back off."

"And I think you need to realize my sister isn't someone you sleep with on the first date and use until you've made a name for yourself," Wyatt shot back.

Deacon let out a long breath. "One, it wasn't our first date. We've been together since she left Keeneston. Second, it's none of your business. In case you haven't noticed, Sydney is a grown woman. And third, I love her. I'll never use her for any reason."

"That's what they all tell her. Well, I learned better even if my sister hasn't. You love her now, but when she cuts off your funds or doesn't let you use her jet, then suddenly you're out of love."

Deacon really wanted to roll his eyes. Sydney was definitely wearing off on him. "I don't need your sister's money. Google me and then see if I have any reason to use your sister. But I'll tell you something. I do love her, and I will protect her. I won't have you and your father hurting her by making her feel bad for having found love," Deacon told him as he worked to unclench his jaw.

Wyatt stared at him for a moment, then slowly held out his hand. "Truce?"

Deacon breathed in relief. "Truce," he said, shaking Wyatt's hand.

Ten minutes later Deacon held open the door to the

Blossom Café for Sydney. He had smelled the cooking from the time they parked along a very crowded Main Street. Sydney had said it was her favorite place to eat, but as he looked around downtown Keeneston he noticed it was the only place to eat.

"Syd, welcome home. How ya doin', hon?" a curvy, reddish-blond knockout asked as she wrapped Sydney up in a hug.

"Thanks, Poppy. I'm hanging in there."

Another woman came from the back of the café and held out her arms to Sydney. This one was more svelte and her hair a little more blond than red. "We've been thinking about you, hon. Now, who's the hunk?"

"Zinnia, I'm wounded you don't recognize me." Deacon turned to the deep southern drawl coming from behind him. Wyatt sauntered in with his hands over his heart.

Zinnia smacked him on the shoulder with a wooden spoon. A trickle of what looked to be a sauce of some kind was left behind. Wyatt swiped at it and smiled. "You even made my favorite."

The woman sent him a wink, and all eyes turned to Deacon. Wyatt's distraction only lasted so long. Sydney came and put her arm through his. "Poppy and Zinnia Meadows, this is my boyfriend, Deacon McKnight. Deacon, Poppy and Zinnia are sisters. They filled in for the Rose sisters and are now running the Blossom Café and the bed-and-breakfast up the street."

"Ma'am," Deacon said as he shook each woman's hand. He sent them a smile that made them blush. If there was one thing he knew how to do, it was flatter a group of women. Debutante balls were certainly good for learning that.

"And these are the Rose sisters and their husbands," Sydney told him as she pulled him to a table filled with white-haired seniors. Well, seniors may be too generous. Dinosaurs may be more accurate. But there was a twinkle in their eyes that made him smile. They looked like they knew how to get into trouble.

"Afternoon," Deacon said as he was introduced to the shorter woman sitting next to the man with a jolly belly.

"This is Miss Lily and her husband, John Wolfe," Sydney introduced. "And that is Miss Daisy and her husband, Charles Lastinger."

"Sir, ma'am. It's a pleasure," Deacon said to the slightly taller, thinner woman and man smiling up at him.

"And this is Miss Violet and her husband, Anton Vasseur," Sydney ended.

"So, young man, are you going to save that young Bailey?" John asked.

Deacon stared at him for a second. How did he know about that?

"While you're thinking about it, how about our Sydney here? I know you busted in and protected her from that Vic character, but you better keep a closer eye on her. He shouldn't have been able to attack our girl in the first place."

Deacon's mouth dropped open, but no words came out.

"Oh hush, John. Can't you see the boy's in love with her? He probably feels horrible about it," Miss Lily said as she swatted her husband's arm.

"How . . .?" Deacon stuttered.

"Aliens," Sydney whispered as the door opened. "But here are my friends. We'll see you later," she said louder to the group.

Deacon gave them a weak smile as they all beamed back at him. Then Miss Daisy held up some money, and Poppy ran over. The rest was a blur of money and dates. He was so lost. "What's going on?" Deacon asked.

"Oh, they're just placing bets on when you and my cousin are going to tie the knot," a tall man with Sydney's hazel eyes and dark brown hair said with a grin. "Ryan Parker. And this is my wife, Sienna."

"Hello," the pretty auburn-haired woman said as she held out her hand. "It's so nice to meet you. Even if I haven't heard anything about you."

Sydney stuck her tongue out at Sienna and the two laughed. "Sienna's my best friend. And this is Nash Dagher; he's the second in command of security for Dani and Mo," she told him as she pointed out a lightly tanned man with large muscles, black hair, and almost black eyes. He didn't say anything, only gave a quick nod of recognition and headed for a table in the back of the café.

"And this is Zain Ali Rahman. One of Dani and Mo's twin sons." Sydney introduced the tall serious man in a suit. His hair was dark brown—cut short and perfect. His jaw and nose had sharp angles that screamed power.

"Nice to meet y'all. I'm Deacon McKnight. I appreciate any help you can give me on the case."

As the group smiled at him and moved to the table where Nash was already seated, Deacon turned to Sydney. "Who are Dani and Mo, and why do I feel as if I should know them?"

"They're the Prince and Princess of Rahmi. Zain is in line for the throne, albeit a way down the line. But he has a lot of resources, to say the least. His twin brother, Gabe, is also a diplomat, but he's currently spending this month in Rahmi with his uncle, the king. As I said, we're a small but mighty town."

"I think that's an understatement. Who's Ryan, the president's son?" Deacon asked sarcastically.

"No, he's the head of the Lexington FBI office. And Sienna is a sports psychologist who works for the NFL's Lexington Thoroughbreds. Her father, Will Ashton, and Zain's father own the team. And her mother, Kenna, is the local prosecutor," Sydney explained in whispers as they walked toward the table.

"And Nash?"

Sydney just shrugged. "Nash is a badass and doesn't mind going outside the law if it's for a just cause. Diplomatic immunity has its perks."

Deacon pulled out Sydney's chair and then took a seat between her and Ryan. Sydney filled them in on Bailey's disappearance, Vic's assault of her, and then turned it over for Deacon to tell them what he found at the shipping yard.

The table was quiet for a moment. Then Sienna spoke up. "The championship game. That's where you think she is."

"That's right. But as both the photographer, Patrick, and the designer, Teddy, pointed out, it's a sold-out game with exclusive parties," Deacon said.

Everyone at the table just smiled. "We have more

tickets to the game than we could ever use. Between our fathers, that's easy," Sienna laughed as she pointed to Zain.

"I can get you into any political party," Zain told him with a shrug. "I can easily believe some of those men would sink to that level."

"You don't need help getting into the other parties," Wyatt said as if it were obvious.

"I don't?" Deacon asked.

Nash shook his head and pointed to Sydney. "You have her. No one will turn away a supermodel."

"I'm not a supermodel anymore, Nash. I'm retired. No one cares except on the business front," Sydney said with frustration.

Nash took out his phone. He typed something quickly and then smiled. "Not anymore. One of the gossip sites just got a tip that Sydney Davies is coming out of retirement and unveiling a new look at the football game."

Deacon saw Sydney's eyes grow wide. "I'm nowhere near model-ready! How am I going to lose thirty pounds and get a new look in two days?"

"You don't need to lose a single pound. You're stunning," Deacon said instantly.

Wyatt looked quickly at him and then took his sister's hand. "As much as I hate to agree with your *boyfriend,* I do. You're beautiful just the way you are."

"But—" Syd started.

"May I make a suggestion and not be attacked by your brother and your boyfriend?" Nash asked casually as if he weren't really concerned about it. "You've put weight on in all the right places. I would suggest a less-is-more theory when picking your wardrobe. You'll get in everywhere and keep them distracted while Deacon and I work."

Deacon bit back his snarl. He didn't like the way Nash's eyes went to Sydney's generous breasts. Those were his. "Wait, while you and I work?"

"Yes. As Zain said, we could be looking at a very large ring spanning both the political and entertainment worlds. Syd knows the entertainers. I know the politicians. Plus it's always good to have someone on hand with diplomatic immunity."

"And I can contact the local FBI and alert them to your presence," Ryan told him. "I'll have them reach out to that detective of yours for the case file. Everyone will be on the same page and will be looking for Bailey and her handlers. You know they will be close by, controlling their girls. They're the ones we must get our hands on."

Deacon looked around the table at Sydney's friends and family. "This is a good plan. Thank you all for helping."

"Of course, you're one of us now." Sienna smiled at him.

Wyatt grunted under his breath, "We'll see about that."

"Now that's taken care of, I have a couple questions for you," Zain said with a mischievous grin.

Chapter Fifteen

Sydney tried not to blush when Sienna gave her the thumbs-ups sign before fanning herself as the group left the café. Ryan stopped his wife and kissed her so passionately that it was Syd's turn to blush.

"I'll have to find other men attractive more often," Sydney heard Sienna tease as she and Ryan got in their car.

Sydney shook her head and then looped her hand through Deacon's arm. He had held up well. Her father had pointed a gun at him, her brother had punched him, and her friends had interrogated him. If he didn't run screaming from the Davies monthly family dinner tomorrow night, he might just be the one.

"So, what's next?" Deacon asked as they strolled down Main Street in the cold February air. The sun was bright and warmed her through as they walked.

"I need to stop at Aunt Paige's shop. She's Ryan's mom and owns Southern Charms right down there." Sydney pointed to the shop at the end of Main Street. "I need to see if she has fabric for my new look. My phone has been vibrating nonstop since that gossip site picked up the news of my supposed return."

"What are you going to do?" Deacon asked as he

pulled her against his side.

"I'm thinking something inspired by my great-grandmother. And that requires one hell of a hat. And I just so happen to know a woman who can make one for me. As for all the phone calls — that's what voicemail is for. I'm going to be unreachable. I may post something on social media about the game just to fuel the fires."

"Hey, Deacon!" Sydney turned her head to see Nash pulling to a stop next to them. "Want to come back to the farm and see what we can find out about Vic and the others you mentioned?"

Deacon looked to her first, and Sydney gave his hand a squeeze. "I'm going shopping." The pained look on Deacon's face made her giggle.

"I don't like leaving you alone while this is going on. I worry about Vic coming back," Deacon confessed.

"I know, but I promise to go straight home from Paige's."

"Text me to let me know you're safe," Deacon said before lowering his head for a kiss. The warmth of his lips on hers was a sharp contrast to the blistering cold air blowing across them. And when Deacon pulled away, the heat lingered as a memory, even after he'd disappeared from sight.

Sydney pushed open the door to the cute shop on the end of Main Street. Paige Davies was a renowned Derby hat designer, but she also stocked some of her own clothing designs as well as Sydney's. Her aunt sat behind the counter. Her light-brown hair had turned a lighter shade as she got older, but the Davies hazel eyes still shone bright as she worked on a tiny hat that could fit a baby.

"What are you working on?" Sydney asked as Paige looked up. She quickly hid the hat under the counter and smiled innocently at her.

"Nothing! It's good to see you again. Come give me a hug," Paige ordered as she looked behind Sydney. "Where's the boyfriend? Katelyn told me all about him. I hoped I could meet him before he fled the family dinner in terror like your other boyfriends have."

"Seriously, couldn't you go easy on him for once? Is it any wonder none of us cousins bring dates anymore. I mean, Uncle Miles made Layne's date cry, and that was nothing compared to what Uncle Cy did to Reagan's date."

Paige smiled serenely and patted Syd's arm. "Honey, if they break after just a couple itsy-bitsy minutes with us, then are they really husband material? We do it out of love. Now, what can I do for you today? It this about you coming out of retirement?"

Sydney's eyebrows rose in surprise. "You already know about that?"

"Oh, it's gone viral. Everyone wants to know what your new look is."

"That's what I want your help with. I need some material and a new hat. Great-grandma Wyatt has inspired me. I want an all-white outfit with her shocking red lipstick. I want simple, elegant, and sexy. Do you have any material that fits that?"

Paige nodded and headed for the back of the shop. "I have a beautiful laser-cut silk. It cost a fortune, but it's stunning. It's sheer where it's been laser-cut."

Paige held up the fabric, and Sydney drew in her

breath. It was perfect. Edgy and sophisticated at the same time. "Can you make a hat to match?"

Paige took in Sydney's hair, face, and the silk. "I'd stick with white. Are you going for 'look at me' or something more subtle?"

"Subtle, but still a statement."

"I have an idea. It will highlight the red lips. I can have it finished in two days. Is that soon enough?"

Sydney hugged her aunt. "That's perfect. I don't know if we are leaving that night or the next day yet. Thank you so much!"

"Anything for you, hon."

"Anything?" Sydney tested. "How about going easy on Deacon tomorrow. It's not just the guys who are bad. Jackson's last date ran from dinner after you had a little girl talk with her."

Paige smiled with satisfaction. "She was all wrong for my boy. Jackson is an FBI hostage rescuer. He's a tough man and needs a tough woman who won't just roll over and do whatever he says. A little challenge is good for my boys. Sienna certainly doesn't give in to whatever Ryan says, and look how happy they are. And if I remember correctly, you were also there and asked if she had any intention of trying to change your cousin. I only stepped in when she mentioned his job was too dangerous."

Paige may have a point, but terrorizing said dates was not the best way to go about it now that she had a serious date of her own. So far, only Sienna had survived. But that wasn't a good example since she'd been coming to Davies family gatherings her whole life, and everyone already considered her part of the family.

Sydney paid for the fabric, thanked Paige again, and headed for home. She hadn't meant to stay out so long. She turned down her driveway and pulled into the garage. Sydney picked up the material for her new outfit, headed inside, and froze. It was quiet. There were no little puppy howls coming from Robyn's crate near the back door. There also wasn't the sound of snoring. The little wrinkly pup could wake the dead with her snores.

Sydney set down the material and raced to the sunroom where Robyn's crate was. The door was open, and the crate was empty. Oh no, not again! Robyn was a little Houdini. Of course, Robyn's great-great-grandfather was Bob, Sydney's childhood dog, and he could climb trees. It was no wonder a simple thing such as a locked cage couldn't hold Robyn.

"No, no, no," Sydney chanted as she raced upstairs to her bedroom. "Don't do it! Robyn, I'm sending you to obedience school if you're eating my Pradas!"

Sydney rushed into her room, and there in the middle of her bed was the cute puppy with her ears perked, her head tilted, and one former silver strappy high-heeled Prada hanging from her mouth.

"How did you . . .?" Sydney sputtered. "That shoe was in a box a good five feet up in my closet."

Robyn didn't answer. She just stared back with a look that conveyed exactly what she thought of Sydney's attempts to hide her Pradas from her.

"I warned you. I'm calling Bridget." Robyn's ears went down, and she dropped the shoe. She rolled over onto her back, her lips falling into a sweet smile as she thumped her tail on the bed. "Oh, no. You're not getting out of it by being cute."

Sydney pulled out her phone and sent a text to Bridget Mueez. She trained police and military dogs for a living. And she had known Bob. Her husband, Ahmed, the retired head of security and all-around badass for Mo and Dani, had been afraid of Bob. He had said the dog knew too many secrets. And Robyn was turning out to be just like him. Except she didn't climb trees. She climbed shoe shelves.

Her phone pinged and Sydney smiled. "Someone starts school tomorrow."

Robyn narrowed her eyes and peed on the bed.

Deacon looked in contemplation at the three large screens that lined a wall of the security room at Desert Sun Farm. He hadn't met the prince and princess but had met Nabi, the current head of security for Dani and Mo. Deacon thought it was pretty cool that royalty were so down to earth, and he couldn't believe how helpful Nash and Nabi were. Nabi was older than he was, probably around forty-five. His dark hair had a few strands of gray, but that was the only tell. He still looked like he could take a man down without blinking.

Nash was checking with his underground contacts to see if they had heard of Tristan Models or a man named Vic who worked for them. Nabi had pulled up all he could on the model Emily Tamlin, the photographer Patrick Mawler, and the designer, Teddy Brown. They were the images Deacon was reviewing.

"Emily told Sydney she was out of the country for the

next few weeks," Deacon told Nabi as his fingers flew over the keyboard pulling up pictures and information on the model.

Nash hung up his cell and headed over to another computer. He typed in some commands and the picture of Patrick Mawler shrank and an itinerary popped up. "These are the parties Mawler is going to Sunday. I had no problem securing invitations for Sydney. You and I are acting as her security. The bigger you are, the more security you have. Do you have a black suit?"

"I do. What about Brown, the designer? Is he going to these same parties?" Deacon asked.

Nash hit a couple more keys and Brown's itinerary came up. "Mostly. However, he has these two that Mawler isn't going to. I've secured invites to those as well. Further, Zain has talked to his contacts. Here are the 'it' parties to be at if you're young and famous. Most of them are after the game, while almost all of the others are within the football stadium in private rooms and suites. And here are the political parties—you know, the exact opposite of the 'it' parties. These are mostly before the game at nearby hotels."

Deacon chuckled. Sydney had some great friends. He'd been in Keeneston for such a short time, but he felt as if these people were his own friends already. They were more honest and open than any of the people he had grown up with in Atlanta.

"The invites to the political parties took a little more finesse to get. Zain's executive assistant called and got us into those," Nash told him as the center screen turned into one long list of parties.

"How are we going to make it to all these parties in one night?" Deacon asked.

"You stay no more than ten to twenty minutes at each party," Nabi said as he took in the list. "I would say you could cut out the 'it' parties afterward, but nowadays the young are just as likely to hire a prostitute or buy a girl as the older crowd. It used to be about power, but now it's just about ego. They think it shows off how much money they have. With social media and the Internet, anyone can lure a girl to them. Sadly, it's a growing market."

"Okay, so we have three days to learn everything we can about these three people, all those parties, and who is hosting them." Deacon crossed his arms and looked at the screens. It was a needle in a haystack. "Have you learned anything about Vic?"

Nash shook his head. "Not yet, but I have my feelers out. By tomorrow I'll have heard something."

"And I'll put a couple of guys from my team on it as well," Nabi told them. "They can get you a handbook with pictures and event details. It will help when you're searching the parties."

"That would be great. Thank you both for all your help," Deacon said sincerely. "I'm going to see what I can find in the public forums. There's a staggering amount of ads for the sale of women and children right out in the open."

Nabi nodded. "I'll check the dark web. I'll see what's being talked about outside the reach of everyday people."

"Sounds like we all have work to do tonight. Let's meet back here tomorrow after breakfast and see if we've found anything that will help us," Nash said as he grabbed his car keys. "I'll give you a lift home, Deacon."

"Thanks." He smiled. He didn't bother to correct him that Sydney's home wasn't his. He was already beginning to feel like part of the town and a part of Syd's life.

Deacon opened the door as he and Nash headed out of the building. The sun was out, and the horses were running and playing in the pastures around him. There were Derby winners, colts, and fillies for as far as he could see.

"It's beautiful, isn't it?" Nash asked as they approached his car.

"Very."

"People have a tendency to come for a visit and stay. Both Nabi and I were only supposed to be on temporary assignment here, and well, you can see we've asked the king if we could stay longer. It's a special place."

Deacon slid into the car and looked at the man driving it. "I'm glad the king has agreed to let you stay. You're a good friend to Sydney."

"She's a wonderful lady. But alas, my king hasn't agreed to allow me to stay forever. I must return home soon."

"Why?" Deacon asked.

Nash gave a humorless laugh. "I've been trained too well by Ahmed and Nabi. I am now indispensible as an operative, and it's time for me to return to serve my country."

Chapter Sixteen

Sydney had her head bent over the sewing machine when she heard Robyn give a yip of excitement. She turned her head and saw Deacon leaning against the door, watching her. Those jeans hugging his thighs, that black V-neck sweater clinging to his chest, those chestnut brown eyes molten with desire as they traveled her body — she was in serious trouble.

Tomorrow night Deacon would run from her life in fear. Her father hated PIs and had no doubt told his brothers. Goodness knows what the uncles would do. She was sure that the innocent cleaning of weapons would be involved. Crap, she couldn't remember if Dylan was in town. He was Tammy and Pierce's son. A few years younger than Syd, he was built like a well-crafted tank and scared the crap out of most of the men her cousins brought to dinner without even opening his mouth. He just narrowed his eyes at them, flexed his hand into a ball, and the dates went running.

Jackson was going to be tough enough. He was Ryan's younger brother and his silver eyes could freeze a man where he stood. And now the cousins in their younger twenties like Dylan's younger brother, Jace, and Cade and

Annie's kids, Colton and Landon, were getting in on the action of tormenting dates. The twins! Cy and Gemma's twin boys, Porter and Parker, were the worst. They would team up on the unsuspecting fools . . . dates, that is. Sydney went back through all the conversations with her aunts and uncles. Everyone would be away at college except Jace. He had graduated nine months before but was overseas, helping build a school in the middle of Africa. He was in charge of the project and would be gone for another four months. Oh thank goodness, maybe there was a small ray of hope tomorrow wouldn't be a total disaster. Who was she kidding? This was her last night with Deacon, and she didn't want to spend it clothed.

"Darlin', you planning to sew an outfit out of air?"

Sydney blinked and looked away from Deacon. The needle in her sewing machine was running wildly with not a stitch of fabric nearby. Her material had long since fallen to the floor as she had sat ogling Deacon and simultaneously fearing the family dinner.

Deacon bent down and picked up a wiggling Robyn. He held her in his arms as the puppy lapped at his face. Deacon chuckled at the puppy's antics, and Sydney felt like crying. She'd finally found someone to love and who loved her for all the right reasons. And she was so scared she'd lose him tomorrow.

"Deacon?"

"Hmm?" Deacon responded as he scratched behind Robyn's ears.

"Make love to me," Sydney whispered. Her heart ached, knowing tomorrow everything would change between them. Even if he managed not to be scared off, he would find her family overwhelming and too much work. She'd seen it over and over again with dates.

Sydney picked up the destroyed Prada shoe and tossed it to Robyn as Deacon set her down. "What's the matter, Sydney?"

Sydney shook her head. "I just love you so much. I'm scared of losing you."

Deacon cupped her face with his hands and waited for her to look him in the eyes. "I'm not going anywhere, darlin'." Then he lowered his lips to hers. He took his time tasting her, and Sydney savored every sweep of his tongue, every caress of his hands, and every sweet word he murmured as he kissed his way through undressing her.

Sydney took her time undressing him. She pulled his sweater over his head, and as his hands cupped her sides right under her breasts, Syd started unbuttoning his shirt. Deacon teased her by fluttering his fingers across the soft underside of her breast before moving them to gently trace her breasts in languid circles. Sydney's breathing came faster as the heat built. She was pressing herself into his hands, silently begging him to take her nipples between his fingers as she removed his pants.

Without saying a word, Deacon bent forward and kissed her again. She sighed into his mouth as his tongue mimicked what she wanted his lower body to do. He took a step backward, and Sydney followed him without breaking the kiss. Deacon took a seat on her sewing chair and pulled her onto his lap. With their bodies pressed tightly against each other, they moved as one. Sydney felt tears well beneath her eyelids as she looked into Deacon's eyes. All his love and passion for her were right there looking back at her. And she knew. She knew she would do anything to keep him in her life.

The next morning, Deacon drove a very un-Sydney-like pickup truck to meet with Nash. He had left Sydney asleep in bed and hadn't stopped smiling since. It had been a very good night. A very long night, but that didn't keep the bounce out of his step. Instead, he'd left a note on the pillow next to Sydney, telling her where he was and that he'd taken Robyn with him. He'd found the keys to the old beaten-up pickup hanging by the door leading to the garage and taken off.

Robyn sat proudly in the front seat as she looked out the window. He thought the little pup would enjoy running around the farm. She was such an angel he didn't think Nash or Nabi would mind.

Deacon pulled into the farm and drove to the security building designed to look like a small but very secure barn. If you didn't know what was inside—high tech computers, a holding room, and a lot of weapons—you would think it was just another barn on the farm.

He clipped Robyn's leash onto her tiny collar and carried her from the truck. As soon as he put her on the ground, she gave a shake and then happily followed as he rang for entrance at the steel barn door. A buzzer sounded, and Deacon wound his way through the hallways to the computer room.

An older man with his head bent over a computer was the only person in the room besides Nabi. He looked everywhere for Nash but didn't see him. The older man straightened and turned with a tight look to his face. Shit. This man was serious. His dark hair had only a few gray hairs at the temples. He was muscled, and the way his jaw tightened, Deacon knew this man would kill and think nothing of it.

"Who let you in with the Spawn of Satan?" the man asked with such menace Deacon wondered if he was about to be shot.

"Excuse me?" Deacon asked, not fully understanding.

The man pointed at Robyn who was happily wiggling around at the end of the leash. "That thing. She's the Spawn of Satan. Just last week she attacked one of the police dogs my wife was training. Sent the poor thing running to his crate."

Deacon was pretty sure this man was delusional. "Were you training a Chihuahua? Robyn's a smushy little puppy." Deacon laughed before he saw Nabi's grim face as he tried to wave Deacon off the subject.

The other man snarled. "That *puppy* broke into a training exercise, latched onto the leg of the man in the bodysuit, and took him down. When Magnus tried to assist, that *puppy* snarled and smacked him on the nose with her paw, sending him running to his crate. By the time my wife got to them, Magnus was back at the kennel and Satan's Spawn was sitting on top of the trainer. Just look at her," the man pointed. "She *knows things*."

Deacon looked down at Robyn. Robyn smiled up at him. "Sure, buddy. Look, I'm Deacon McKnight," he said, holding out his hand. The man looked at Robyn dubiously before reaching out and shaking hands.

"Ahmed Mueez."

Deacon almost snorted with laughter. *This* was the big, bad Ahmed? This man who was afraid of a little puppy? The door opened, and a woman with beautiful long, strawberry-blond hair, wearing all black, sauntered in.

"There's my little spawn. Your mommy said you'd be here," she cooed to Robyn who rolled over on her back to get her round belly rubbed. The woman stood up and turned to him. "Hi. I'm Bridget Mueez, Ahmed's wife. Sydney said you had Robyn. I'm here to take her to obedience school for the week."

Robyn narrowed her eyes and moved closer to Deacon's leg as she lifted her lip in a snarl. "I don't think she wants to go," Deacon said with surprise as the little pup made it very clear she didn't want to go and expected Deacon to do something about it. It was like she knew what they were saying.

Bridget bent down and looked at Robyn. "We're going to learn a lot of cool things. How would you like to find drugs? Learn to take down the bad guys? Find stolen Prada?"

The little puppy yipped in excitement and jumped into Bridget's arms. Deacon shook his head as he watched Bridget tell the puppy all the things she was going to teach her.

"Why is she talking to Robyn like she can understand?" Deacon asked as the door closed.

"Because she can. That whole line going back to Bob could understand you. It's not natural. They just sit there looking at you like you're *their* pet." Ahmed shivered.

Deacon had to bite his lip to keep from laughing.

"Just you wait. You'll see," Ahmed said ominously.

"Okay. Well, is Nash ready?" Deacon asked Nabi.

"He gave me his report. Nash had to leave very early this morning," Nabi said with sadness. What had happened?

"Why?" Deacon asked.

"The king wanted him to come home. He had a mission for Nash," Ahmed said tightly. "He is sending some imbecile to replace him—the ambassador's son. He's a spoiled nitwit who is in some distant way related to the king."

Deacon didn't know what to say. "He just left? I know he didn't tell Sydney or she would have been very upset. He was a good friend of hers and many others."

"He was the best. We have groomed him to take over here, but now our plans must change. He was called away immediately. He didn't have time to inform anyone outside of security. He wouldn't anyway. Nash wouldn't appreciate the fuss but he filled me in, and I'm here to offer any assistance I can," Ahmed said as his jaw finally relaxed. "Nash said he was able to find a Victor Tamboli from Hungary who has ties to Durante Ingemi and Tristan Models, mostly in Europe. Beyond that, he's a ghost."

Deacon felt somewhat panicked. He and Nash had understood each other. But he couldn't get a feel on this Ahmed guy. Besides knowing he was afraid of a puppy and that he looked like he'd killed three terrorists before breakfast, he knew nothing about Ahmed.

"Then let's make the best of it," Deacon said as they got down to business. "I found over seventy ads for women and children for sale during the big game. I narrowed it to ads featuring young women since the girls

KATHLEEN BROOKS

we found in Atlanta weren't over twenty years old. I found thirty-seven that referred to girls as *fresh, new to town,* and *college freshmen* looking for dates. I narrowed it further by seeing which ads had the same phone number or a phone number trying to be concealed from automated searches, like the letter *o* instead of a zero. That cut the list down even more." Deacon handed the printout of seventeen numbers to Ahmed and Nabi.

"College freshman roommates new to the area who are open to new experiences, love sports, and are looking for a party," Nabi read slowly.

Deacon nodded. "That's the one that looks the most suspicious to me. And if you look at the bottom of the page, there's another one that's very similarly worded and the phone number is the same if you change the letter *l* for the number 1."

Ahmed's jaw was back to being tight as he typed into the computer. "The phone number is a burner phone out of Florida. Very strange for an ad in Indianapolis. What about the other fifteen?"

"They all reference football, sports, or watching sports. That's why I think they're girls who have been moved in specifically for the event. I just don't know how to track them down," Deacon confessed.

Nabi stood and went to a row of drawers. He opened one and pulled out phones, tossing one to each man. "We call them."

Deacon looked at his five numbers to call and felt his stomach tighten in disgust. He turned on his phone and dialed.

Thirty minutes later, Deacon lifted his hand from the desk he'd splintered. Some of the numbers he dialed were answered by a woman and some by a man. But they all only cared about the money. Deacon had told them he worked in the oil business and would be at the game and desired some barely legal, *wink-wink,* dates who wanted to party with him and his friends. He had negotiated prices, times, and locations. Some demanded Deacon host the party at their place; others were happy to bring the girls to him along with *security* for the girls' protection. But he knew better. That security would be there to keep the girls from escaping. Talking with these people had made him so angry he had smashed his hand onto the table, breaking it.

Ahmed and Nabi looked as awful as he did. "Which ones gave you the worst feeling?" Ahmed asked quietly. "Although they all deserve to die."

They discussed their calls and by the end had four parties set up that would come to them with girls matching the descriptions Gentry had sent.

"The party with the 555 number and the woman answering gave me the worst feeling," Deacon told them. "She told me they would call with the details, but I would have to have my *date* after the game. They would be at a private party during the game."

"That sounds like a solid lead," Ahmed said as he circled the number.

"If I can't find them before then, at least I will—I hope—get to them sometime that night," Deacon said more to himself than to the two men.

"If that's the one your gut is telling you to be at, then we should call Ryan. We can hand over all the information on these numbers to the FBI. At least they can make our appointments we have set up for the other numbers and provide back-up for your appointment," Nabi said as he picked up the phone to call.

While Nabi talked to Ryan, Ahmed pulled Deacon into a separate room. "Did you have to give them your name?"

"I only gave them a first name—Dean—and said I was coming in from Louisiana. I didn't need to give more since I said I was paying with cash."

"Good, but just in case, I'm giving you a fake ID. Sit." Ahmed gestured to the chair against the white sheet hanging from the wall. A camera flashed, and a minute later Deacon stood staring at a Louisiana license so good it could fool a cop with his picture and the name of Dean McCarthy on it.

"The FBI will stake out all the other appointments. They told Ryan that some of them were already on their radar, and they would organize stings to take them all down. They'll also keep an eye out for Bailey," Nabi called from the door. "And they'll work with you on the one where we think Bailey is. Ryan vouched for you, and you'll meet a contact from the local FBI when you arrive at your hotel to lay out plans for the party they can't get into. We'll find her."

"Now that we've narrowed it down to a few ads, let's see what else we can find," Ahmed instructed as they headed back into the main room.

Chapter Seventeen

Sydney flopped down on the couch with a tired sigh. She had woken up this morning to find her man and her dog gone. When Bridget called, Syd found the note. Knowing Deacon would be with Nabi and Nash for a while, Sydney decided to head out to Wyatt Estate. That was seven hours ago.

She had put away the dresses Allegra had shipped and then she had gotten down to treasure hunting. Syd had searched every room and found nothing. No little box, no big box, no trunk, no locked cabinet—nothing. Now it was time to prep Deacon for tonight, but he had texted and said he'd meet her at home at five. That only gave them an hour and a half to get ready, get prepped, and get to Grandma Davies's house.

Sydney groaned as she opened her eyes. There were only two creepy places left that she hadn't searched—the attic and the basement. Deciding to wait until it was sunny out to do the attic, Sydney pushed herself up and headed for the basement stairs near the kitchen. Like most old houses, the basement had an earthen floor, exposed stone foundation, and thick wood beams with concrete pillars supporting the house above.

There were always critters down there. Spiders, rats, snakes . . . it didn't matter that every month Critter Capture came in to set traps and clean out the area as best as they could. It still gave her the creeps. Especially since there was only one light dangling from a cord at the bottom of the stairs to light the whole area.

Sydney flicked on the light and stared down at the basement. She turned her phone's flashlight on and slowly started down the rickety wooden steps as the door closed on its own behind her. She should have propped it open. She didn't care if she was a grown woman; the basement scared her to death. The light played on the boxes and cast strange shadows where critters could hide. Mysterious cobwebs with no spiders hung in the corners and old metal toys from long ago sat staring out at her from open boxes. Not to mention the spine-chilling draft from the old coal chute that always seemed to be blowing air into the earthy darkness, even though the thick metal door was latched shut.

Sydney stepped onto the pressed-dirt floor and took a fortifying breath. She could do this. Just look for a trunk or something with a lock. She turned to the right and headed for the boxes stacked against the far wall. Cardboard boxes filled with old Christmas lights and a plastic Santa were all she could see. She pushed aside a box and found an old metal trunk. This could be it! Sydney held up her key in one hand and the light in the other. She inserted the key into the lock and sighed. The key was way too small.

Sydney started to stand up when the creaking sound of old hinges froze her in place. She tried to tell herself she was just imagining it, but the goose bumps running down her arms told her otherwise. The sound stopped, and Sydney begged for there not to be a big snake slithering around the old farm equipment. She went to turn when there was the sound of a light bulb shattering and then darkness.

Sydney whirled around with her flashlight just in time to see a black-clad arm snaking out from the darkness to knock her phone from her hand. The phone fell and the light was lost to the dirt floor. The basement was in complete darkness, and she wasn't alone. Her breath came in shallow gasps as she tried to hear where the other person was.

A strong breeze from behind rippled her hair as the intruder ran his hand behind her. She spun with her hand held out, but he wasn't there. The only sound as she fumbled, hands outstretched through the darkness, was a soft, taunting laugh that seemed to echo around her.

"What do you want?" Sydney demanded as she struggled to keep the panic at bay.

"I told you I would come for you." The man's malicious threat sent Sydney running blindly.

She stumbled in the dark and fell forward. She grasped at the object in front of her and it grasped back.

"Eager to be in my arms again?" He tormented her as he hauled her onto her feet.

"Vic," Sydney cried as she struggled to pull away.

"I love an enthusiastic partner. Keep fighting, Sydney. I like it rough." Vic laughed.

Adrenaline and fear caused Sydney's brain to switch off and her baser instincts to kick in. It was fight-or-flight time, and her body was screaming for her to let loose. She pulled her knee back and plowed it into the region she hoped contained his balls.

Sydney felt her knee connect, and Vic howled in pain. She leaped back as he released her to grab his balls. With a foul curse he lunged at her, but Sydney twirled away when she felt his fingertips against her side and slammed into the back wall. Her hands felt the cool stone and something else. She smiled in the dark as her fingers wrapped around the hilt of some antique farm tool.

Sydney spun around and lashed out with the long tool. It was heavy on the end and could be anything from a shovel to an axe. The thump coming from the darkness as the tool bashed Vic made her baser self smile. She darted away with the tool in front of her as Vic cursed again. Too bad she hadn't killed him.

The end of the tool thudded against wood and Sydney knew she had found the stairs. With her hand outstretched, she felt the stairs and fled up them. She reached out for the door and found the knob. She flung the door open and then slammed it shut, throwing the old lock on it before dashing to her great-grandfather's office. Inside was a veritable armory of guns. Granted, most were antiques, but they worked nonetheless.

Sydney didn't bother looking for the key. She grabbed a small statue from his desk and threw it through the glass doors of the gun case. She reached inside and pulled out a shotgun, searching for the correct shells as she kept an ear open for Vic trying to beat down the basement door.

With shaking hands, Sydney loaded the gun and stuffed some shells into her pocket before lightly stepping her way back to the kitchen. The door was still bolted as she reached for the phone hanging on the wall. She picked it up and dialed 9-1-1 with the shotgun aimed at the door.

"This is Sydney Davies, Sheriff Davies's daughter. I'm at Wyatt Farm in Keeneston and have been attacked by an intruder who is now locked in the basement," Sydney stated as clearly as she could while she rattled off the address. "Yes, I'll stay on the line. And yes, I think I'm safe. I have a shotgun aimed at the basement door."

Sydney heard the first siren just four minutes later, but it had been the longest four minutes of her life. The front door was hurled open and crashed against the wall as booted steps ran toward her.

"Syd!"

"Matt! I'm in the kitchen," Sydney called as she hung up with the dispatcher and the Kentucky state trooper rushed into the room.

"Is the perp down there? Did he hurt you?" Matt Walz fired off questions as he looked her over with his gun aimed at the basement door.

"He's still down there. I'm okay, just shaken up."

The young trooper nodded his head and moved toward the door. Matt was around her age with dark blond hair and navy blue eyes. Keeneston became divided with Matt's arrival a few years before. The women under forty called Matt with emergencies. The over-forty crowd called Syd's father. Her mother found it amusing. Her father was just relieved to no longer be called to fights at the PTA meetings.

"Stay here, I'm going down," Matt ordered as Sydney heard the sounds of a second set of sirens drawing near.

Matt pulled out his flashlight and unlocked the door. He disappeared slowly down the stairs, and Sydney moved closer to see the beam of light sweeping the basement.

"Sydney!" she heard her father call out as he and Annie sprinted into the kitchen. "Matt?" he asked, nodding toward the open door.

"Yes, he just went down there."

Her father leaned over and kissed her cheek before pulling out his own flashlight. "Stay with her, Annie. Matt, I'm coming down," Marshall called down the stairs.

Annie had her gun drawn and looked Sydney over. "You hurt?"

Sydney shook her head. "No. Just scared out of my mind. It was the same man from Atlanta. He found me, and I don't think he's going to stop until he has me or he's dead."

Two beams of light appeared near the bottom of the stairs and soon she could make out the forms of her father and Matt.

"He's gone," her father called out. "It looks like he got in and out from the old coal chute. I'll call and have that welded shut."

Matt held out her cell phone. "Did find this, though."

"Thank you. I don't know why he's so fixated on me." Sydney took her phone and shoved it in her pocket.

"You've challenged him by not giving in to him. Men like that want to dominate women. He sees it as a challenge that you fight him. On some level he's turned on by the chase," Annie told them as her father ground his teeth together so hard she could hear them.

Her father wrapped his arms around her and pulled her head to his shoulder. "It's okay, baby. I'll stay with you until this man's caught. I won't leave your side, not for one minute."

Deacon, Ahmed, and Nabi stared at the agenda they created. It highlighted all the parties Sydney and he were to attend in order to find Bailey. As a fallback, they would rely on the yet-to-be-scheduled appointment. Nabi had created a fake profile and website for *Dean* as well. But that threw a kink in their plans to have Deacon serve as a bodyguard.

The door to the control room opened and Zain angrily stalked in. "Nash is gone? I can't believe my uncle would do this. I could kill him!"

Nabi shook his head. "Calm down. You just committed treason because of your anger. You are better than this. We've taught you how to control your emotions."

"I'm sorry, but someone berating me, arguing with me, or provoking me is completely different from learning my uncle ordered one of my best friends away during a sting to help protect one of my other friends. And all without a word of goodbye. Now what are Deacon and Sydney going to do without Nash for backup?" Zain asked as he stopped to look at the computer screen.

"I'll just go it alone. The plan has to change anyway. I think I have an appointment with Bailey under the assumed identity of a rich oil baron. We were just discussing it," Deacon explained.

Zain let out a frustrated breath. "That's the real reason

I'm here and how I found out about Nash. I got a call from a 'friend' that there are going to be some models at this elite party in a suite at the football game. Only the worst of the rich will be there. And if Barrett Bischoff is going to be there, then it's not going to be good. He's part of a group with the mindset that money makes you invincible and above the law. They believe life is only about their pleasure, their wants."

Ahmed looked up at the master list of parties they had learned about. "Which one is it?"

"It's not on there anywhere. This is a secret, know-the-password, nothing-written-down party. Barrett only told me about it since I'd asked around for some unconventional fun during the game. When he called to see what I meant, I told him I just wanted to get laid and watch a game without all these women expecting to become a princess. I told him I'd pay a fortune for some young girl to, well, you know. And I just did pay a fortune for it. I agreed to bring $50,000 in cash to be able to join this party," Zain told them with his anger shifting away from his uncle and onto Barrett.

Deacon smiled. "I have an idea. I think your good friend Dean McCarthy, Louisiana oil baron, needs to go with you."

Nabi shook his head. "No way. I'm not letting someone in line for the crown of Rahmi go to a place where your security is unable to go. No way."

"But I will have security. I'll have Deacon. And I have all the training you've given me over the years. You know I would have gone into the military had I not been in line for the crown," Zain argued.

"I don't like it. Besides, there's no guarantee Deacon can get in," Nabi told him.

Deacon watched as Zain whipped out his phone and placed a call. "Barrett, my good friend is coming in tomorrow to visit, and I want to bring him with me."

Zain paused and then laughed. "Dean McCarthy. He's got his hand in all the oil in Louisiana and the Gulf. He has more money than I do. I've partied with him before; he likes them young and good at taking direction, if you catch my drift." Zain waited and then smiled. "Great. Thanks again; this is exactly what I need. See you then."

Zain hung up and shot a triumphant smile at Nabi. "Deacon's in. Apparently you put together a great profile online. Barrett liked the pictures of him with the porn stars."

"Porn stars?" Deacon asked.

Nabi just smiled. "I had to show you weren't an angel."

"Sydney's father will kill me if he sees that. Speaking of which, I have to get going. I'm going to the Davies dinner tonight."

The three other men sucked in air. "Don't mess this up or you won't be alive to find Bailey," Ahmed warned.

"It's just dinner," Deacon said with a shrug of his shoulders.

"Oh, you poor son of a bitch. You have no idea what's in store for you," Zain said with a smirk.

"Think how awful waterboarding is," Nabi said as he fought to find the right words, "then multiply that by 100."

Deacon didn't know whether to laugh or cry. Were they joking? If not, then he was worried—very, very worried.

"All units, we have an assault with suspect still on site. Wyatt Farm in Keeneston," the dispatcher said on the police scanner sitting on the side table of the security room. Deacon felt his heart stop as the dispatcher rattled off the address.

"Be advised, the victim is on scene, armed, and guarding the suspect. The victim is Sheriff Marshall Davies's daughter. Handle with care," the dispatcher said.

Deacon was out the door before he could hear the rest of the dispatcher's information. All he knew was Sydney was hurt, but at least she was well enough to call in the attack. Deacon felt fear's icy hold as he sped out of Desert Farm and tried to remember the way to Mrs. Wyatt's farm. He tried to call Sydney, but the phone rang and went to voicemail.

Deacon gunned the old truck and shot down the narrow country road. He flew past a gated entrance and slammed on his brakes a mile down the road as Marshall Davies went flying by him in the opposite direction.

"Shit," Deacon cursed as he bounced through the grass to turn the truck around. The cruiser was already out of sight as he coaxed the old truck to go faster. He should have slowed down to read the name on the gate. He turned into the driveway and the gate slid open.

By the time he arrived at the old house, a Kentucky state trooper and a sheriff's cruiser were parked by the front door. Deacon didn't even bother to turn off the truck as he jumped out and raced inside.

"I won't leave your side, not for one minute," he heard Sydney's dad say as Deacon rushed into the room.

"Sydney, are you okay?" Deacon asked as he tried to pry Sydney from her father's grasp. He was pretty sure Marshall growled at him as he tightened his grip on his daughter.

"Dad, I can't breathe," Sydney said, mushed against her father's chest.

Marshall loosened his grip and Sydney tried to turn toward Deacon, but her father didn't let her. "And where were you? How do we know it wasn't you that assaulted her?"

Deacon felt his eyes go wide. "Me?" he gasped. He didn't even know what to say to that.

"Knock it off, Dad. It wasn't Deacon and you know it. Deacon, it was Vic. He found me here," Sydney said as she tried to step out of her father's grasp. "Dad, will you please let me go to my boyfriend?"

Her father growled again. "I should have known better than to trust a PI with my daughter's safety."

"Don't worry, sir. From now on I won't leave Sydney's side," Deacon said as he mimicked Marshall's early statement.

Annie shook her head as Sydney was finally enfolded in Deacon's arms. "I can't wait for dinner tonight! Speaking of which, we need to get going. Matt, you got this?"

"Sure do." Matt held out his hand to Deacon and Deacon shook it. "Wish I had a chance to get to know you," he chuckled before heading back down into the basement.

Annie dragged Marshall to the cruiser and finally Deacon could focus on Sydney. "I don't think your father likes me."

"My father doesn't like anyone who's interested in me," Sydney sighed.

"Are you up for tonight? Will you tell me what happened?" Deacon asked.

"You don't know my family. If I don't go, they'll just hunt me down," Sydney said before filling him in on what happened and then listening as Deacon told her about Bailey. "But I can't get into that party," Sydney complained.

"I know. You'll take half of Zain's security guards and hit the other parties going on at that time. But, after this incident, I think you should stay here with your dad."

Sydney stopped walking toward the car. "Are you serious?"

"Yes. If Vic is after you, then you should be protected."

"I can't believe it. You're just like him. I'm surprised you aren't best friends."

Deacon opened Sydney's door for her before turning off the truck, grabbing a box from the back, and sliding into the driver's seat of Sydney's SUV. "We need to find a new way to explain my being around you at the parties until Zain and I go to this private party."

"I'll think of something. But the more pressing matter is I have ten minutes to prep you for the longest night of your life," Sydney said seriously.

Deacon chuckled before leaning across the console and placing a quick kiss on her lips. "It's just dinner. Why is everyone being so dramatic about this?"

Chapter Eighteen

Deacon pulled Sydney's SUV to a stop in front of the white wooden farmhouse. Her grandparents' house was always a special place. Every week, the entire family would gather. Extra tables had to be put up since the dining room table only fit her parents' generation. Since then, their grandfather had bought banquet tables and extended the dining room table all the way into the living room. It was a free-for-all to get one of the ends—that's where Grandma Davies would set her pies after dinner.

It was a place of happy memories, freshly baked cookies, and slumber parties with the cousins when they were young. But tonight the brightly lit house was savage. It didn't smell of fried chicken and pies. It smelled of the pending death of her relationship. Her family was plastered to the window, staring out at them in eager anticipation of tearing her boyfriend to shreds and sending him screaming into the night.

"Let's go," Sydney said quickly as she put her seatbelt back on.

"Let me just get the box I brought and then we can go inside," Deacon said as he went to open his door.

"No, I mean leave here. Let's go home," Sydney said

with forced excitement. When Deacon just shook his head and grinned at her, she sweetened the pot. "I'll do kinky things. I have lots of scarves."

Deacon's eyes melted as they traveled her body. She thought she had him until he sent her a wink. "I'll look forward to that after dinner." And then the dumb bastard got out of the car, opened the back door, pulled out a box, and walked around to open her door.

Sydney took his hand as he helped her from the SUV. "Just don't show any fear. They feed on that."

"Darlin', if I can handle the debutantes and their mothers at the Daughters of Atlanta Ball, then I think I can handle a family dinner filled with people who love you just as much as I do. Besides, from all of Mrs. Wyatt's letters, I feel as if I'm already part of the family," he said as he smiled at her. Bless his heart.

The front door was flung open and her grandparents stepped out onto the porch to greet them. Sydney slid her hand into Deacon's for support as he walked toward his death, smiling cheerfully.

"Grandma, Grandpa, this is Deacon McKnight. Deacon, these are my grandparents, Jake and Marcy Davies," Sydney introduced. Her grandparents were usually the nice ones. It was the pack of wolves behind them that weren't.

Deacon let go of her hand to shake hands with her grandfather before reaching into the box and pulling out a small bouquet of gardenias. "Mrs. Davies, Mrs. Wyatt told me what a special friend you were to her. I'm so pleased to finally meet you in person," Deacon said sincerely as he handed the fragrant flowers to her grandmother.

Marcy beamed. Sydney's father stood in the doorway behind her and frowned. "Oh, what a nice young man you have here, Sydney. It's such a pleasure to meet you, Deacon. Welcome to our home."

Sydney breathed her first sigh of relief. He'd made it through the first round. But he was about to run the gauntlet as the aunts, uncles, and cousins lined the entrance into house. Sydney narrowed her eyes and stared them down. Deacon wasn't like the others. He really loved her, and she didn't want to lose him.

"Mrs. Davies, it's so nice to see you again," Deacon said with a smile that had her mother blushing as he handed her a bundle of roses. "And Mr. Davies, I'm looking forward to hanging out with you tonight. We haven't had much time to get to know each other. Sydney tells me you enjoy shooting. We'll have to go sometime."

Sydney almost choked. Her father was squeezing Deacon's hand so hard his knuckles were white, but Deacon just smiled before turning to Annie. "It's good to see you again, Annie. Is it okay if I call you that, or would you prefer Mrs. Davies as well?" Deacon asked as he handed her a bouquet of daisies.

Annie took the flowers and smiled. "Annie is fine. This is my husband, Cade."

Layne, Miles and Morgan's only child and one of Sydney's closest cousins, leaned forward and whispered, "Oh, he's smooth. The aunts are melting. Hell, so am I."

Sydney nodded at her cousin. Tonight Layne's long black hair was hanging loose and made her look soft — exactly what she wasn't. Her father was an ex-Special Forces leader. While Layne was a physical therapist, she

KATHLEEN BROOKS

knew more ways to kill someone with her hands than how
to heal them, thanks to Miles.

"I know. There might be hope for him yet."

Layne shook her head. "Don't count on it. The men
look aggravated that he's winning over their wives."

Sydney watched as Deacon handed flowers to her
remaining aunts — Paige, Gemma, and Tammy — before
setting his box down. He turned to Sydney's cousins and
quirked his lips in an apologetic smile. "I'm sorry, ladies. I
didn't bring enough flowers for all of you. I'll remember it
next time. I'm Deacon," he said, holding out his hand to
them.

"I'm Riley," the redhead said, sticking out her hand.
"This is my twin, Reagan. We belong to Cy and Gemma.
Our mom's the one you gave gardenias to. Our dad is the
one that already ran a background check on you, right
down to the results of your last STD test."

Sydney would kill them. But Deacon just laughed as he
shook her hand.

"Aw, bless his heart, he thinks you're joking," Piper
said as if Deacon was too dumb to realize he was being
made fun of. Piper was Tammy and Pierce's oldest child
and a lab geek like her father. She was always trying to
invent something new. Unlike her father, though, she
didn't build things. She played with genes and viruses.

Deacon sent her a wink. "I've been told I am blessed,
but it wasn't my heart they were talking about."

Piper snorted and turned to Sydney with a grin on her
face. "Okay, I like this one," she said before sauntering into
the dining room to help set the table.

"Deacon," Sydney said as she placed her hand on his

arm, "I want you to meet Layne and Sophie. Layne is Miles and Morgan's daughter. Miles is the one glaring at you. Oh, I guess I should be more specific. He's the taller one glaring you. His wife has black hair and you gave her irises. And Sophie is Cade and Annie's oldest daughter."

"Ladies, it's nice to meet you. Sydney has told me all about you both." Deacon shook their hands and Sydney dared to breathe a little easier as Ryan and Sienna joined them.

Ryan shook Deacon's hand, and Sydney heard someone whisper, "Traitor." Ryan just shook his head and turned to the group of men circling like sharks behind them. "I've already met him. Give me a break. I have to save my interrogation for when Greer brings someone home," Ryan said about his little sister who was graduating from college in a couple months.

Sydney's grandmother clapped her hands and her grandfather let out a shrill whistle. "Chow's ready!" Grandpa called out as everyone hurried to find a seat.

Deacon had Sydney's hand in his and one second later he didn't. Suddenly he found himself being shuffled into the dining room by a wall of men while Sydney was shut out of the dining room altogether.

"Dad!" Sydney yelled warningly from her place at the far end of the table.

"What?" Marshall replied innocently.

Deacon looked at where he'd been escorted. He was the third seat in from the end. The first belonged to Cade, then Miles. On his other side were Marshall and Pierce. Across from him were Cy and two younger men who wore the same Davies glare as the older men. Deacon's hand tightened on his fork. He knew an ambush when he saw one.

"So, which cousins are you?" Deacon asked as he let go of his fork and tried to casually scoop some homemade macaroni and cheese onto his plate.

"Does it matter?" asked the muscled one with a hard glint to his eye and the hint of a tattoo peeking out from under the V-neck of his tight black shirt.

Deacon shrugged as he passed the macaroni and cheese to Marshall. "*Hey You* is easier to remember."

The other young man's silver eyes shone with amusement, but he quickly banked it. "So, Uncle Cy, what did you find out about our friend here?"

"I'm so glad you asked, Jackson. Our *friend* here is a trust fund brat who escorts debs around at *society* events," the man with the short light brown hair said with distaste.

"Guilty. Or at least I used to be. Haven't done that in years. Although, the dance lessons my mother forced me to take paid off. Do you know how much women love a man who can dance?" Deacon asked as he casually moved his hand from where Marshall was dangerously close to stabbing him with his dinner knife. "Is that all you've got? For a super-spy, that's pretty lame. But, I guess you are retired."

Cy's lip rose in a snarl. "Oh, I know a lot more. All the way down to the fact you got a C+ in Algebra in the ninth grade and that your dentist thinks you need to floss more."

Deacon took a bite of the fried chicken and groaned. "Mrs. D, this is amazing. And everyone needs to floss more. Did you find the four parking tickets, three speeding tickets, my concealed-carry permit, and the fact I'm really hoping to meet Trey Everett while I'm here? Oh, and don't forget my clean blood test from last month when I donated blood."

Deacon dug into his dinner as he felt the men beside him move into action. He leaned forward and sent a smile to a very worried-looking Sydney. She didn't look reassured.

"What are your intentions toward my daughter?" Marshall asked.

"How much money do you make? Can you support her?" Miles asked.

"Will you sign a pre-nup?" Pierce asked as he leaned forward.

"Of course he won't. If he does, he won't be able to access her money when she ditches him," Cade sneered.

"It must be emasculating to know no matter how much money you do have, she'll have more," *Hey You* said.

"And if you're with Sydney, you will stop being Deacon McKnight and just be the guy that super-smart, beautiful, and powerful Sydney is dating. It would suck to know your name will never be remembered, and the only time people will talk about you is to wonder why Sydney would be with someone like you," Jackson smirked.

Deacon took a bite of his dinner before clearing his throat. "I love your daughter, and I want to be free to explore what kind of future we have together." He turned to Miles. "I don't make much money, but then as Cy said, I don't need it. While I do get paid, and paid well for my high-profile cases, I then turn around and use most of that money to work on cases for people who don't have the money to pay my regular fees." Deacon looked to Cade and then Pierce. "And yes, I'll happily sign a pre-nup. When Sydney and I get to the point of marriage, a pre-nup will be a moot point anyway. When I finally decide to marry someone, it'll be forever."

Deacon took another bite of dinner and took his time enjoying it before looking across the table at her cousins. "And I don't give a flying shit in space what others think about me. I only care what Sydney thinks. Further, only a self-absorbed little twit with no confidence in himself as a man would care that the woman he loves makes more money than he does. You don't care, do you, Cy? Your wife has sold three books that have been turned into movies and has made a fortune off of them while I believe you just enjoy a normal government pension every month."

Deacon turned in his seat toward Marshall. "And we don't even need to address the fact that you, a small-town sheriff, married a supermodel. You didn't care. I don't care." Deacon smiled at him then. "Maybe Sydney was right."

"Right about what?" Marshall asked reluctantly.

"Oh, she was just surprised at how much we had in common. And don't get me started on Pierce and Tammy's relationship and how he was too dumb to recognize the perfect woman standing in front of him until he almost lost her. I'm already miles ahead there; I realize how special and perfect Sydney is."

Deacon turned to his left and looked at Miles and Cade. "Further, if I leave dinner tonight with the family's blessing, I'll gladly roast the next poor bastard who's in this seat, and who will probably belong to one of your daughters." Deacon turned to a highly amused Marcy. "Ma'am, if dinner was this fantastic, I can't imagine what dessert is like. Is it one of your famous apple pies?"

"It sure is, young man. But first, how do you feel about babies? I can't die happy until I've held a great-grandchild in my arms. And since Ryan isn't cooperating yet . . ."

Marshall groaned along with his brothers. "Mooooom, really?"

Marcy lifted a delicate shoulder. "I couldn't let you boys have all the fun. So, what is it, young man?"

"Well, I fear this may mean I don't get dessert—" Deacon started.

"Yes!" Marshall cried as he pumped his fist.

"But," Deacon said, ignoring Sydney's father who clearly thought that meant there was no hanky-panky going on, "I love children. I want as many as I can get. However, that's for Sydney and me to decide, no matter how much we love and respect you and your desire for great-grandchildren."

Miles sucked in his breath next to him and whispered, "You're a dead man."

Marcy stared at him and then gave a brief nod before silently getting up and leaving the table.

Cade laughed from where he sat at the end of the table. "We could have skipped this whole production if we just had Mom go first."

"That's too bad," Cy said a little disappointed. "I was just beginning to like him."

Miles smiled at Marshall. "Oh, come on, Marsh. You were starting to like him, too."

"Maybe, but it's a moot point now," Marshall said, and Deacon detected a little remorse.

"I still don't like him," *Hey You* muttered.

"You don't like anyone, Dylan," Jackson teased.

Deacon looked up as Marcy came back into the dining room with two hot apple pies. Was his time really up? Marcy set the pies down without looking at him. Crap. He had blown it. She grabbed a knife, cut the pie, and slid a big piece onto a plate as her husband brought out ice cream. Marcy scooped out a spoonful and topped the pie with it.

"I always get the first slice," her husband said gleefully as he reached for it.

"Not tonight. Tonight Sydney's boyfriend does. Here you go, Deacon. I'm so glad my grandbaby found such a special man."

Sydney almost collapsed against the back of her chair when her grandmother handed the first slice of pie to Deacon. She saw her family's shocked expressions and wanted to jump up and do a happy dance. Somehow Deacon had survived. By the way her father casually shook Deacon's hand, she knew the worst was over.

Sydney took a calming breath as her mom sent her a wink from across the table, and Sophie gave her a discreet nudge under the table.

"He did it. It's a first. Did someone document this?" Sophie whispered from where she sat on one side of Syd.

"Look, even my dad is shaking his hand. Or maybe he's trying to steal his pie. Either way, they're smiling. *Smiling!*" Layne said, stunned as Miles, Deacon, and Cade all laughed.

"Maybe there's hope for us yet," Sophie said optimistically.

Two hours later, Sydney hugged her parents goodbye and waved to her family as she and Deacon walked toward the car. Deacon had fit right in once the macho tension had been sliced along with the apple pie.

Deacon walked next to Sydney with his arm around her, keeping her warm. The stars were clear in the cold sky above as she rested her head against his shoulder. She was both exhausted and excited. The day had been long, scary, and stressful, but at the same time her family had accepted Deacon. Mostly. Her dad wasn't thrilled, but he also had stopped reaching for his gun. That was a pretty big win for the first family dinner.

"So you survived." Syd grinned up to him as he opened the car door for her.

"It wasn't so bad. You have a really great family. I think after your dad gets over wanting to shoot me, we'll get along great." Deacon smirked at her before closing the door.

"Now you see why I always come home. My whole family grows and leaves the nest, but they all come back again. I've just reached that part of my life where I'm coming home to stay. I still have my houses elsewhere, but this is home."

"What about your new house in Georgia?" Deacon asked casually, although there was nothing casual about it.

Sydney felt the closest thing to panic she thought possible. She'd had nerves of steel growing up in the modeling world and then breaking into business. But the thought of being separated from Deacon, of going back to the way they were before they met was just too much.

"I'm going to keep it for now. Beyond that, I don't know. I guess time will tell."

"I'm glad you're going to keep it. It's such a historic place. You know, the Daughters of Atlanta had been begging Mrs. Wyatt to open the house to visitors. Since I was living there, I appreciated that she didn't," Deacon said wryly as he drove toward her house.

"I bet there have been plenty of Daughters of Atlanta in that house," Syd teased back.

"Jealous, darlin'? I wouldn't have guessed it," Deacon said amused as he pulled into her garage. "Don't you worry, there's only one woman I want in my house and in my bed."

Sydney felt a giddy rush of pleasure as Deacon sent her a wink. He opened her door for her and slung his arm over her shoulder. "It's just too bad she isn't here."

Sydney gasped and smacked his stomach.

"What? I'll miss that little squirt of a shoe-eating pup while she's at obedience school," Deacon sighed dramatically.

Sydney stepped into the kitchen and kicked off her shoes as she shook her head. She tossed her jacket onto the barstool and began to slide out of her jeans. She felt Deacon stop as soon as he entered the kitchen. She could feel his eyes on her as she pulled the sweater from her body and dropped it onto the floor. Sydney grinned to herself as she started to walk out of the kitchen.

Sydney reached behind her and unhooked her bra

before looking over her shoulder at Deacon. "It's just too bad you have to sleep alone tonight," Sydney said sympathetically as she dropped her bra to the floor.

"Like hell I am." Deacon grinned as he shot toward her, pulling his shirt over his head as he ran. Sydney screamed and darted up the stairs. It didn't take him long to catch her. "I love you, Sydney."

Sydney didn't have a chance to respond before he covered her mouth with his. And when his hand disappeared beneath the satin of her panties, she didn't care if they even made it to the bed.

Chapter Nineteen

"This is torture," Sophie whined as Sydney pinned the material she'd bought from Paige.

"Try doing this for a living," Sydney mumbled around a mouthful of pins. "Now hold still. I just need to make one more adjustment."

"I've been standing here forever," Sophie complained as she took a drink of white wine. "I have to leave late tonight, and I'm not even going to have time to get some bread pudding from the café, especially at the rate you're going. It's dinner time!"

Sydney tried not to roll her eyes. Her cousin has been standing there for all of five minutes. "Where are you off to this time?"

"Washington," Sophie sighed.

"What do you have to do there?" Sydney asked but was met with silence. "Oh, right. Some super-secret lab geek stuff. I swear you and Piper should be sisters."

Sophie shifted, and Sydney poked her to stand upright. "Piper likes to play with viruses. I play with biometrics. Completely different."

"If you say so," Sydney muttered as she made the last tuck. "Okay, now hold very still while I get this off you."

Sydney carefully extricated Sophie from the top and then helped her shimmy out of the short skirt. She'd been working all day on sewing the outfit. While Sophie was a little shorter than Sydney, she was close to the same size, and it helped to see how the finishing touches would look when the material was draped on a real person.

"Is that the hat Aunt Paige made?" Sophie asked as she pulled on her black slacks and cream sweater.

"Sure is." Sydney opened the hatbox and gently brought out the large white hat.

"Oh, I love how she used some of the material from your dress as the band," Sophie exclaimed as she set the hat on Sydney's head. "How mysterious! It's so large that it's hard to tell it's you. But the way it curves is so feminine at the same time. You're going to kill it with this dress. Just don't let Nash kill anyone," Sophie laughed.

"Haven't you heard?" Sydney asked with dread. While her cousin had never admitted it, the whole town knew there was something between Nash and Soph, or there could be if they'd allow it. It didn't matter how much they denied it or seemed to avoid each other; something was definitely there.

"Heard what?" Sophie asked as she put the hat in the box.

"The king ordered Nash back to Rahmi," Sydney said carefully.

Sophie shrugged. "He's always sending Nash on assignments. Not that Nash will ever tell me about them. It's his job. Just like mine, it involves a lot of travel."

Sydney shook her head. "No, Soph. It's more like a permanent assignment. Nash isn't coming back this time."

Sydney reached out to comfort her cousin, but Sophie shook her off as she downed her wine. "So he's gone, and he didn't bother saying goodbye?"

"He didn't get a chance. From what Nabi told Deacon, Nash was called away immediately."

"He could have called or something," Sophie fumed as she poured another glass of wine and downed it.

"I know you care about him. I'm sure he'll call," Sydney said as she tried to sound optimistic.

"Why? There's nothing between us. I don't care about him. I could have any man I want. But you know what I want? Bread. Freaking. Pudding."

Sydney had to scramble to keep up with Sophie as she marched toward her car. "Soph, let me drive. Deacon can pick me up from the café when he's done with Ahmed and Nabi." Sydney grabbed the keys. As Sophie got into the car, Syd texted the girls to meet them at the café.

Minutes later, Sydney hurried after Sophie as she slammed into the café. For once, the patrons were quiet. Everyone ducked their heads and took great interest in their food. Poppy saw them coming and placed glasses of ice water on the center of the round table.

Poppy saw them coming and placed glasses of water were at the round table in the center.

"I have a special hot drink Miss Lily taught me. I'll bring it right out. And chocolate. What else do you need, hon?" Poppy asked Sophie, who dropped into her chair.

"Nothing. Why would I need anything? I'm hunky-dory, peachy-keen, in fact. I have a great job, an apartment in DC, and a small house here that I'm never at. But it's here when I want it. And shoes, you should see all the shoes I have. What else does a woman need?"

Poppy nodded. "So, more chocolate then?"

"Yes," Sophie said with a sigh.

The bell over the door tinkled as Sienna, Layne, and Piper rushed in. The three women were completely different. Sienna was average height and curvy, with auburn hair. Raven-haired Layne was a little taller and athletically built. Piper was the shortest, with dirty-blond hair pulled back into a sloppy bun. But the looks of concern were the same on all their faces as they sat down.

"So, you heard about Nash?" Piper asked slowly.

"Why should I care about Nash?" Sophie asked nonchalantly as Poppy set down the warm drinks that were probably laced with a healthy dose of Kentucky bourbon.

"Sophie, you don't have to pretend with us. We know something happened between you two," Sienna said kindly as she took a sip of the drink and coughed.

"I don't know what—" Sophie started only to be cut off by Layne.

"Oh, knock it off, Soph. You wouldn't be upset and on your second cup of whatever this drink is if you weren't upset. Now, talk," Layne ordered. It was easy to see that her father and mother had rubbed off on her. Miles was the head of a company and a former leader in the Special Forces. Morgan was a take-no-prisoners-in-business type as well.

The bell over the door to the café tinkled, and Sydney glanced quickly to see who came in. "Crap on a cracker," she muttered as she saw Nikki Canter and her Keeneston

Belle squad saunter in as if the café were a catwalk.

The Keeneston Belles had started as a charitable organization for seniors at Keeneston High. They were the pretty, popular women in high school who wanted to do good and had no trouble getting others to help them with a bat of their lashes. Sadly, the power went to their heads, and every other generation or so, the Belles forgot their charitable purpose and instead were busy husband-hunting from the crème de la crème of Keeneston bachelors. When they married, they joined the Keeneston Ladies, the real power behind the town. Now the seniors they recruited in high school were more like pledges of a sort. The ones in charge were the girls who were back from college where they perfected their claw sharpening on frat boys and professors.

The queen bee of the Belles was newly elected Nikki Canter. She sashayed into the café in skinny jeans, knee-high leather boots, and a jacket so tight she couldn't button it over her newly enhanced boobs. According to Ryan's sister, Greer, who was one year younger than Nikki, Nikki was the ignored girl in school, always number two. It was her best friend who was the prom queen and the most popular girl. Nikki took it as a challenge when she went away to college to come back and take over the Belles.

Nikki had lost fifteen pounds and moved that weight to her tits, along with injecting her lips and dyeing her brown hair mahogany red. Furthermore, she refused to remain in the background any longer. She had swept into the Belles and demanded they bow down to her new rule. She ousted the last president in a negative campaign that made national elections seem friendly. Nikki had her eye on the prize, and that prize was the most powerful bachelor in Keeneston, Zain Ali Rahman. Nothing was going to stop her until she was a princess.

Within the Belles was also a secret list ranking the most eligible bachelors. So while Nikki focused on Zain, her followers had targeted the others deemed most likely to hold power, money, and prestige. Most of Sydney's friends and cousins were on that list, including Nash. And by the way Nikki zeroed in on Sophie, there was no doubt what was on her mind.

"Oh, Belles! Look how sad." Nikki exaggerated a pout that made her over-injected lower lip cover her chin. "There's poor Sophie drowning her sorrows in chocolate over losing Nash. Too bad she doesn't even know what she lost out on, huh?" Nikki winked and held out her hands to demonstrate how much of Nash she had missed out on.

The patrons of the café gasped. The women tittered for it was no small measurement Nikki had held up. Sydney started to look up Kenna's number because her friend was about to be arrested for murdering a Belle and would need a lawyer.

"I'm sorry, Nikki, but I couldn't hear you. Your lips melted into your boobs and all I heard was a muffled cry for attention," Sophie said with a chilling smile.

Nikki turned red as she narrowed her eyes. "It's so pathetic to see a woman chasing after a man she could never get. Someone like Nash needs an exciting woman to keep his interest. Something a boring lab rat would know nothing about."

Sophie nodded her head. "You're right. It is pathetic to see a woman chasing after a man she could never get.

Someone like Zain, for example, needs a woman with class to get his attention. Something an over-injected bimbo like you would know nothing about."

Nikki shrieked and came toward the table with her claws out. Then she yelped like a puppy and dropped to the ground in a passed-out heap of boobs, lips, and hair. Her followers all looked at her just lying there, not knowing what to do. Sydney looked at her friends who all stared opened-mouthed except for a smiling and serene Sophie who closed her purse and started eating her bread pudding.

"Mmm. Poppy, this is excellent," Sophie said, breaking the silence as the patrons all stared at Nikki.

"Sophie, what did you do?" Sydney whispered as Nikki's minions started poking her with their sharp-toed shoes.

"Me?" Sophie asked way too innocently. "Why would you think I had anything to do with that? Besides, she's fine. She'll probably start waking up in ten minutes or so."

"You have to tell me how you did that. I want it, whatever it is." Layne winked as the table erupted into giggles when Nikki farted loudly. Then whispers were no longer needed as the patrons all started talking at once.

The bell over the door rang again, and Sydney saw Andy, Deputy Sheriff Dinky's son, come in. Nikki farted again and Andy grinned. Bless his redheaded heart, Andy wasn't on the Belle's bachelor list. He was around five-foot-seven with shocking carrot-orange hair and freckles. And he had been the high school's mascot. It had doomed him to uncool status all throughout high school, even if he was one of the nicest guys in town. He was also just one year older than Nikki. By the smile on his face, he was enjoying the scene as only a guy scorned could.

Andy stepped around the Belles and stopped at Sydney's table. "So, what's going on there?"

"She just yelped like a lap dog and went down. Maybe it's a seizure," Sophie said gleefully as she motioned to Poppy to refill her spiked drink.

"Please tell me someone is videoing this," Andy chuckled.

"Oh, I'm on it." Piper grinned as she recorded Nikki who had now added moaning to the farting.

"Man, as much as I love this, these damn southern gentlemen manners won't let me leave her there," Andy groaned as he headed over to the Belles. "Ladies, may I be of assistance?"

Nikki let one rip in response, and the Belles looked as if they were thinking of abandoning their leader. They grabbed on to Andy's offer and had him carry a very musical Nikki out the door a minute later—a door that was held open by a very sexy man.

"Hey," Sydney whispered to the girls, "who's that?"

She saw all their heads turn to look at the newcomer. He was around five-feet-eleven inches, with light brown hair and a runner's build. In his late twenties, he looked pretty damn good in those jeans and a black leather jacket.

"He's not from here, but I likey," Sophie grinned as she slammed down another empty cup.

Sydney shook her head as Sophie came to a wobbly stand. "What are you doing?" Sydney asked.

"Getting some. Do you know how long it's been since I've had sex?" Sophie asked rather loudly.

"I'm sure your father is happy about that," Miss Lily called out from across the room. Cade Davies would be thrilled to hear the news. And by the way Miss Lily was tweeting, he would be hearing it pretty darn soon.

The stranger obviously heard, too, smiled to himself, and took a seat at a nearby table. Poppy hurried over and took a drink order before handing him a menu. As she passed him walking toward the back of the café to get his drink, Layne called her over.

"Do you know him?" Layne asked.

Poppy shook her head. "Never seen him before."

"I call dibs." Sophie ran a hand over her hair and licked her lips. She stood up and walked as straight as possible to the newcomer.

Sydney and the girls grinned at each other. "It's like watching a train wreck. You know it isn't going to be pretty, but you can't look away."

Piper shrugged. "Maybe she'll get to have sloppy-drunk sex and leave town happy."

"I guess it's a good way to get over Nash," Sienna said unconvincingly.

Sophie stopped in front of the table, and the man stood up to greet her. That had to be a good start. At least he had manners.

"I'm Sophie Davies, and who might you be?" Sophie all but purred.

The man held out his hand. "Ben Jacobs. It's nice to meet you, Miss Davies."

Sophie smiled predatorily. "Can I have a seat?"

"Of course." Ben motioned to the empty chair across from him as he sat down. But Sophie had another idea. As soon as Ben sat, she took her seat . . . in his lap. The man was obviously surprised but was too nice to say anything.

"So, what brings you to Keeneston?" Sophie asked as she looped her hands around the man's neck.

"I'm starting a new job this weekend. In fact, that's what I'm doing here. I'm getting ready to meet the man I'm replacing. Are you all right? Do you need any assistance?" he asked.

"You know, I do. And I have the perfect idea for how you can help me."

The man took her meaning at once and smiled kindly at her. "I don't think I can be that kind of assistance for you."

"Why not?" Sophie asked as she trailed a finger down the man's chest. "Are you gay?"

"No, not gay."

"Married?"

"Not technically."

Sophie pouted. "So you have a girlfriend?"

The man shook his head. "No girlfriend."

"Then I don't see the problem." Sophie smiled.

"Ah, Miss Sophie, I see you've met my replacement," an older man's voice said from the door to the café.

"Holy —" Sydney gasped along with everyone in the café.

"Shit." Sophie finished what her friend had started as she looked up into the kind old face of Father James. Father James grinned at her as he walked over to the table. Sophie looked between him and the man whose lap she was sitting on. "Replacement?" she stammered.

"That's right. I start this Sunday," Ben, rather, Father

Jacobs said.

Sophie jumped up so fast that she would have fallen backward had Father Jacobs not caught her. "I'm going to hell."

Ben smiled kindly at her. "No, you're not. At least, not for hitting on a priest. Do you need a ride home, Miss Davies?"

Sophie shook her head as she looked at the clock on the wall. "No, thank you, Father. I have to catch a flight. Um, sorry about that. I'm not normally like that. It's just that I haven't had sex in a while and then Nash . . ." Sophie snapped her mouth shut. She was in the Blossom Café, not the confessional.

"Ben is fine," the young priest assured her. "And I'm sorry there seems to be a personal issue upsetting you. You're always welcome to stop by to talk if you need to. I'm good at keeping secrets."

Sydney took mercy on her cousin and leapt up. "Look at the time! We need to be going. Father, Ben, um, I'm Sydney Davies, and that's Sienna Parker, Layne Davies, and Piper Davies. We'll see you around. Welcome to Keeneston."

And in a flash, Sydney and her cousins had Sophie bundled up and out the door.

Chapter Twenty

D eacon had spent the next day with Zain going over the details of their cover. Nabi's men had given them a notebook full of pictures, facts on the people involved, and a map to each party. On the other hand, Sydney had spent all day finalizing her outfit and sending anonymous tips to the media about coming out of retirement. She had planted leaks about who was escorting her: all the way from Hollywood's sexiest star to the quarterback who would be playing in the big game that night. Syd sat quietly in her living room, tweeting and submitting these anonymous tips as she listened to Deacon and Zain. Every now and then, she would give her advice to the men. But as the night grew dark, the only unanswered question had been how to keep Sydney close without drawing attention.

Sydney had smiled and turned her phone for them to see. The gossip sites were all trying to figure out who her date for the evening was and what her new look would be. Sydney had been notoriously private as a model and now her long bleached-blond hair had grown out to her natural golden blond. Her curves were more pronounced, and instead of the natural makeup that made her look fresh-faced, she was going to look shocking in bright red lipstick.

On top of that, she had been seen in nothing but business attire for years now.

"It's easy. Zain will be my date. Who better than a prince to escort me? Then after the first party, his bad influence of a friend can show up and try to hit on me," Sydney had winked.

And that was the plan they went with. The group reviewed the cover story as they drove to Indianapolis. After arriving at the hotel, Deacon and Zain had quickly donned their tuxedos for a series of dinners with politicians. Sydney came out of the bathroom in a bathrobe with her hair pinned up to say goodbye to them.

"You two behave. Find out everything you can, and let me know if you find Bailey. I'll meet you back here in three hours. Hopefully, I'll be ready by then." Sydney smiled as she leaned forward and gave Zain a quick hug.

"You need three hours to get ready?" Deacon asked.

Sydney leveled him with a glare. "No, it usually takes four. But someone made us late."

Deacon grinned. He'd done that, and he didn't feel one bit guilty about it either. "You're beautiful already. Stay in here with the door locked. There's security outside if you need anything."

Deacon pulled Sydney into his arms and kissed her goodbye. She might be on Zain's arm tonight, but it was him she was kissing. Deacon couldn't wait for this to be over so he could do a little more kissing afterward—naked kissing. However, right now Zain was tapping his Italian leather-covered toe impatiently.

"I'll see you soon. Text me if you need anything," Deacon said as he pulled away from Sydney.

"I will. I love you. Be safe." Sydney smiled tightly at them as they followed a horde of security guards who were under Nabi's orders to protect them at all costs.

Deacon opened the digital file for the first party as soon as they were ensconced in the limousine. Senator Albert Bucks, the five-term senator from Indiana, was hosting the first party. He had cleared the background check with only the normal political skeletons in his closet—bribery, prostitutes, and corruption. The party was for high-ranking Indiana politicians: the governor, the mayor of Indianapolis, the other US senator, and the congressmen from their state. And of course, the politicians were surrounded by their allies and *yes men*.

"This isn't my area of expertise, but nothing really sticks out to me here. What should I be looking for?" Deacon asked Zain as they drove toward the restaurant.

"Nothing in particular. Just the usual. Politics is all about power. There are some good people who really want to change the world for the better. But the dark side of politics usually beats them down. Look closely at their dates. Lots of times they tell their wives it's a men-only party. Or if their wives are back in DC, they will bring their 'secretary' or maybe an 'aide' or 'intern.' If they say it with a wink, then you know they're prostitutes. The high-priced escorts who aren't being forced into these situations will take every opportunity to talk down the cheap, unprofessional girls that are likely being forced into the line of business. They take their jobs seriously, and getting rid of the competition increases their own bookings," Zain explained.

Deacon took a moment to really look at Zain. His face

was impassive, but there were tight lines around his mouth and eyes. He hated this. "You don't like politics, do you?"

"Despise it," Zain answered quickly.

"Then why are you a diplomat for your uncle and father?"

"Because I'm one of those who still thinks he can make the world a better place. Stupid, isn't it?"

Deacon shook his head. "No. It's not. Maybe the better question is, how do you know so much about high-priced escorts?" Deacon teased.

Zain finally smiled. "Some of them are really nice. Some of the women are trying to save money to pay for school or to pay off student loans. Some really enjoy it and would have gone into politics if they could. But it's such an old-boys club that it's hard for someone new to break into. However, their dates don't realize this and usually talk freely around them. I'm nice to them, and they trust me. I learned a lot about what was going on in politics from them. Plus they don't hit on me, aren't trying to become a princess, and generally don't give a shit who I am. They are surprised and relieved when I'm a nice person."

"You've hired them before, haven't you?" Deacon asked with surprise.

Zain grinned. "I don't need to hire women for sex."

"Not for sex but as a professional date for all these dinners."

"I'll let you in on a secret. I bring my advisor for foreign affairs to these things. We're a good team. Plus, she's a lesbian. I take her with me when I need a date, and she brings back all the information from the ladies' room. You won't believe what they talk about in there."

The limousine came to a stop before Deacon could crack one of the greatest mysteries in the world. The door was opened, and Zain climbed smoothly out into the flashing lights of cameras. He buttoned his tuxedo jacket and smiled as the journalists tossed out questions.

"Your Highness, what are you hoping to accomplish with the international summit you're hosting this summer?" a reporter asked as a microphone was shoved forward.

Zain turned to the reporter and gave a nod of acknowledgment. "I'm hoping that with open discussion among several world leaders, we can find a way to work together to support each country facing troubles stemming from infectious disease outbreaks, health crises, and cyber attacks. While it seems some of those issues are the problems of one country alone, in fact they are global, and we need to find a way to put aside geopolitical tensions so we can be better prepared to secure and help those citizens and leaders who require assistance. That can't happen until we're in the same room together," Zain said with a slight smile before moving on to the next reporter.

Deacon fell back into the pack of assistants and bodyguards as the politicians moved down press row, each eating up the limelight, except for Zain. While he appeared calm and collected, he was clearly not getting off on the attention like some of the others were. Especially when the third reporter in a row asked about his personal life.

Zain smiled mysteriously in reply to the question and fueled rumors by saying they may find out later tonight. Deacon had to take a deep breath as he walked through security and into the private room at the restaurant. The

KATHLEEN BROOKS

media would be all over Zain and Sydney later. It made it easier, knowing them both as he did. He trusted Zain and he trusted Sydney. However, it would still be hard to watch when all Deacon wanted to do was shout his love for Sydney for all to hear and claim her as his. But that could wait. He didn't know how he hit the jackpot of earning Sydney's love, but right now he needed to focus on Bailey. After that there would be plenty he and Sydney had to work out before they could continue on as a couple.

The room Deacon entered was full of cigar smoke, deep chuckles, and high-pitched giggles. Considering most of the men in the room were over fifty-five and all of the women in the room were in their early twenties, Deacon guessed Zain had read the situation correctly. There wasn't a wife to be found in the room. He was sure the girls had arrived early and had slipped in through the kitchen.

A moment after entering the room, Zain came to a stop beside him. He casually looked over the guests as he picked up a drink from the tray circulating around the tables. "They're all escorts," Zain said before taking a sip of his drink.

"I guessed that," Deacon said dryly. "Know any of them?"

Zain nodded right before a pretty woman disengaged herself from an older man and sauntered over to them.

"Zain," she smiled before placing a kiss on his cheek. "It's good to see you again. Who's your friend?" the brunette bombshell asked. She was dressed conservatively. They all were, but it was the way she carried herself with a quiet confidence that was the reason most of the eyes in the room were on her.

"Jessica." Zain smiled as the woman smacked him on the arm.

"Don't say that too loud. I don't want these old goats to know my real name. You and your mysterious network—I still don't know how you found out my name," she said as she looked cautiously at Deacon.

"Don't worry," Zain said softly, "he's with me. Jessica, meet Deacon McKnight, a PI from Atlanta. But tonight he's like you, undercover. Call him Dean. Deacon, this is Jessica Samburg, tonight known as Jackie. She's a third-year law student at Georgetown."

Deacon held out his hand, and she shook it, looking relieved. "Well, Dean, what brings you by tonight?"

"We're looking for a girl," Deacon said softly as some of the men started inching closer. "An eighteen-year-old girl named Bailey. A man named Vic, who claims to be a modeling scout, convinced her to leave her mother so he could make her famous. We have reason to believe she's at the game, and we're trying to find her."

Jessica shook her head. "You think she was trafficked?"

Deacon nodded.

"She's not here. I know that. High-priced or low-priced?"

"We don't know for sure, but there's a private party later tonight Barrett Bischoff is hosting. A party that cost me fifty grand to get into with supposedly high-class entertainment," Zain explained.

Jessica made a sound of disgust. "Barrett is sickening. He thinks women are objects made to please him. None of the women I know will accept jobs from him anymore.

He's too rough and doesn't know the meaning of the word *no*. It's a good place to look for her. Let me check in with some of my sources, and I'll let you know in a couple minutes."

Jessica sent them a wink and then turned to schmooze her way through the crowd. Deacon kept an eye on her as Zain introduced him to politician after politician. Ten minutes later, Jessica and some of the girls excused themselves to powder their noses.

"I'm a big supporter of the oil business," a politician Deacon had met droned on. "We could be of mutual help to one another if you have anything that needs to get a vote through. I have an election coming up next term."

Deacon saw Jessica come back out and smile at him. He turned his attention to the politician he remembered seeing on the news talking about the evils of oil just last week and smiled. "We'll talk later. For now, I see something a lot more interesting than oil." With a wink, Deacon headed over to Jessica.

"How do you tolerate these idiots?" he whispered, causing her to laugh.

"You get used to it. It's just a big production. You fluff their ego, and they pay for you to go to law school. Plus, they won't be able to turn me down when I ask for a recommendation for a clerkship on the Supreme Court. Oh, they'll huff and puff when they find out there's blackmail involved, but knowing they'll cave is what puts a smile on my face," Jessica said so innocently that Deacon chuckled behind the glass of bourbon he pretended to drink.

"So your girl, we don't know if it's her specifically, but

the rumor is that this Vic character is trouble. Plenty of our girls have been approached by him to become a model. One went with him, and the last time anyone saw her was in a mug shot in the paper for prostitution. That's the trouble with trafficking. The victims are often arrested, and the officers look no further."

Deacon nodded. "That's what I found, too. It's also a way the traffickers manipulate the girls into staying put."

"We found out he has a new batch of models with him tonight. Good luck. I hope you find her," Jessica said before placing a kiss on his cheek. "You and Zain are the good ones. Senator," Jessica said loudly as she beamed a killer smile at the man who had been making his way toward them. "I was just saying how amazingly sexy your filibuster was."

Deacon watched as Jessica slid her hand down the senator's arm and walked away. Zain approached with his still full drink and watched as Jessica focused all her attention on the older man.

Deacon filled him in on what Jessica had told him. Zain handed his glass to a waiter walking by. "We've found out enough here; let's hit the other parties."

An hour and a half later, Deacon had lost all hope in politicians. Their spouses, however, were a barrel of information. Zain had learned from the wives that a junior congressman, who got elected by his daddy's famous last name, was going to a private party later. Deacon stood nearby talking to the husband of a congresswoman as he heard the women confiding in Zain.

"See, over there. That's not even his wife. She's a

hooker, and a cheap one at that. But what do you expect from someone whose daddy had to cover up a rape charge when he was a juvenile?" the wife whispered loud enough for Deacon and the man he was talking with to hear.

"Is that true?" Deacon asked the husband.

He tossed back his drink and nodded. "He's friends with that Swiss banker's asshole son. What's his name? Bischoff. Entitled doesn't even begin to describe those two. That jerk over there slapped my wife's ass. She's a damn senior member of Congress, and the party leader yelled at her for filing an internal complaint against him. They forced her to drop it. His daddy donates too much money to the party. Oh, excuse me. I see my wife signaling me."

Deacon watched the dirty junior congressman slip his hand up the slit of his date's dress in front of everyone. Zain came to stand by his side as they watched the spectacle. "His name is Sebastian Oliver. Let's head that way and stop at the bar to have a little guy talk," Zain winked.

Deacon casually poured his drink into the potted plant and headed toward the bar. He slammed his empty glass on the bar top. "Bourbon. The good stuff this time," Deacon ordered as he saw Sebastian take notice from the corner of his eye. "Zain, come on, man, you're a freaking prince, and I have more money than most countries. Why," Deacon groaned, "are we stuck at these parties? I want some action." He elbowed Zain and sent him a wink. "You know the kind I'm talking about."

Zain let out a sigh. "This is the last one I have to show my face at to appease *His Highness*. We'll be rewarded at Barrett's party soon enough. I hope he found some good entertainment this time."

Deacon ignored Sebastian as the man stumbled over toward them. "Hey, you know Barrett Bischoff?"

"Yeah, who are you?" Zain asked with such royal indifference that Deacon nearly laughed.

"Sebastian Oliver," he said cockily.

Deacon couldn't help himself as he looked at the short man, slightly bloated from alcohol abuse. "Who?"

Sebastian turned red. "I'm a congressman. My father is Kurt Oliver, the actor."

"Oh. So you're friends with Barrett?" Zain asked with a hint of disbelief.

"Barrett's my man." Sebastian grinned. "We party together all the time. But I haven't seen you there, Zain."

Deacon bit back his grin. Sebastian obviously knew the power players in the room. No introductions were necessary as Sebastian rattled on, trying to prove he ran with the party crowd.

"You wouldn't. I only go to select private parties. The last one I went to in Abu Dhabi was a disappointment, though. The women," Zain shook his head, "just weren't up to my standards. I hope tonight is different."

"Haven't you heard?" Sebastian crowed. "He hired a modeling scout to find him some new girls."

"I wonder how the scout found them. It was probably some guy he found online," Deacon snorted.

Sebastian shook his head. "No. Vic works with Tristan Models. They're like, famous." Sebastian lowered his voice. "And he even has an inside track in the industry helping line these girls up. It's how they can find the best of the up-and-coming models."

Deacon smirked. "I guess we'll find out tonight, huh, boys?"

"Cheers to that," Zain said with a smile as Sebastian fed on being included. "Crap. Dean, we have to go. I have one more job to do before Barrett's party."

"You have to go?" Sebastian all but whined. "What do you have to do?"

"A friend of mine is a model, and she needs me on her arm. You know, to get even more attention. Luckily, I can ditch her after a couple of parties," Zain explained as Deacon held his tongue.

"Why would you want to ditch a model?" Sebastian asked.

"She's one of those women who thinks she's equal. Dumb blond just doesn't know when to shut her mouth and put it to better use. Like I told Barrett, tonight I'm just looking to unwind."

Sebastian nodded his head. "I'll catch up with you soon and see you two there."

Deacon and Zain casually said their goodbyes and headed out of the party hotel. As soon as they left the room, security swarmed them and they made their way to the car.

"I'm calling our FBI contact to let them know it's definitely Barrett's party. I wish Barrett would send the freaking location, though," Zain said as he pulled out his phone.

"I guess we can tell Sydney she doesn't have to come out of retirement," Zain said after hanging up.

Deacon shook his head. "I'm not so sure about that. Sebastian said Vic used people inside the industry to find these girls. We know we can find Bailey and take down Vic, but I want to bring the whole operation down."

"So, we can cross off the nonfashion industry parties and focus on who has connections to Tristan Models and, more importantly, to Vic," Zain said.

Deacon watched the cityscape and lights pass by as he pulled at the strings in his mind. It still came back to who had told Vic that Sydney was asking questions about him. The answer had to rest with Patrick Mawler or Teddy Brown.

Chapter Twenty-One

Sydney looked in the mirror. All that was left was her great-grandmother's lipstick. Sydney had grabbed one from the house and now opened the package and pulled out the black lacquered tube. The door to the suite opened, and she heard Deacon's and Zain's familiar deep voices.

"Syd, are you about ready?" Deacon called out.

"I'll be out in a minute," Sydney said from behind the closed bathroom door. She twisted the tube of bright red lipstick and took her time tracing it along her lips. The color was sexy and made her think of a seductress biting her lip as she looked at her lover. It was a powerful color that emboldened her as she settled the hat on her head.

The tight laser-cut white lace highlighted all her curves and gave peeks at the skin beneath. The bright red lips demanded attention and the hat hid her eyes mysteriously. Sydney opened a large, rectangular box and pulled out the black leather over-the-knee boots her designer friend had shipped to her. She slid her legs into the supple leather, loving the embellishment of stitching around the heel and knee. Her skirt stopped at her upper thigh and the band of silky skin across her mid-thighs drew the eyes downward to complete the picture she presented.

Sydney took a deep breath and stood up. Tonight her body was the distraction. Under the cover of her hat, she would be taking in every detail, every person, and she would help bring down anyone participating in this trafficking ring.

Sydney opened the bathroom door, and for the first time in a long time, was nervous about how she looked. She wasn't eighteen anymore, and the only person whose opinion she cared about was standing across the room talking to one of her best friends. The guys had changed from their tuxes to jeans and fitted shirts that showed off their chests and flat stomachs.

"I'm ready," Sydney said softly as she watched Deacon and Zain turn to look at her. Zain grinned, but Deacon just stared, his brow creasing and his lips turning into a frown.

"Is something the matter?" Sydney asked self-consciously.

Deacon shook his head. "I'm trying to decide if I'm in heaven or hell. Heaven, because I'm lucky enough to have you as my girlfriend. I still don't know how that happened, by the way. It's hell because I'm going to sit back and watch as other men drool over you all night long. It's going to be torture keeping my hands to myself. You're simply stunning. An elegant, sexy, classy seductress."

Sydney smiled, embarrassed that Zain overheard Deacon's praise as Deacon stepped forward to kiss her cheek. "I'll just think of it as foreplay. And tonight, when we're finally alone . . . well, I'll just let you think about that every time you see me tonight," Deacon whispered in her ear before stepping back and giving her body a slow once-over.

"You don't happen to be armed under there, do you?" Deacon asked.

Sydney laughed. "Where would I put a weapon? Besides, we are going to be going through security, aren't we?"

Deacon shook his head. "I have just the thing." He hurried over to his bag and pulled out what looked like a large tube of lipstick.

"What's that?" Sydney asked as he handed her the red tube.

"A stun gun. Just take off the top and press that button. It's all charged and ready to go." Deacon showed her. "You can put it in your purse and most security wouldn't think about asking a model about an extra tube of lipstick."

Sydney pressed the button and saw the volts of electricity dance at the end of it. She knew she would be surrounded by Zain's security, but she felt better having something she could rely on. She unzipped her boot and slid the tube into the top of it. "Thank you. So, are we ready to do this?"

"That's my cue to leave. I'll meet you at the second party. Zain can fill you in on all the details, but we learned some fashion insider is feeding Vic the names of up-and-coming models. There's a good chance Bailey will be at the party tonight. Now, be safe. Let us know if anything seems off, okay?" Deacon ordered.

"Okay. But I feel I might not be the most help. You two are the ones who are going into the nest, so I want you both to promise to be careful, too," Sydney said, pinning both the men with a look until they agreed.

"Love you," Deacon said before kissing her on her cheek once more.

"Love you, too," Sydney said softly as she watched Deacon stride out the door.

"Aw, aren't you two cute?" Zain teased.

"Don't make me test my stun gun," Sydney said as she pulled a black fitted jacket from the closet and slipped it on.

Zain gave her an elegant bow that made her laugh before holding out his arm to her. "Your prince awaits."

Sydney slipped her hand into the crook of his arm. "Then let's do this."

The limo pulled to a stop at the VIP entrance of the stadium. Fans mixed with athletes and celebrities as journalists snapped pictures and asked questions. Sydney saw the heaters lining the red carpet and unbuttoned her jacket.

"You ready for this?" Zain asked with an encouraging smile.

"Of course," Sydney said with more determination than she actually felt.

Zain's security surrounded the door before it was opened. He slid out first and waved before turning and holding his hand to help Sydney out of the limo. The old trick of getting out of a car while wearing a short skirt and a ready smile instantly came back. The poses that were made to look like natural movements designed to get the best photos were like riding a bike. With Zain's hand at the small of her back, Sydney smiled, posed, and worked her way along the red carpet.

"Sydney, are you back?" a reporter yelled.

Sydney smiled mysteriously and stopped in front of him. "I didn't think I had gone anywhere. I've been busy putting my clothes on catwalks instead of myself, that's all." She laughed before moving to the next reporter.

"Are you and Prince Ali Rahman dating?" was shouted from multiple directions.

Zain smiled down at Sydney and expertly laid out the standard "We're just friends," line and added a wink to it that left the reporters with neither a confirmation nor a denial.

"Sydney, over here!" A woman waved and Sydney recognized the name of the most popular magazine on the woman's press pass.

"This is the last one," Sydney said to Zain without moving her lips — a talent you have to perfect if you walk enough red carpets. She and Zain stepped forward and allowed the cameraman to snap off a series of photographs.

"It's wonderful to see you're out of retirement," the woman led off.

Sydney smiled. "Well, I don't know if you would say I'm out of retirement. I'm just here to enjoy what I hope to be a good football game."

"Is this one of your creations?"

Sydney smiled and slipped out of her jacket to give the photographer a chance to snap her dress at all angles. "It is, thank you for asking. But now I am freezing, so we're going to head inside. Thank you so much for your questions, though."

Zain expertly slid her jacket back on as they walked

the rest of the way into the stadium where they were met with a tour guide. Sydney kept her eyes out for people she knew as the guide drove them on a golf cart to the football field for the pregame show. It was another formality that they had to go through to blend in. They signed footballs, took pictures with fans, and shook hands with other celebrities and athletes before they were finally guided back inside.

"There's a row of suites and conference rooms hosting the parties you expressed interest in. The first couple are right next to each other," the guide explained as he drove them through the underbelly of the stadium to the elevators.

The doors opened on their floor, and a smiling hostess was there to greet them and direct them to the parties. Sydney looked around and saw the line of swag, posters, and photo ops lining the hallway for the different magazines, businesses, and sports channels.

"Okay, this is the first party where Patrick appears," Zain whispered as they walked in right behind a well-known actor.

Sydney pasted on her smile as she took in the room. "I see him. Ready for a show?"

"What do we do first?" Zain whispered as he sent a wink to a singer eyeing him from across the room.

"Get all the people staring at us to pose for pictures in the photo booth over there. It's hooked up to social media." Sydney did the fake surprised gasp as she saw some acquaintances. Once she made eye contact, they were swamped. Rappers, athletes, and even a few actors rushed over.

"I've missed you so much," Syd cried as she hugged some former models who had done nothing but backstab her during her entire career. "Selfie!" And that was all it took to get everyone into the photo booth.

As Sydney tumbled out a couple minutes later with a grinning Zain, she saw that she had gotten Patrick's attention. "Why are you grinning like that?" she asked Zain as she pretended not to notice Patrick walking her way.

"Because your old competition got jealous and tried to give your fake boyfriend a thrill in the photo booth. Remind me to be your date more often."

Sydney rolled her eyes before Patrick got to them. "Amazing, just amazing. I have to shoot you right now," Patrick gushed in his overly eager artistic way. "And while I do, I'm going to yell at you for not telling me you were coming!"

"Patrick! I was hoping you'd be here. Do you know Zain Ali Rahman?" Sydney introduced them as a feeling of guilt and worry turned her stomach. Patrick was a friend, and she felt horrible thinking he could be part of this. But if he actually was . . . well, that feeling was even worse.

"So, you like my design then?" Sydney laughed as Patrick turned his attention back to her.

"Love. Love. Love. They set up a black room and a white room for me to take pictures for a huge spread in their magazine. You have to let me shoot you. You think your man candy can fend for himself for a minute?" Patrick asked as he shot Zain a wink.

"I'm kind of insulted I won't make it into your photo spread. I guess I'll console myself with that hot brunette over there." Zain shot them a half smile before ambling away while Sydney rolled her eyes at him.

"There is so much we have to get caught up on," Patrick gushed as he took her arm and led her to the attached room being used for photo shoots. Sydney saw two of Zain's guards discreetly take up position on either side of the door. "So, you think you still have it?" Patrick goaded as he pointed her to the black backdrop.

"I don't know. I may have forgotten everything in my old age," Sydney quipped as she posed for shot after shot.

"I know, you're almost like, thirty. But the camera still loves you. Here, look at these." Patrick came to Sydney and handed her the camera before dropping his voice. "I found your email strange, asking about Durante and that Vic guy. I thought something might be going on so I've been asking around for you."

Sydney could have sworn her heart stopped beating. She tried to keep her hands from shaking as she stared blankly down at the camera. If anyone came in, it would look like they were discussing the pictures. "What did you find?"

"The models don't seem to know anything, but while they've been getting ready, I've chatted up some of the agents. It seems that no one really understands how Tristan Models works. Their specialty, foreign models, is what keeps them afloat, but it shouldn't bring in the money they are flashing around to pick up major talent. What I found most interesting was one agent's story of a man trying to get a sixteen-year-old girl to meet him. He promised to make her a big star. Wanted to meet her at the mall. He didn't give an agency name, but just said he worked with a modeling agency. He didn't know she'd just signed with QYN. She told her agent who told this man to back off. The next day, his social media account was gone and his phone disconnected."

"Did the agent get a name?" Sydney asked.

"No, all she got was that he sounded European. However, the model did get something. She asked how he discovered her. The man told the model that an industry insider saw her at a Teddy Brown open-casting call," Patrick said seriously.

"Teddy? Do you think . . .?" Sydney stopped herself from accusing their friend.

"I hope not. But Teddy hasn't been acting himself since last year's spring collection bombed. I feel horrible even suggesting it. But when I asked Teddy about it, he snapped at me. Told me there were thousands of people there, from established models to agents and photographers. It could have been anyone."

"That's true," Sydney had to admit.

"Now, can you tell me what this is about?" Patrick asked as he quickly glanced at the open door.

Sydney had to decide if Patrick was involved or not in a split second. She looked at his spiked hair, thick black-framed glasses, and decided he couldn't be. He was Patrick. He was bullied in high school, worked his way up to become a well-known photographer, and always treated his employees and models with respect. "A sex trafficking ring. I emailed you all about that man, and then he showed up in my room and attacked me in the middle of the night. He knew I had been asking about him."

"It wasn't me. I didn't tell anyone . . . Teddy. I talked

about it with Teddy. I just can't—" Patrick couldn't finish as the horde of models fell into the room with glasses of champagne in their hands.

"Patrick, don't we get our pictures done?"

Sydney leaned forward and kissed his cheek. "Thank you. You're a good friend. Come visit me soon."

"Only if I get to exclusively shoot your next collection as modeled by you," Patrick teased, but the laughter wasn't there. His eyes were as troubled as hers.

"I wouldn't have it any other way," Sydney told him as she squeezed his hand. Patrick turned to placate the models as Sydney headed to find Zain. Two security guards fell into line behind her.

Zain looked up from where he was talking to a group of women and immediately excused himself. "What is it?" he asked as he escorted her from the room.

Sydney filled him in as they smiled and took their leave of the party. The next one was where Deacon was . . . and also Teddy.

Chapter Twenty-Two

D eacon had arrived at the party for the large department store that carried Teddy Brown's designs. He had spotted the designer talking quietly with a man upon entering the room. Deacon watched as the man nodded to Teddy and then left. Deacon made his way around the room, pretending to drink the signature drink while talking football and money. Good manners said you were never supposed to talk money, but somehow if you said "investments," it became perfectly acceptable economics.

Deacon knew the minute Sydney walked into the room. He felt her before he saw her. When he turned, he saw her smiling, but her eyes didn't light up like they did when she smiled for him. Something was wrong.

"There's my buddy Zain. Excuse me." Deacon grinned to the man he had been talking to, a perfume designer for a big name brand.

"Zain!" Deacon waved. Sydney looked briefly relieved before her fake smile resettled on her face.

"Dean. There you are. Let me introduce you to my friend, Sydney Davies," Zain said loud enough to draw the attention of most everyone in the room.

"A pleasure to meet such a beautiful and talented woman." Deacon smiled as he took Sydney's hand and placed a kiss on her knuckles.

Deacon spoke softly and quickly before anyone else joined them. "Teddy is acting strange. A man came in and they went over to the side of the room, whispered, and then the man left. Look, here he comes again."

Zain, Sydney, and Deacon watched the middle-aged man in jeans and a black sweater make eye contact with Teddy, who smiled and quickly excused himself from the group to talk to the man. With their heads close together, it was hard to hear what they were talking about before the man nodded his head and turned to leave once again. Deacon observed Teddy in his worn jeans and a torn T-shirt, layered under a super-fitted sports jacket as Zain told him what Patrick had said. Teddy's red hair was slicked back, and his face seemed worried beneath the fashionable beard he sported as he looked around the room.

"Time's up. Teddy just saw Sydney," Deacon murmured before stumbling forward to wrap his arm around her shoulder as he pretended to hit on her.

Zain grinned and said loudly, "I was just teasing, Dean. We went to college together, and he had the biggest crush on you. He didn't believe me when I told him we were friends."

"And it only took you how long to introduce her to her future husband?" Deacon laughed. He wasn't laughing when he felt the way Sydney's breathing hitched at the word *husband*, though.

"Sydney! I didn't know you were coming." Teddy smiled somewhat tightly.

"I couldn't spoil the surprise of the first of my new line." Sydney smiled as she kissed both of Teddy's cheeks.

"And it's gorgeous!"

"Thank you, Teddy," Syd said sweetly. Deacon saw Teddy looking to Zain and then himself. "Oh, let me introduce you. This is my friend from home who is nice enough to escort me to some of these parties, Zain Ali Rahman. This other man is Zain's friend, Dean, and apparently he's going to be my husband."

The group laughed, but Deacon took pleasure in hearing the word *husband* come from Sydney. Teddy didn't waste any time in grabbing Sydney's hand. "Come see my new line, and tell me what you think."

Deacon watched as Sydney walked over to the wall where a display had been set up. Teddy whispered a lot and Sydney's lips grew taut. "You think it could be him?" Deacon asked Zain as they slowly made their way to the bar to pretend to have another drink.

"He sure isn't acting normal. Let's see what he and Patrick are like at the next party we go to." Zain looked at his watch and cursed. "We need to get to it, or it will look like we're following them."

Deacon kept an eye on Teddy and Sydney. "It doesn't look like they're in a hurry."

Deacon toyed with his drink as he saw the mystery man walk back into the room. He slowly approached Syd and Teddy. Once Teddy saw him, he smiled at Sydney and excused himself. Sydney took her time posing for pictures and chatting up the owners of the large store before making her way to the bar.

"We have to go," Zain said through smiling lips.

"We're way behind schedule." Zain slipped his arm around Sydney as they made their way out of the room and farther down the hall.

"What did Teddy say?" Deacon asked once they were out of earshot.

"It was weird. He was asking me about Patrick and if I had talked with him. He said he heard someone say they saw us together. I told Teddy I just saw Patrick at The Glitz party and that he seemed to be doing well," Sydney said, sounding distracted. "But then he asked about a model he had discovered at his clothing casting. He said he sent her to Patrick for some photographs and never heard back from her. Then he asked about the email I sent. He wanted to know what it was about."

"So, he's casting blame on Patrick, and Patrick's casting blame on Teddy," Zain said with wonder.

"Who was the guy who came up at the end?" Deacon asked as they slowed their steps so they wouldn't be overheard by a group of people in front of them.

"I don't know. But as soon as Teddy saw him, he told me he had to go."

Deacon looked at his phone. "Both of them should be at the party we're going to now. Then Zain and I have to leave you once the game starts." Deacon nodded to the security guard carrying a small satchel containing $100,000 of traceable money. Zain and Deacon had fronted it, but the FBI had marked it and even tagged the bundle with a GPS chip that was less than half the size of a dime.

"If it is Teddy, I played it up that I was just using you for attention tonight and that Dean is some sleazy rich guy who just wants to earn a trophy on his bedpost. Sorry,"

Sydney said with a wink to him. "I'll be at the two parties we planned, and I will have security with me. Okay, game time." Sydney placed a smile on her face as they walked into the next party.

"Sydney Davies!"

"Amanda!" Sydney said in a voice Deacon was starting to recognize as fake. The two women hugged and gave each other air kisses as they strode into the room.

Zain pulled out his phone, and his lips tightened. "Barrett sent a text. It's just the floor, not the suite. Damn, Sebastian just walked in, too, and he is heading straight for Syd."

"I'll wrangle him in." Deacon hurried from the room, trying to catch Sebastian's eye.

"Sebastian, just the man I wanted to see," Deacon called out as he pulled the drunken man out the door. "I went to pull out my cigar, and it was gone. Darn thing must have smoked itself. But as soon as I saw you I knew you could hook me up." Deacon's speech became slightly slurred.

"You know I can, man. I was dying for a smoke, too. Come on, there's a place right over here." Now he could try to get some more information from Sebastian and give Zain and Syd a chance to learn something as well.

Sydney looked back and saw Deacon hurrying from the room. She pried herself from Amanda, who had been a really nice girl when they started out modeling together. She promised to email and made her way over to Zain.

"Where did Deacon go?"

"He saw Congressman Oliver and wanted to give us

time to cruise the room," Zain replied.

Sydney didn't have time to worry about it. Teddy was walking in the door and had already spotted her.

"Syd, long time no see." Teddy laughed as he made his way over to her.

"Sydney. Teddy," the hesitant voice of Patrick said from behind Teddy.

Sydney tried to laugh off the tension. "The three amigos together again, huh? It's just like old times."

"Well, I only stopped by for a moment. I have a private party to go to," Teddy said while ignoring Patrick. "I'd better make my rounds."

Patrick sighed. "I told you," he whispered. "Unfortunately, I can't stay long either. I too have a party I'm committed to. I'll see you soon, though."

Sydney smiled at her friend as he kissed her cheek and headed off into the crowd. "Well, that's a bust."

Zain's security guard tapped him on his shoulder. "It's time for us to go. Text if you need anything. I'm leaving two guards with you. Deacon or I will let you know as soon as we have Bailey."

"Take care of him, Zain," Sydney said softly.

Zain chuckled. "I think it's supposed to be the other way around."

"How about the both of you just stay safe. I'll text you if I have any updates."

Zain kissed her cheek and headed out of the room after both Teddy and Patrick rapidly departed. Sydney went to the bar and got a drink. She was on her own. Well, except for the two big guards standing by the door.

"Sydney!"

Sydney pasted on her smile and went to work.

Deacon was having a disgusting conversation with Sebastian when Zain and his two guards found him. Sebastian liked rough sex with young girls. Barrett had promised him all his wishes would come true tonight. Deacon ground out the cigar Sebastian gave him and turned his attention to Zain.

"Men, our obligations are over and the game is about to begin," Zain said with such unpleasantness it made Deacon blink. Gone was the smile and in its place an evil smirk that, combined with Zain's dark complexion, made him look sinister.

"By all means," Sebastian said happily as he took off for the elevator.

"Close off all your emotions. I have a feeling nothing can prepare us for what we're about to see," Zain whispered before stepping on the elevator.

The door opened, and when they got off, they had to show their tickets to a group of security guards and everyone was checked for weapons. A man in a black suit greeted them after they passed through security. "Gentleman, your phones, please."

Deacon and Zain turned off their phones and handed them over. He was sure Zain was cursing under his breath as much as he was. This was not good.

The group walked down the hallway lined with private security until they reached a suite. Outside were chairs filled with private security. Some worked for Barrett and some must have belonged to the men inside. Deacon counted eight men. Some of the men stepped forward, asking for the code word to enter.

"The money please, gentlemen," a young man in a suit said.

Zain gave a nod to his guard who opened the bag. The moneyman looked it over and took it before moving on to Sebastian.

"There's only enough room for twenty people; that's why it costs so much," Sebastian explained as if he were a tour guide.

"Okay, gentlemen. You're good to go," the moneyman announced as he took the money and placed it with another guard.

One of the goons, who had to be six-foot-seven and four hundred pounds of bulging muscle, opened the door. There was a makeshift holding area for security. A privacy screen had been placed, blocking the view into the suite from the hallway. Only after the hall door was closed was the screen opened. Deacon tried to relax as he saw the suite for the first time.

Sleek round coffee tables with chairs, couches, and a fully stocked bar with an attached buffet were visible, along with ten women. They were in beautiful dresses, but some had their dresses pulled down to expose their breasts and some had their skirts hiked up so the men could see what was underneath. Barrett was behind the bar and called out Zain's name. Deacon counted the men — nine, including them. There was still one missing. He tried to casually look for Bailey, but some of the women's faces were turned away as they sat on men's laps or did other things that caused Deacon to force himself to unclench his jaw. He also only counted nine women.

"Barrett, this is my friend Dean. Dean, Barrett," Zain introduced as he poured himself a bourbon. Sebastian had already leapt onto the young woman who had stepped forward with a fake smile and glazed eyes.

"Welcome to my party, gentlemen! It's nice to meet you, Dean. When I found out you were from the South, I put aside a nice little southern belle for you."

Dean smiled and shook the bastard's hand. "Much appreciated."

Barrett motioned with his hand. "Here she is now. Enjoy my gift, and as always, sharing it is encouraged." Barrett winked before heading toward the row of seats facing the large tinted windows that overlooked the field.

Chapter Twenty-Three

Sydney tried not to roll her eyes and strangle the ditzy woman talking to her about . . . well, she wasn't exactly sure what the woman was talking about. Sydney had tried to keep up, but after hearing about the woman's reign as Miss Cornfield, Sydney gave up. Instead, she kept her eye on the game and on the clock. Somewhere above her, Deacon and Zain were surrounding themselves with danger. Sydney only hoped the undercover FBI agent following Zain and Deacon had discovered the location of the party and was waiting with backup.

"And so there I was with my ass up in the air and a pig covered in grease in my arms!"

"What?" Sydney asked as she searched desperately for an escape. "Oh, my friend is about to leave. I need to say goodbye. It was great meeting you."

Sydney took off across the room to where Amanda was leaving with a group of newbies. "Amanda!" Sydney called out to her old friend.

"Hey, girl. We need to head out to another party."

"Care if I join?" Sydney asked as she dragged Amanda from the room.

"It's a private party, but who would care if Sydney

Davies came?" Amanda smiled as she arranged her hair just so.

"What kind of party is it?" Sydney asked as the five models got into the elevator and rode down a floor.

"It's a meet-and-greet for potential models, clients, and agencies."

"Which agency? GYN? Denrees?" Sydney asked as the elevator opened and they stepped into the hallway. These were the internal conference rooms. No big windows overlooking the field here.

"I don't know who is here. Très Mia is hosting. They're pretty new. But they take people from within the industry and match them with agents, designers, and so forth. I'm sure there will be tons of people you know." Amanda took a minute to reapply her lipstick and fluff her light blond hair.

The room was packed with girls in football jerseys who had been granted an invite by the "scouts" walking around the stadium, along with obvious models who were active in the business. Along the wall were tables with banners behind them. Teddy Brown Designs had a table along with a couple other smaller brand names. One whole side was selling nutrition. Along the back was a long line of young women leading to Becker Agency.

Sydney tried to remember who the Becker Agency was but couldn't. It must be a new boutique agency. She couldn't see the recruiter, but then the crowd shifted and Sydney was looking straight at Emily Tamlin behind the table next to Becker. Sydney smiled at her friend and waved. Emily looked surprised but then squealed with excitement as she hurried from behind the table.

"Sydney! I didn't think I would get to see you." Emily wrapped her in a hug and Sydney laughed.

"Me too. I thought you were overseas."

"I was. But I finished a job and just had to be here to represent my new business. I'm not getting any younger, you know," Emily teased. Her short, brown hair was spiked and looked to be a complete contradiction to the business suit she wore.

"What new company? You didn't tell me about it last time we talked," Sydney chided.

"Très Mia. I work to bring people together. All these girls sign with me and companies pay a fee to get the right match," Emily whispered with a smile. "And I help match them up. So if Becker is looking for a model of a certain type for a European campaign, I send them a list of my girls and they sign any they like. Similarly, designers may be looking for something very specific, so they send me the same wish list they send the agencies. If any of my girls fit, I pass the list along to them and they go. Instead of a percentage like an agent, I just get part of the booking fee if there is one. But I don't review any of the documents or negotiate like an agent."

"That's fabulous. I see you asked Teddy to help," Sydney said as she watched Teddy holding up an outfit to a girl.

Emily rolled her dark brown eyes. "As if I could keep him away. Ever since his spring line failed, he's been a bear to work with. He's determined to find the perfect person to be the new face of his designs."

"Hey, I have some girls looking to sign up. But let's chat soon, okay?"

"Sounds good. I'm proud of you. This is really amazing."

"Thanks. You really inspired me to do something after modeling. After all, it's a short career for most of us." Emily gave a lop-sided smile and hurried back to her table.

Sydney tried to see Becker but couldn't get a good look over the crowd. Instead, she decided to head to the bar while her two security guards took position close to the door. Sydney smiled at the girls trying to get drinks at the bar. They couldn't be over eighteen, but the bartender didn't seem to care as he served them each a Sex on the Beach.

Sydney ducked her head and hid behind her hat while sipping champagne. For now she was content to eavesdrop.

"I can't believe it!" Girl With Pink Hair cheered. "We meet in line and now we're both going to Europe as models!"

"It's so exciting. That man is an angel. I told him I have nothing left. My druggy mom is in jail, and I don't want to go back into foster care. I turn eighteen next week, and he's putting me up at a hotel until I can get all my documents. Then I'll be meeting you in Europe," Girl With Tattoo said.

"I know what you mean. I'm a foster kid, too. Maybe we'll be roommates in Paris!"

"Or Milan!"

Girl With Tattoo looked up. "Oh, there he goes. I wonder if Mr. Tamboli will be our agent?"

"I sure hope so. He's dreamy, and I think he was flirting with me," Girl With Pink Hair giggled.

Sydney pulled out her phone and sent a text to Deacon

asking if they'd heard anything about Becker Agency or a man named Tamboli. When she looked up, she saw Emily approaching the girls.

"Leah," Emily said and Girl With Pink Hair lifted her head in response.

"Oh, Ms. Tamlin. Thank you so much for putting this together. I signed with Becker!"

"I know. Will you come over here for a second?" Emily smiled at Girl With Tattoo and Sydney kept her head down, looking at her phone. She was starting to get worried that Deacon wasn't texting her back.

"Mr. Tamboli was so impressed with you. There's a private party upstairs for some very important men. He believes you'll be the perfect fit."

Sydney's head popped up as she overheard Emily. She couldn't be talking about . . . Teddy moved away from his table and slowly walked toward Emily with the mystery man beside him. No. It couldn't be.

"Mr. Tamboli has gone up to the suite to tell them about your arrival. Don't tell anyone, even Stella. This is a special honor to the girl Mr. Tamboli thinks has the greatest potential." Emily leaned forward and whispered to the girl. The specific location was lost in the noise of the room.

Sydney looked to where Stella was pounding back another drink, oblivious to Leah turning to leave. Sydney looked to Emily and then to Teddy casually heading toward Emily and Leah.

"Leah!" Sydney called out, stopping the girl, Emily, and Teddy in their tracks. They all turned toward her. "Is that you? It's me, Sydney Davies. I think I got an application from you to model some of my clothes."

Emily frowned, but quickly turned it into a practiced smile. "Syd, dear, what are you doing?"

Leah looked confused, but one look confirmed it was the Sydney Davies, and the young hopeful headed back into the room.

"Leah, you need to go now or you'll miss your appointment." Emily smiled but the order behind her words was clear as Sydney came to stand next to her. "What do you think you're doing?" she hissed.

"It's you, isn't it?" Sydney accused, not bothering to lower her voice.

"I don't know what you're talking about," Emily said dramatically. "Now, go along, Leah."

The girl looked as if she were being bounced around in a pinball game. She stopped again and turned to do as she was told.

"Don't move one step, Leah!" Sydney yelled and then did the only thing she could think of to prevent Leah from leaving. She pulled back her hand and slammed it into Emily's face.

Zain followed Barrett as Deacon waited for his girl to turn around and head toward him. When she stood up, he saw that her hair was dyed platinum blond, and she wore a tight dress with five-inch heels. Then she turned around and headed toward him with a determined smile. The slit of her dress came to her upper thigh and the top of her dress looked as if a gentle breeze would pull it down.

Even with the dyed hair, he knew instantly he had just

found Bailey. Deacon tried to nonchalantly get Zain's attention, but instead he only gained Barrett's.

"Does my choice meet with your approval?" Barrett asked as he kept his eyes on Deacon. Bailey stopped in front of him and ran her hand down his chest.

"She exceeds expectations. You sure know how to throw a party," Deacon grinned as he eyed Bailey. "Care to lead me to our seat, sweetie?" Deacon purred in his heaviest southern accent. When Bailey turned, he swatted her on the butt, and Barrett gave him a nod of approval before turning his attention toward his own entertainment.

"I'm Magnolia. Would you like a drink?" Bailey asked as she kept her eyes downcast.

"No thanks." Deacon took a seat, and when he finally got Zain's attention he winked. Zain looked toward the girl and gave the slightest dip of his head to indicate he understood this was the girl they were looking for.

Barrett looked back at Deacon, and Deacon pulled Bailey down into his lap. Zain was talking to the girl in front of him as Barrett made sure all of the guests were being entertained. When Barrett returned his focus to the girl giving him a lap dance, Deacon once again caught Zain's attention and held up his hand with his fingers splayed and flashed them twice. Zain tapped his watch in return, understanding that in ten minutes they'd make their move. They were on their own now that their phones had been taken.

"Shit!" Emily screamed as her nose cracked under Sydney's punch. Women screamed all around them, but no one moved. They all stared at Sydney and then at the blood trickling down Emily's face.

Sydney saw her guards rush forward. "Take the girl to safety. Grab Teddy and the man with him!" Sydney screamed as Emily shook off the shock and lunged at her.

Sydney let out a whoosh of air as she and Emily went down hard onto the floor. "You bitch!" Emily yelled as she straddled Syd and pulled her arm back to let loose with a wild punch.

Sydney blocked the punch and used Emily's momentum to shove her off. Sydney rolled and grabbed Emily's hair as she scrambled to stand up. "You're selling these girls! You're working with Vic, aren't you? How could you?" Sydney grunted as Emily screeched and tried to remove Syd's hand from her hair. The room was full of people, but instead of helping they just stood in a circle around the two women watching and filming with their phones.

Emily slammed her elbow back and hit Sydney in the ribs. Sydney let go of Emily's hair as the wind rushed out of her. She gasped for air as Emily spun and lashed out with a punch. Sydney felt the blow to her cheek as pain lanced across her face.

"Where did he go? The agent?" Sydney yelled as she evaded another punch. The pain had triggered all the lessons her father had taught her. No longer off guard, Sydney waited until Emily swung again and then made her move. She countered Emily's punch with one of her own that sent Emily sprawling back to the ground.

Slowly, Sydney rose to her feet as Emily darted away. Syd stalked her as she tried to take cover, but the crowd wouldn't let her escape. Sydney surged forward and landed a right hook that brought Emily to her knees. "Who else is in your trafficking ring?" Sydney threatened with her arm primed for another punch.

"I don't know what you're talking about!" Emily screamed.

"I don't believe you," Sydney said, letting loose with the punch. Emily crumpled, and Sydney reached down and grabbed a handful of spiky hair. She dragged her back up to her knees and stared her down.

"Tell me," Sydney ordered as she threatened another punch. "How many girls have you sold for sex? How many girls have you taken from their homes only to leave them to die if they didn't bend to your will and agree to be used by those men?"

"I don't know what you're talking about," Emily sneered. She opened her mouth to say something else, but Sydney had had enough. She hammered a punch into Emily's cheek as she heard the shocked silence of a roomful of people.

Emily fell to the ground on top of her small clutch purse, and Sydney strode mercilessly to the fallen model. With a shove from her leather boots, she pushed Emily onto her back. With her hands on her hips, Sydney lifted her boot-clad leg and placed the spiky heel of her boot to Emily's neck. "Talk," Sydney said calmly as the crowd gasped.

"I don't—" Emily started to say.

Sydney twisted the heel just enough to indent the skin. Emily clawed at Syd's leg with one hand, but it was protected in the leather encasing her from foot to thigh.

"What about the twenty dead girls in the storage container in Atlanta? What about Bailey Vander? Where is she?" Sydney asked as she twisted her heel just a little harder. Emily fought and Syd pressed harder until Emily gulped and went still. Sydney released the pressure as Emily glared at her. "Talk. Now. Where is Bailey Vander?"

Emily looked up at the ceiling. "Upstairs in a suite," she mumbled.

Sydney forgot to breathe. She searched the crowd and saw the security guards holding Leah and Teddy. The one holding Leah pulled out his phone, and Syd guessed he was texting the FBI agent they were working with.

"Which suite?" Sydney asked angrily.

"I know," a voice squeaked out as Leah held up her hand. "Suite 50."

"Who else is involved?" Sydney demanded.

"My brother. He's behind it all. He made me do it. I'm just a victim," Emily cried as tears streamed down her face.

"What about him?" Sydney asked as she glanced at a surprised Teddy.

"Teddy? He didn't have anything to do with this."

Sydney took her foot from Emily's neck as she watched someone she had known for years curl into a ball and sob. Sydney didn't even know Emily had a brother. What had he done to her that she felt participating was her only option? At least Teddy wasn't involved. The thought of being close to someone who had done such horrific things made her want to throw up. Sydney stepped closer to offer a hand when Emily looked up from where she had buried her face. There were no tears. Instead there was nothing but a flinty glare and a second later, pain shot through

Sydney's leg.

Sydney shouted out as Emily scrambled to her feet. Sydney looked down at a pair of tweezers sticking out from her thigh, right about where her boots ended.

Emily charged, and Sydney waited for just the right moment. Everything seemed to move in slow motion as Emily sprang forward with arms outstretched, reaching for Syd's neck. Sydney let out a breath, ducked down, and came up with her hand fisted. She delivered the uppercut straight to Emily's chin. Emily's eyes rolled back, and she dropped in a heap to the floor.

"Sydney!" Teddy yelled as he struggled to break free from the security guard.

"Let them go," Sydney called out as FBI rushed into the room.

Teddy ran forward and wrapped her in his arms. "Are you okay? She stabbed you! With tweezers! Who does that?"

Sydney relaxed into his arms as she shook her head. "A model. I'm sorry I thought you had something to do with this."

"I'm not a very good friend either," Teddy admitted. "I thought it was Patrick. I even had my assistant following him. But after we had a blowout and both confessed we thought each other were involved, it got me thinking who it really could be. I pulled up the group email you sent and saw Emily's name. It reminded me that Emily was also at my open-casting call. I didn't have anything to go on, but I thought I would watch her. And when she approached that young girl right after that agent left . . . the modeling agent!"

Sydney reached down, and like ripping off a bandage, yanked the tweezers from her leg and handed them to the FBI agent approaching her. "He's her brother," Sydney said more to herself than to the people around her before turning to Teddy and the FBI agent, who was putting the tweezers into an evidence bag. "He's upstairs in Suite 50 with Bailey."

"I'll tell Agent Helms. He's in charge."

Sydney pushed past the agent who was a little slow in connecting the dots.

"Ma'am, stay here," he yelled after her. But as the blood ran down her leg and into her boot, she ignored the agent and sprinted for the elevator.

"Miss Davies, wait," her guards shouted, but she didn't listen as she jumped into the elevator with Teddy right behind her.

"Patrick! Suite 50 and hurry. It *was* Emily. The agent from Becker is her brother, and they have a missing girl," Teddy shouted into the phone before hanging up. "What's our plan?" he asked her.

"I don't have one," Sydney said as the doors to the elevator opened.

Chapter Twenty-Four

Deacon settled his arm around Bailey as she went through the motions of trying to be seductive. She rubbed her hand on his thigh, wiggled her bottom against his crotch, and kissed his neck. Deacon struggled not to toss her off his lap. He felt sick and dirty. Everything about this whole scene was wrong. But when Bailey bent her head to kiss along his neck again, he used one hand to clamp down on her neck and hold her there while using his other to pin her to his lap. He was about to risk his life with nothing more than a whisper.

"Bailey, I'm a friend," Deacon whispered as he used her head to shield his moving lips from Barrett's view. The girl stiffened and instantly tried to get up, but Deacon held tight. "Don't move or they will know something's wrong, and it won't just be me they hurt."

Bailey sagged back against Deacon with a whimper. "Who are you? How did you know my name?"

"Your mother sent me. How many men here are involved in hurting you?"

Bailey shook her head as Deacon felt a tear drop onto his neck. "My mom won't want me back. She'll never be able to look at me again after . . ."

Deacon squeezed her tight. "Your mother knows everything, and that's why she sent me. She begged me to find you. She loves you so much and wants nothing more than to tell you that. She's not angry with you. She doesn't blame you. She only loves you and wants you safe. I want you safe, too. Help me out, and we'll both get out of here alive."

"The guards outside will stop us. And Barrett, he's the main agent. He's the host. There's another guy, Vic, who is the pimp. Then there's a woman. She's the one in charge. She's the one who tells Vic who to get and then tells Barrett who to sell us to. I don't know her name, though. I'm going to jail, aren't I? Barrett and Vic told me if I ever told anyone what happened, my mother would be disgusted and kick me out, and the police would arrest me for prostitution." Bailey's voice became shaky again and Deacon moved to hug her. She was no longer a flight risk. She needed comfort and someone to fight for her. And he would. So would Zain.

"We have two men outside and two inside, including me. Your mother is not disgusted. She's scared and worried you are dead. She just wants you home. And don't worry about the police. They are working with the FBI and us. You will not be arrested. I promise," Deacon swore.

"What do you want me to do?" Bailey asked, then gasped and buried her head in his neck. Her whole body trembled uncontrollably.

"Bailey, what is it?" Deacon whispered as he stroked her hair.

"Vic just walked in. He'll beat me if I'm not doing my job. He said he loved me. He said he was proud of me. He said I was beautiful, but then he . . ." Bailey became stiff as she wiped the tears from her face. "If he sees I was crying —"

"He won't." Deacon needed to get her talking. It calmed her down. "Are the other girls here like you?"

"Yes," Bailey responded.

"Sit up and tell me who they are. I'm going to rub my hand down your back to make it look like you're pleasing me. May I touch you?" Deacon asked as he tried to give some semblance of control back to Bailey.

She nodded her head and even gave him a little smile before sitting up. Deacon could feel eyes on him as he brushed his hand up her leg and let it disappear under her skirt. He left it on her leg as he shouted at the game. Then he whispered, "Tell me what you know."

"The girl with your friend came from Des Moines, Iowa. She's sixteen. I don't know her real name. We all have these stupid names. I'm Magnolia. She's Bambi. The girl who is with Barrett is Diamond. She's seventeen. Then there's Dallas. She's called that because she's from there. Then the girl who is naked and dancing for that old man is Starr. She's twenty and was taken from a strip club in Seattle. The rest are new tonight. I haven't worked with them before," Bailey told him as she stood and moved to straddle him.

"Do they want out? Will they help us?" Deacon asked.

"Diamond won't. She's too scared of Barrett. She's his pet. Dallas and Starr will. I don't know about Bambi. She's so young," Bailey said sadly.

Deacon didn't want to process the fact that Bailey at eighteen was almost as young. "Is there a restroom or anywhere that you can talk to them without being overheard?"

"I'll try. But I need a reason to go. I'm not allowed to go unless I'm given permission."

Deacon leaned back. "Zain! How about a little group action?"

Zain came over with Bambi looking timid and scared on his arm but a fake smile on her lips. "Sounds great. What kind of action?"

"Barrett," Deacon smiled, "can we borrow some of the girls and have them do a little group number for us?"

Some of the men smiled approvingly at the thought of the women together. "Of course, who would you like? We can see if their dates are willing to spare them for a moment."

Deacon pointed out Dallas, Bambi, and Starr. When the men eagerly agreed, Deacon sent a wink to Bailey. "You gals go clean up. When you come out, we want a show."

Used to taking orders, the girls hurried to the bathroom as the men who were going to enjoy the show moved to refill their drinks. "What's going on?" Zain whispered as he grabbed a bottle of vodka and casually kept it dangling by his side.

"Bailey thinks they'll fight their way out of here with us. Our phones are gone so we can't notify anyone. We're on our own until we get past the guards out front." Deacon looked at the open bar and selected a bourbon in a heavy square glass bottle.

He poured himself a drink as the girls came out of the room less than a minute later with fresh lipstick on. He held his breath until Bailey winked at him. "They're in,"

Deacon whispered as they moved toward the girls who were kissing each other. "Barrett and the new guy who came in are the two directly involved. Vic is the new guy, and he's the one who attacked Syd. He's mine." Deacon tightened his hand on the neck of the heavy bottle. Now he was ready to enjoy himself.

"I never did like Barrett. It will be a pleasure." Zain smiled before breaking away from Deacon and heading over to the side of the room where Barrett was sitting.

Deacon saw Zain stand slightly behind Barrett, waiting for Deacon to make the first move. Barrett would be easy. He was watching the girls in action while Diamond was on her knees pleasing him. Deacon had a little more trouble getting to Vic. The man kept moving, and Deacon had to stop and wait for him to come nearer. He didn't want to make the man suspicious. He also didn't know if Vic would recognize him from Atlanta.

Deacon watched as Vic made his way around the room before stopping and whispering something to Barrett, who immediately turned toward him. Shit. Vic *did* recognize him. Deacon pretended not to see him, but when Barrett pushed Diamond off of him, surprise was no longer an option.

"Now!" Deacon yelled as he shoved past the men enjoying the show. Zain lifted his arm and swung the bottle down onto Barrett's head. Diamond and the girls not in the know shrieked as Barrett slumped unconscious in his seat a moment before Zain was confronted by some of the men in attendance.

Bailey and the girls yanked off their stripper heels and formed a circle. Any of the men who tried to grab them were stabbed with a flurry of cheap stilettos. Deacon saw Vic make a move for the door to call security. Deacon shoved a man aside, jumped onto a chair, and vaulted into the air. He slammed into Vic's back, and they tumbled to the ground in a tangle of limbs as his bourbon bottle went skidding away from him.

They fought for power and control, each trying to gain the upper hand. As they grappled on the ground, Deacon landed an elbow to the solar plexus, leaving Vic gasping. It's what allowed him to see Sebastian slinking past him. Deacon sat up and used all the leverage he had to bash his fist into Vic's face. Vic went still beneath him, and Deacon unfolded himself to his full height and stalked forward.

Deacon bent and picked up the bottle of bourbon that had slid out of his reach. "Sebastian," Deacon warned as the man jumped toward the door. Deacon planted his feet and threw the bottle. The amber liquid glinted in the lights as it went end over end through the air. A second later the heavy bottle struck Sebastian full force in the back. He tumbled forward, tripped over his feet, and went sprawling to the ground.

Deacon bent and picked the whiny diplomat up by the back of his collar. He flung Sebastian away from the door and back into the mêlée of the room. Speaking of diplomats, Zain had one hell of a punch.

"Stop!" Deacon yelled. The room froze. The women stopped crying, and Deacon noticed some of them had even joined the circle of women Bailey was leading in attacks against their dates. "You're outnumbered now, fellas. Hands up or we can continue to knock you out." Deacon tossed the bourbon bottle menacingly in his hand.

"Either way works for me. It's just a matter of whether or not you want to take a chance one of us hits a little too hard and leaves you dead."

Deacon stopped at Vic's head as the remaining men raised their hands in surrender. "Girls, please escort the men to the bathroom and empty their pockets. Dallas, Bailey, drag Vic in there, please. Diamond, get Barrett." The girl hadn't moved from her spot on the floor. She stared back and forth between the man who had complete control over her and the group of women finding their own power. Slowly, she got up and grabbed Barrett by the feet, pulling as hard as she could. The unconscious man slid from the chair, hitting his head on the edge of the seat and then again on the floor. Diamond gave a slight smile as she heard the thump.

Zain stood behind the girls, giving a threatening glare to any of the men who thought about making a run for it as Deacon searched for a way to lock them into the bathroom. At last, Sebastian, Vic, and Barrett were shoved in the bathroom and the door was shut.

"How can we lock them in?" Bailey asked.

Deacon looked at the piles of objects from everyone's pockets. "Get me twelve pennies." The girls started sifting through the piles, collecting pennies.

Zain looked at him confused. "Pennies?"

"You never locked your brother in his room with this old penny gag?"

"No. How can you lock someone in with pennies?" Zain asked.

Deacon just smiled as Bailey ran over with a handful of pennies. "I'll show you." He headed over to the door and pushed against it above the handle. "Bailey, slide the pennies in the gap, as many as you can until they won't fit anymore. Stack them up; that's right," he said, as Bailey started pushing pennies into the narrow slot between the door and the doorjamb.

"I can only fit four," she said worriedly.

"That's fine. Now, do the same thing down here." He pushed the door beneath the handle as Bailey shoved in four pennies.

Zain crossed his arms. "Seriously? That jams the door?"

Deacon smiled. "Sure does. Now, ladies, here's the plan. Grab bottles and anything else you can find to defend yourself. Stay with either Zain or me. The FBI is aware of what's going on; they just don't know our exact location. No one is going to be arrested for prostitution, so there is no need to run from the police. They will help you. I promise. Now, let's bust out of here."

"I need your ticket, miss," the security guard said with his face in a permanent frown. Teddy had handed his over and been permitted to pass.

"It's in my purse and I don't know where I left it. But can't you look up my name? It's Sydney Davies." Sydney gave her sweetest trust-me smile.

"No ticket, no entry. This is a secure area. We have lots of important men here."

Sydney put her hands on her hips. "Men? Is that what you think of women? That since I'm not old and wrinkly and don't have a penis, I'm not important."

The guard stuttered, and Sydney pressed her advantage. "Now, just call your boss and have me checked out. I believe you will change your sexist mind about who is important."

The guard pulled out his phone and sent a text. A second later, his shoulder's slumped. "I'm sorry, Miss Davies."

Sydney patted his shoulder. "I know. You were just doing your job. Trying to keep good people safe and bad people out. I hope you remember that in the future," Sydney said ominously as she and Teddy headed down the hall.

"Remind me to send that man an apology card," Sydney smiled as they counted off the suites.

"Teddy! Sydney!" a harsh whisper from behind them called out.

"Patrick, thank goodness you're here." Sydney hugged her friend and Teddy did the same. "We need all the help we can get. See that door with all the men standing outside it? I think that's our destination. I see two of Zain's guards. I should have waited for mine. I didn't think there would be that many of them. Can I borrow a phone?"

Teddy handed over his, and she sent a text to Sienna, one of the few numbers she knew by heart. She would relay the info to Ryan and Nabi, who would relay it to the FBI and guards. "In just a minute, those two big guys in black, well . . ." Sydney realized all the guards were dressed exactly alike. "Um, the two standing across from the door with black hair. When they get a text, we'll make our move. Now, let's just act normal and stop nearby. You all have any weapons?"

Patrick nodded. "I have my tripod and my camera."

Teddy looked worried as he dug in his bag. "I have some sewing needles, but that's all."

"Bunch them together and stab the neck or face," Sydney told him.

Teddy and Patrick turned white. "Who are you?"

Sydney smiled. "I'm my father's daughter. Now let's kick some ass."

Sydney and her group started chatting about who was wearing what as they slowly moved closer to the group of guards. She was worried they wouldn't make it. Teddy and Patrick were so stiff. Their voices trembled, and they laughed nervously. She needed to do something to distract the guards. She saw one move to stand up from his chair by the door at the same time both of Zain's guards pulled out their cell phones. They looked down and immediately looked up at her. Sydney sent them a wink before turning on her full smile for the guard.

"Ugh, do you have a bandage?" Sydney asked as she lifted her foot onto the seat the guard had just vacated when he stood up. "Some bimbo dropped her glass of champagne and the darn thing nicked me." The guard stood staring as Sydney's skirt slid so far up her leg that she nearly exposed herself. But it worked. The guard didn't pay attention to her unzipping the top of her boot. She pulled out the tube of lipstick and pretended to put it on as she got ready to use it.

"Can you take a look at it? Do you think it needs stitches?" Sydney asked worriedly.

"Sure thing." The guard hastened to his knees so he could examine it. Sydney waited for him to bend forward and casually brought the lipstick to his neck and pressed the button.

Zzzzt. The guard fell forward as Sydney swung her leg from the chair. At the same time, Zain's two guards sprang into action. Patrick spilled everything from his camera bag as he pulled out a tripod. He extended it and swung with as much force as he could at the guard approaching a frozen Teddy. "Who else can I hit?" Patrick yelled frantically as he stared at the ensuing melee.

"Anyone but the two guys I pointed out a second ago," Sydney yelled as she ducked a punch and zapped a guard in the crotch.

She went to stand back up but was too slow. A guard rammed her to the ground. He was huge, and she felt her ribs crack under his weight. He had to be close to seven feet tall and as heavy as a massive boulder. Even if her stun gun hadn't gone skittering off when she hit the cement floor, it wouldn't have impacted this man. The breath was pushed from her lungs as his weight pressed down on her. She gasped for air, but her lungs didn't have room to expand. Sydney tried to push past the panic and keep calm as she struggled against the weight squeezing the life from her.

Light danced in front of her eyes, and the sounds of Teddy and Patrick screaming her name became muffled. Her arms fell to her side as her heart slowed. Through the fog came a war cry. Sydney forced herself to be present — forced herself to fight. And into her narrow field of vision came a ghost of designer vengeance. Teddy, screaming madly as fear drove him, jammed a handful of razor-sharp needles into the giant's cheek. The man pushing the life from her reared up with a shout at the same time Patrick swung his tripod into his face.

Sydney gasped, dragging in breath after breath of air as the world came back into focus. With needles sticking out of his cheek and a busted nose pouring blood down his face, the massive man staggered to his feet. Sydney scooted away from him and jumped to her feet just as the door to the suite was flung open.

The man turned, and Sydney pulled her skirt up over her hips and ran straight at his back. She took a deep breath and jumped.

Chapter Twenty-Five

D eacon and Zain stopped by the door leading to the hallway. The girls were standing behind them, armed with everything from stools to liquor bottles. He stopped with his hand to the door when he heard a strange cry.

"What is that?" Deacon whispered.

Zain shook his head and leaned forward to press his ear to the door. "There's a lot of movement out there."

An angry roar penetrated the door, and the girls started to look nervous. "Don't worry, ladies, reinforcements are here. Shall we help them?" Deacon asked with a smile. Thank goodness, the FBI must have found them.

Bailey tightened her grip on the gin bottle and nodded her head. "We got this. Girls, it's payback time."

Suddenly emboldened, the girls let out a war cry. Deacon threw open the door and rushed into the fight. He expected to see guns drawn, maybe a few punches, and some fighting as the guards tried avoid arrest. What he didn't think he would see was Sydney in a thong hurtling through the air and landing on the back of the behemoth guard who had a batch of needles sticking out of his cheek and not a single FBI agent in sight.

Deacon didn't have time to take it in before a man landed a punch to his face. His head snapped to the side as he saw Zain's guards move to surround the prince. The three fought as one against Barrett's guards and the other guards. Deacon shook off the punch and was about to throw his own when the ladies swooped in, clubbing the man with their bottles and crashing a chair over the guard's head, leaving him unconscious.

Deacon hurried to help Sydney but couldn't get to her before another guard engaged him. He caught a glimpse of the giant who was spinning round and round trying to shake Sydney off of his back.

"Sydney!" Deacon yelled. He watched helplessly as the guard slammed her into the cement wall.

Sydney made an *oomph* sound but held on. Her arm was wrapped around the man's throat. Her elbow was under his chin as her hand held tightly to her opposite bicep. Her other arm was locked onto the back of his neck, pressing forward as the arm under the guy's chin pressed back. If done right, a chokehold could take someone out in under ten seconds, but that seemed a lifetime as the man spun and slammed Sydney again.

The entire scene was now utter chaos. The ladies beat guards into submission as a group. Zain and his guards systematically took other men down. And Deacon fought with the guard who had demanded the money when they first arrived. They traded punches as Deacon tried to keep an eye on Sydney. He saw the colossal man suddenly drop to his knees. Sydney held on for dear life as Deacon saw the guard's eyes roll back.

He wouldn't be out long; he'd wake up as soon as

blood flow was restored. The sound of the fight had brought stadium security, which had finally amassed and were running down the hall toward them. "Hey! We need to detain him!" Deacon yelled as the stadium guard, now backed up by other stadium guards from the floor, stopped to stare at the scene.

"Hands up!" he ordered Deacon who was busy pinning the moneyman to the floor.

Deacon stared at him. There were no guns, tasers, or weapons for stadium guards. "Come on, I'm the good guy. He's the dick."

The man shook his head. "I don't care. We're detaining everyone."

Sydney let out a frustrated sigh. "Do you remember me?" she called out from where she lay on the goliath's back, ready to choke him out the second he came back around. "Keep the good people safe and the bad out. Well, we're the good people, and they're the bad people. Call the FBI agents already in the building. Please. In the meantime, do you have any restraints for this guy?"

The guard looked conflicted, but then the gargantuan man started to groan. The security guard reached into his utility belt and pulled out a zip tie. He struggled to pull the man's arms together. Deacon went to help slide the ties on as another stadium guard held on to Moneybags.

"Freeze!" A group of FBI agents rushed forward with Zain's other two guards. "Prince Ali Rahman, explain," the lead agent called as the group kept their guns trained on everyone.

"Agent Helms. Sorry for the delay in contacting you. Our cell phones were confiscated, and we had a little distraction once we got out of the suite," Zain said from between his two guards with a pile of unconscious and injured bad guys on the ground in front of them.

Deacon let Zain take the lead as he turned to wrap Sydney up in his arms. "Are you okay?" Deacon asked. He pulled away to look at her when she gasped in pain. He saw the blood trickling down her leg and the bruises forming all over her body.

"I think I have a broken rib or two. Maybe three." She smiled as she leaned against him.

Deacon wrapped his arm gently around her and casually pulled her skirt down. Sydney chuckled and then groaned. "It took ten years off my life when I saw you leap onto that man's back. What were you thinking?" Deacon asked in disbelief.

"I had to stop him. He was big and strong enough to take everyone down. Once he was distracted, I saw my chance. My dad taught me that move when I was eight years old. I just remember him telling me size didn't matter; it was about the technique. All I had to do was get the chokehold right, and I could take the big guy down," Sydney told him as she slumped against him.

The FBI moved in and secured the beast of a man with cuffs. They also called for leg shackles and more assistance when he started to wake up. Zain continued to tell Agent Helms the events that had transpired on their end, and Deacon took the opportunity to check on the girls who were huddled together, looking petrified.

"Ladies, you were fantastic. This is Sydney Davies. She's part of the group responsible for finding you. Sydney, this is Bailey Vander and her friends." Deacon smiled at the group of young women who rushed to hug them.

Sydney laughed through the pain of her injuries when Bailey squeezed her and cried. Deacon had never been around so many sobbing women. He hugged them all as, one by one, they introduced themselves with their real names.

"Agent Helms," Deacon called out. The girls stepped closer to him and Sydney as the agent made his way over to them.

"Deacon McKnight. It's nice to finally meet you. Detective Gentry had a lot of nice things to say about you when we checked you out." The agent turned to Bailey who stood trembling with Syd's arm around her. "And you must be Bailey. It's good to see you. I'm Agent Daniel Helms. I'm going to be talking to you about what happened and making sure you get home as soon as possible." The girls gave him a quivering smile but visibly relaxed once they realized he wasn't going to arrest them. "May we take these ladies back to our hotel and let them shower and get some food while you wrap up here? Then you can talk to them there. There's no need to traumatize them further."

"Of course. I'll have one of my guys escort you in one of our vans. That way you can all go together," Agent Helms said gently. The girls clung to each other, and Deacon appreciated the agent's handling of the situation.

"But what about the woman?" Bailey asked. "She's still out there. She can find us."

Sydney tightened her grip on the scared child at her side

who didn't look old enough to drive. On her other side, Bailey stood rigid as fear overtook her. "Woman?" Sydney asked.

Bailey nodded. "The head of the organization is a woman. I don't know her name. She spoke with Vic in a language I didn't understand. But Vic and Barrett did what she said. She is in charge, and she can still find us."

Sydney felt the girl start to shake. "Vic? Vic was here?" Sydney asked Deacon who nodded.

"He's locked in the bathroom suite with Barrett and the other guys who paid for the girls," Deacon said. His arms were still stretched out with girls huddled under each one.

"What about Mr. Tamboli? He was on his way up here right before us."

"Mr. Tamboli is Vic. Victor Tamboli," Deacon explained. "He's from Hungary and has a link to Tristan Models in Europe. He runs their European department that goes by the name Becker."

Sydney had always heard the expression of a light bulb going off. But it was more accurate to say an image slammed into her head as she gasped and then laughed with relief. "You don't have to worry about that woman ever again," Syd told the girls. "After I knocked her out, I left her with Zain's guards, and she was put into FBI custody. Agent Helms, I believe you will find that the model who goes by Emily Tamlin is the mastermind behind this ring."

Teddy and Patrick gasped, and the girls cheered with relief. Teddy stepped forward with a hand still shaking from adrenaline. He took Syd's hand in his. "Let me help. I have hordes of clothes downstairs I can give to these girls."

Sydney smiled her thanks and squeezed his hand. She gave him the hotel name and room number. Agent Helms got Teddy's information and arranged to interview him at the hotel.

Patrick gave a startled gasp, and Sydney looked over at him as he picked up the GoPro he'd been using to shoot behind-the-scenes images. "What?"

Patrick smiled and shook his head. "Nothing. Just glad my camera isn't broken. My tripod, however . . ." He shrugged as an FBI agent wearing gloves took it from him.

"Why don't you get the girls out of here before we arrest the men inside," Helms suggested as Zain, his guards, and an agent formed a protective circle around them.

"See you in a little bit. Come on, girls. Hot showers, new designer clothes, and lots and lots of room service await." Sydney took Bailey's hand and led the way toward the elevator. She turned around and saw the girls, especially the younger one, glued to Deacon's side with hero worship clearly on their faces. Sydney was pretty sure she had the same look on her face when she looked at him. What made her heart beat even faster was he had that same look when he looked at her.

"Don't think for one second I haven't noticed your leg," Deacon chided as they all got into the elevator.

"I've already texted for a doctor," Zain grinned from the back of the elevator. "And if you ladies give me the information on your parents and loved ones, I can make arrangements to get them here immediately."

The young girl who looked like a lost child looked up

at Zain. "I'm so lucky I was assigned to entertain you. But, who are you? I was only told you were extremely important."

"Zain Ali Rahman, at your service." Zain smiled as he held out his hand.

"Well, thank you, Mr. Ali Rahman, and you too, Mr. McKnight, for saving our lives."

"Your Highness, the doctor will meet you in your suite. Miss Davies, food has been ordered as well," one of the guards whispered.

It wasn't soft enough though. The young girl's eyes grew even rounder. "Highness?"

"He's the Prince of Rahmi—a prince who looks after those in need." Sydney smiled as suddenly the entire group of women turned to stare at Zain with their mouths wide open.

The doors opened, and the agent led the now tittering group to an FBI van. Everyone piled in, and Sydney was finally able to relax. She slid into the seat next to Deacon and laid her head on his shoulder. The voices of the girls giving Zain's men their real names and the names of their parents filled the van.

"Should I call my mom?" Bailey asked hesitantly. "I don't know what to say. Maybe you could talk to her and see if she wants to talk to me."

The other girls similarly nodded. "I'm too afraid to call my parents," the wide-eyed teenager said with embarrassment. "I ran away from home. I left a note blaming them for smothering me. Vic had, well, he had . . . and I thought he loved me."

"Me too. I was on spring break in Panama when I met Vic. He has videos of me," another girl said before tears broke free.

"My mom will never forgive me," another girl said sadly.

Sydney could see the abuse Vic and Barrett subjected them to coming out. The girls literally wilted into their seats. "That is not true," Sydney said forcefully. "You are survivors, and the FBI will find those tapes. You will find power in them and in yourselves. You have the power to stand up and tell the truth. Tell the world that Vic, Emily, and Barrett no longer have any power over you. You no longer need to be afraid of them. And you will do that in a courtroom where Deacon, Zain, all of your parents, and I will be holding your hands as a show of support. Each time you tell your story, you take back your own power and your own destiny. Those things no longer belong to the people who hurt you. With your testimony and the testimony from the survivors the Atlanta police found, your tormentors will never see the light of day again."

"Do you still want me to call your mom?" Deacon asked as they pulled into the hotel.

Bailey nodded. "When we get upstairs, will you please call her for me and see if she wants to talk to me?"

"I will," Deacon promised as he helped Sydney and girls out of the van.

Sydney bit back curse words as she climbed painfully out of the van. Every inch of her body hurt, but she had to make sure the girls were safe before she could give in to the pain. They rode in silence up to the rooms. Zain entered his and opened the connecting door. Between the two suites, there were four showers for the ten girls. But no one moved. Instead they all stood quietly, watching as Deacon pulled out his cell phone and called Eloise Vander.

Chapter Twenty-Six

D eacon put the phone on speakerphone. It only rang once before Ms. Vander snatched it up.

"Did you find her?" asked the panicked mother. Bailey swayed, and with tears streaming down her face, clutched Deacon's arm for support.

"I did. She's alive and with me. Would you like to talk to her?" Deacon asked as he fought back his own tears. Ms. Vander's sobs were clearly heard over the phone.

"More than anything," Ms. Vander choked out.

"Mama?" Bailey said in a voice so small she sounded like a child.

"Bailey!" Ms. Vander shouted, her voice thick with emotion. "I love you. Oh, Bailey, I love you so much."

"I love you, too," Bailey whispered as she gripped Deacon's arm.

Sydney turned her head to wipe the tears rolling down her cheeks.

"I'm coming, baby. Don't move. I'm coming right now," Ms. Vander cried.

Zain stepped forward. "Ms. Vander, my name is Zain Ali Rahman. A private jet is waiting for you at the airport and will leave immediately upon your arrival. A car will meet you at the Indianapolis airport and bring you to us."

"Oh thank you! Thank you! Bailey, hold on, Mama's coming."

After that, everyone rushed to have Deacon and Zain call their parents. Within an hour, every girl had cried until there were no more tears, eaten until they were full, showered, and dressed in the fashionable new clothes. Parents from all over the country, and some from other countries, were in private jets making their way to Indianapolis. The FBI had secured a whole floor for their use over the next week.

Agent Helms and his associates were interviewing the girls, and raids were being organized based on the information the girls gave them. Therapists trained in PTSD and sexual abuse were brought in to meet with the girls individually and with their parents when they arrived.

Sydney had her wound cleaned and stitched, and the doctor ordered her to have X-rays for what appeared to be bruised ribs. She swore she'd do it when she got home. She didn't want to leave the girls since some of them asked her to sit with them while they talked to the FBI agents.

Before Sydney knew it, the door to the suite opened, and Ms. Vander rushed into the room with wide, tear-streaked eyes. "Mama!" Bailey cried as she bounded from the couch and rushed across the room.

Bailey's mother pulled her daughter to her chest, and the two sank to the floor in tears. Deacon stepped to where Sydney sat at the table with the sixteen-year-old girl Bailey had called Bambi. Her name was Lacey. After telling Agent

Helms the horrors she had been through the past month, she was worn out and leaning on Sydney for support.

Deacon placed his hand on Sydney's shoulder and smiled down at her. The door opened again and a petite woman with large round eyes and a middle-aged man with mismatched clothes rushed in.

"Lacey?" the woman called out as her frantic eyes went from girl to girl, looking for her daughter.

"Mommy, Daddy!" Lacey gasped as Sydney helped the girl up. Her tiny body was so overwhelmed with sobs she couldn't move, but it didn't matter. Her parents had her now. They had flown in from Des Moines in such a hurry neither had paid attention while dressing. Her mother was in a night robe over flannel pajamas, and her father was in sweatpants and buttoned-up dress shirt with two different shoes on. They fell to the floor with their daughter cocooned in their arms as they cried, loved, and began to heal.

Over the next six hours, parents and children were reunited. The FBI moved each family to their own room, and finally there was silence. It was four in the morning by the time Deacon and Sydney said goodnight to Zain. Sydney looked dreadful, and Deacon knew he couldn't look so hot either. Now that Sydney had no one else to look after, she let the pain show, and it broke Deacon's heart. He would give anything to take that pain away.

Quietly, he microwaved some pasta he had squirreled away when room service had arrived earlier. "Here, darlin'. Have something to eat. Then you can take the pain pill the doctor gave you."

Deacon placed the dish in front of her and watched as she ate. When she was almost finished, he stood up and went into the bathroom housekeeping had finished cleaning just thirty minutes before and started the shower. Sydney had bled on the bed so the sheets had been changed as well. The room was now pristine, and it was hard to imagine all that had happened in it that night.

He headed back to the table and helped Sydney to her feet. She had long ago taken off her boots, but he silently helped her out of her dress and underwear before stripping himself.

"You were my hero tonight, Deacon." Sydney softly smiled as he held the glass door to the shower open for her.

Deacon laughed. "I don't know about that. I'm pretty sure you were the hero tonight. I can't wait to tell everyone back home about how you took that four-hundred-pound man down. Your father will be so proud. I think even Ahmed will be impressed."

"Is that home, Deacon?" Sydney asked quietly.

"My home is where you are, Sydney. That is, if you want me there." Deacon held his breath as he waited for her answer. They hadn't talked about moving in together. It was crazy, but he remembered all those letters from Mrs. Wyatt saying she knew instantly Beauford was her heart and soul. And Deacon knew Sydney was his. He'd move anywhere for her without hesitation.

"More than anything." Sydney smiled as she cupped his face with her hands and kissed him. And when Sydney's lips touched his, Deacon knew he'd found the peace, the love, and the home he'd been looking for.

Sydney slept the entire drive home. Her ribs were killing her and the stitches on her leg itched. There was nothing she could do about it, so she decided to sleep. She had snuggled up against Deacon's side, rested her head on his shoulder, and fallen asleep as Zain and Deacon discussed their meeting that morning with Agent Helms.

Sydney dreamt of a future she hadn't allowed herself to dream of before. Of a husband, a family, and a life outside of work. And then she dreamt of all the wedding dresses and the letters of her ancestors. Her eyes shot open at the same time the car came to a stop.

"What is it?" Deacon asked quietly as Zain climbed out of the limousine.

"The treasure. I forgot all about it. I have to find the rest of it," Sydney fretted.

"Not until you rest. The doctor in Indianapolis said your ribs were bruised, and it would take four weeks for them to heal."

Zain bent down and looked back into the limo. "Listen to your boyfriend. I've already heard from my father. He wants us to rest for the day but expects us all there tonight so we can tell them what happened. See you all at seven."

Zain shut the door as Sydney fought for reasons to skip resting, go to Wyatt Estate, and search for the treasure and whatever secrets lay hidden in it. Deacon ran a finger over her brow and smiled down at her. "Stop thinking. It's written clear as day on your face that you're trying to come up with a reason to do what you want to do. Let's collect Robyn and go home."

Sydney finally took a breath and then cringed. It hurt to breathe that deeply. "Okay, maybe you're right."

The limo stopped at Bridget's dog training facility, and Deacon helped her stand. The dogs were in training with Bridget standing in the middle, watching. She turned when she heard Deacon close the door and waved them over.

Sydney and Deacon came over to the fence and looked into the training area. A handler was working with Robyn. He held a piece of material in his hand and gave Robyn an order. The little roly-poly puppy sniffed the shirt and then looked up at the handler.

"Find it," he ordered.

Robyn took off with her nose to the ground as she went over obstacles and through tunnels. She wove her way around the training course until she came to a large box. She sat down and yipped at the box. The trainer smiled and Bridget shook her head as the trainer lifted the box to find a person hiding underneath.

"Are you sure you don't want to sell Robyn? The government or a private security firm would pay a fortune for her," Bridget called out.

"I'm sure. She's my girl." Sydney smiled back as Robyn grabbed a chewed shoe from her handler and ran straight for her. She opened the gate and bent down to catch the flying puppy in her arms. Sydney grimaced in pain but held on to the happy puppy.

"If you'll let me, I'll continue having her trained as a search-and-rescue dog. She could come in handy around here with the woods. Remember that child who got lost last year?" Bridget asked and Sydney nodded. "She has one heck of a nose on her. Robyn can track people, pick out explosives, and even detect knock-off luxury shoes. It's the strangest talent I've ever seen."

"Of course you can train her. That boy was lost in the woods overnight. If Robyn can help if that ever happens again, I want her trained and ready to go," Sydney said as Robyn wiggled over to Deacon and demanded to be picked up.

"I know you travel a lot since your headquarters are in New York City, so if you ever need a dog-sitter, just let me know." Bridget smiled at the playful puppy with eyes that took in a lot more than she let on.

"I'm thinking about making some changes," Sydney said cryptically. "But I'm sure Ahmed wouldn't want Robyn running around the house any more than she has this week."

Bridget laughed. "They have come to an uneasy truce. He thinks she's plotting to take over the world, and she's letting him believe it. She found a way to scare him to death every morning. One day when he woke up, she was standing over him. She didn't bark or anything, just stared. Then once he stepped out of the shower, lifted the towel from where it hung, and she was underneath it. He swears she winked at him. Personally, I've never laughed so hard as I did when he came running naked from the bathroom, swearing the dog was trying to kill him."

Sydney laughed and then groaned. Bridget's eyes swept over her and then gave Syd a tight smile. "Bruised or broken?"

"Bruised."

Bridged nodded knowingly. "Hurts like the devil, but just keep breathing deeply. They'll start to feel better soon.

Luckily there are no real physical limitations on you. Wait, are you limping, too?"

"Stabbed with tweezers." Sydney grinned.

"Tweezers? Who does that? Now a switchblade . . ."

"A model does that when that's the only weapon she has on her. Trust me, I'd much rather get stabbed with tweezers than a switchblade."

Bridget shrugged. "Yeah, but then you don't have a cool scar like this one." Bridget raised her shirt and showed off a scar on her side.

"Oh please," Ahmed said as he walked up behind them. He pulled up his shirt a bit and Sydney blinked. Ahmed still had a six-pack. No wonder Bridget always looked so happy. "Now, this is a knife scar."

Robyn rolled her eyes and almost fell from Deacon's arms.

"Spawn, it's such a shame you're leaving," Ahmed taunted.

"She'll be back tomorrow. She's going to have day camp here while we finish her training," Bridget explained.

Robyn's tongue now rested just out of her mouth as though she were mocking Ahmed. Sydney looked between the puppy and Ahmed. They had matching twinkles in their eyes. Some things — Robyn's apparent ability to understand people, her simultaneous ability to demonstrate her belief that humans are beneath her, and Ahmed's pleasure in trying to outwit a dog — were just better to leave alone.

"So," Sydney said while shaking her head at man and beast, "we'll see you tonight?"

"Of course. Wouldn't miss hearing how you got

stabbed. Your father is going to be apoplectic. It'll be hilarious." Ahmed smiled.

"Aren't you the father who sent out a whole armed security team when Abby was five minutes late for curfew?" Sydney asked innocently. Ahmed and Bridget's daughter was four years younger than Sydney and was finishing up a Master's program at George Washington University. She was also the source of all of Ahmed's worries. She shouldn't be, though. Between having Ahmed as a father and Bridget as a mother, Abby knew how to kill someone twenty different ways with nothing but her hands. And if you gave her a fork, well, then things would get interesting. Kale, their youngest, was a computer genius. He was currently at MIT, but everyone from private security to major Internet companies and governments all over the world were already vying for him to come work for them. He got off light on the dating front. Ahmed was too busy sending drones after Abby to worry about Kale's social life.

Deacon smothered a laugh behind a cough. Ahmed's piercing gaze swung to him. "You laugh now. Just wait until you have a daughter." With that warning, Ahmed chuckled to himself and headed into the training facility.

Chapter Twenty-Seven

Ahmed had underestimated Marshall's reaction to his daughter being stabbed by tweezers and then crushed by a gargantuan guard. As the dramatic rescue of the girls was told, Marshall became redder and redder. Deacon feared he'd have an aneurysm.

"Where the hell were you?" Marshall demanded of him. "You were supposed to keep her safe!"

"I was fighting to get to her, sir," Deacon told him. "It stopped my heart when I saw her leap onto that man's back. But, you would have been proud. She held on and choked him out. She put everything you taught her into action."

Wyatt made a strangled noise from his seat at the table. "What is it?" Mo, Zain's father, asked.

"Nothing." Wyatt smiled a second before someone else's cell phone pinged and then another, and another. "Sis, I'd run if I were you," Deacon heard Sydney's brother whisper a second before Katelyn gasped.

"What is it?" Deacon asked.

"You've gone viral," Wyatt said as he tried to hide a smirk on his face. He handed Sydney his phone and Deacon leaned closer.

"Model Mayhem," Sydney read out loud. She scrolled down the screen and gasped at the same time Ahmed smiled.

"That is an rather impressive headlock, my dear," Ahmed said from across the table.

Deacon stared at picture after picture of the fight in the hallway at the stadium.

"Nice thong," Zain quipped.

Deacon shot to his feet at the same time Marshall did. The two of them looked at each other from across the table, and in that instant, Marshall looked at him with respect. Deacon didn't know if it was for him defending his daughter's honor or for the picture that showed him taking down two men at once. Frankly, he didn't care. He was just glad he had it.

"How did they get these pictures?" Sydney asked as she continued scrolling down. "Patrick! He says his GoPro accidently turned on when he reached into his bag for the tripod, and it captured the whole thing."

"Oh, honey," her mother said softly as Deacon and Marshall took their seats. "And you too, Deacon and Zain. I couldn't be prouder of you three than I am right now. It takes good people stepping up to defeat evil like this. Those girls are back with their families and safe because of you all."

Sydney walked around the table to hug her mother, and Deacon picked up the phone. He scrolled past the pictures and scanned the article. It was an interview with Patrick. He told of Sydney's determination to rescue the women taken by Emily and her ring. He told of how Deacon and Zain went into the devil's lair and came out as warriors protecting the innocent victims. And it talked about the responsibility people had to not turn their heads and look the other way when something bad was happening around them.

Deacon sat back and stared at Sydney's parents hugging her. He felt his phone buzz and saw his father was calling. He must have seen the article as well. Deacon quietly excused himself from the table and walked out into the hall.

"Hi, Dad."

"Well, it looks like you've been busy with more than spying on cheaters," his father said sarcastically.

"I've never spied on cheaters, and you know that," Deacon said, suddenly tired of fighting with his father.

"Yes, I know that. You did good, son. Now it's time to come home. I want you to take over the company. With this press, you'll be set for life."

"Dad, I'm already set for life. What I do now makes a difference. I help people, and I want to continue to do that." Deacon paused. "And I'm not coming home. I'm relocating to Kentucky."

"First, you're never too rich. Second, why would you do that? Do you know how many calls I've gotten from my friends wanting to invite you to dinners with their very lovely daughters? It's about time I had a grandchild."

There was something in his father's voice that caught his attention. It wasn't the money; it was the move that bothered him. "Would it make a difference if I told you I'm moving in with Sydney Davies, the woman I'm madly in love with, and that someday soon I hope to marry?"

"Marry?" his father said hopefully before laughing.

"Why, yes, I believe that would make a difference."

"You were never angry that I left the company, were you? You were upset that I gave up on the marriage," Deacon said with realization.

"Of course I was upset. You're my only child, and I wanted you to have what I had with your mother, God rest her soul. Love. And you can't find love while you're solving crimes. Why do you think I pushed you to go to all those dances and parties? Now, tell me about my future daughter-in-law. I always wanted a daughter. I met her once you know. At some charity event a while ago."

Deacon felt silly as tears began stinging his eyes. "She's the most amazing woman in the world. She's the one in the article. I've been living at her great-grandmother's house in Atlanta. Her great-grandmother told me I needed to meet Sydney because she knew that I would love her. By the time I met her, I was already half in love with her after everything Mrs. Wyatt wrote about her. But it paled in comparison to the real thing. She's my everything."

"This makes an old man very happy. I felt the same way about your mother."

"You never told me that, Dad."

"Fell in love with her the second I saw her, married her a month later, and still feel her in my heart. I guess I should have told you that sooner. I just didn't know how. What are you waiting for? Ask that girl to marry you. Now, where the hell is Keeneston?"

Deacon hung up the phone after giving his father directions and setting a date for him to come visit. Deacon had never felt so light, so free, so happy. He was in love, and a family he thought he had lost had returned. Now all he wanted was to make his own family. He could see them sitting around a table: Sydney by his side, children running around with his in-laws, and his father spoiling them rotten—it was all in his reach. And he wasn't going to wait a second longer to make it a reality.

Deacon spun around with all the hope of the future filling his heart and just as quickly, that hope sank. Leaning against the wall with his arms crossed over his chest was Marshall.

"So, you want to marry my daughter?"

"More than anything in this world," Deacon said, his voice tight with emotion. He would marry Sydney with or without her father's blessing, but he sure wished he had it.

Marshall tightened his jaw and looked him over. Deacon held his breath. "Well, I'll be mighty proud to have you as my son." Marshall grinned and held out his hand. Deacon hurried over to shake it.

"Oh, thank goodness. I was afraid you came out here to kill him," Sydney sighed with relief. "What's going on out here?"

"Just had to help give Deacon's father some directions. He's coming up to visit soon," Marshall lied smoothly. He leaned forward, kissed his daughter's cheek, and went back inside the dining room, but not before sending Deacon a wink.

"That's nice about your dad, but I'm exhausted. Are you ready to go home?" Sydney asked.

"There's no place I rather be." Deacon put his arm around her as they made their way to the car.

"Deacon, can you get the door?" Sydney yelled from upstairs. Deacon had kept her down for a couple days, but today she was determined to find the treasure, so he was downstairs making breakfast while she dressed.

"Sure," he called up. He walked to the front door and saw an armed guard standing there. "Can I help you?" Deacon asked through the closed door.

"You can if you are Deacon McKnight," the man answered back.

"I am," Deacon said, looking for a weapon and only finding an umbrella.

"I have a package from your father."

"Oh." Deacon set down the umbrella and opened the door. "And he had to send an armed guard?"

"Sign." The man held out an electronic pad and examined the ID Deacon had to turn over. Deacon signed it, and the man gave him a small box. "Have a good day."

Deacon tore open the box and stared at the dark blue box inside. He pulled it out and opened it. A large, round diamond set in a diamond-encrusted band looked back at him. It was his mother's. His father had sent his mother's engagement ring that had been in the McKnight family for generations. He looked at the ring and was amazed at how something so small had changed so many lives. And it was now about to change his.

"Who was it?" Deacon shoved the ring into his pocket and turned around with a smile on his face.

"Just something I had to sign for Agent Helms. Are you ready?" Deacon hoped to change the subject, but Sydney didn't let it go.

"What did you have to sign?"

"My statement."

"Didn't you sign it while we were at the hotel?"

Deacon nodded. "Signed the wrong place. I told him I'd sign it again."

Sydney shrugged. "Okay. I'm ready to go."

Deacon smiled at her and took her hand in his as they walked to the garage. He was going to get married. Now all he had to do was make a convincing enough argument for Sydney to say yes.

Sydney didn't believe Deacon for one second. Message from Agent Helms, her ass. She watched him as he drove toward Wyatt Estate. She had told Wyatt they were going to spend the day there, but he was booked with four-legged patients all day and wouldn't be able to help them search. Deacon's mind was somewhere else, and that just reinforced her belief that he was lying to her. His eyes were focused on the road as he turned into the drive. They hadn't said one word to each other the entire short trip to the farm.

Deacon pulled to a stop in front of the old house that had been in the Wyatt family for generations. He hopped out of the truck and walked around to open her door.

"Ready to find your treasure?" He smiled but it didn't reach his eyes. What had happened that morning?

"Sure am." Sydney turned and headed into the house as her mind ran wild. She tried to rein it in as she took a deep breath and looked around the house.

"Which room was Mrs. Wyatt's favorite?" Deacon asked her.

"The living room. She felt it was the heart of the

home."

"Then let's start there."

Deacon waited for her to lead the way. As Sydney headed to the living room, she grew more and more nervous. She walked into the warm room and stopped to look around. She paused in front of a painting of her great-grandparents on their wedding day that had to be five feet tall. She missed them so much.

"Sydney," Deacon said quietly from behind her. Sydney turned and Deacon smiled tightly at her.

"What really happened this morning?" she asked. She had to know.

Deacon flushed, and he knew she knew he had lied to her. He looked up at the painting behind her and smiled faintly at it. "You know, Mrs. Wyatt told me she knew the second she met Beauford they would have a grand romance. I thought that was strange. Who knows instantly that they are in love? Your ancestors did, judging from the letters they left behind. And apparently I do, too. I knew the second I saw you, with dirt smeared on your cheek as you dug up my yard in the middle of the night, that I was going to love you. My whole life changed in that one instant. My life before you now seems so inconsequential. It is nothing compared to the future that I can't stop thinking about—a future of holding you in my arms every night, celebrating the joys of life together, and leaning on each other during the hard times. Of children and puppies and family. Of love."

Sydney felt her lips tremble as she fought back tears. Everything Deacon said was what she had experienced. But then he reached into his pocket and pulled out a dark blue box. Sydney's heart soared into her throat as Deacon went down on one knee in front of her and held up the box. He opened it, and the beautiful engagement ring made her catch her breath. Her eyes flew back to his, and in them she saw their future.

"And as I told our fathers last night, I love you with all my heart, and I always will. There is nothing that would make me happier than having you as my wife. Sydney, will you do the me greatest honor of marrying me?"

The question broke her as she gasped, "Yes!" And then Deacon had her in his arms, and she laughed as he twirled her around. She laughed for being so silly. She laughed for the pure joy of being in love. And she laughed because she was so happy she thought she might burst.

"I love you so much," Deacon said reverently as he set her down and slid the ring on her finger.

"I love you, too." Sydney flung her arms around him and kissed him for all she was worth.

Deacon speared his fingers into her hair as he kept her mouth on his. His tongue swept gleefully in as he backed her up against the wall. Sydney was panting by the time he yanked her shirt from her body. The key her great-grandmother had given her rested on a necklace between her breasts. Deacon grabbed her arms and pinned them above her head as he kissed his way down her neck and over her collarbone.

"Yes, Deacon!" Sydney cried as his warm kisses slowly made their way toward her peaked nipples.

"Wait," Deacon said suddenly. He dropped her hands and stared above her head before turning to stare at her breasts.

"Do you want to go upstairs?" Sydney asked between heavy breaths.

"I found it!" Deacon grinned.

Sydney rolled her eyes. Men. "Yes, dear. You've found *it* many times. And you have my eternal gratitude for it."

Deacon reached for her breasts and Sydney arched toward him. But his hand didn't cup her breast as she expected. He grabbed her necklace and stared at it, then at the place he'd had her hands pinned.

"No, darlin', not that. I found your ancestral treasure." He grinned and gently pulled the necklace over her head.

"Where?" Sydney asked as she pulled her shirt back on.

"Look closely at the painting of your great-grandparents."

Sydney faced the painting and looked up at it. "I don't see anything."

"Look at the frame. Right next to where I had you against the wall." Deacon held up the key for her to look at before she stepped to the side of the large gilded frame.

There, at about shoulder height, was a small hole. Sydney felt her eyes go wide as she looked quickly back and forth between the key and the hole. Deacon didn't say a word as he held out the key to her. Sydney reached out and their fingers touched as she took the key from him. He smiled encouragingly for her to complete her promise to her great-grandmother.

Sydney placed the key in the hole and exhaled with relief as the key fit. She turned the key and heard a *click* as the frame opened. She swung the painting open and there, hidden behind it, was a large metal safe.

"How do I open it?" Sydney asked as she looked at the keypad.

"The number has to have importance. Where did you find the key?" Deacon asked.

"In the family Bible," Sydney said as she pushed passed Deacon to grab the tote she had set on the couch. Carefully, she pulled out the Bible and flipped to the inscription on Elizabeth's birth.

"We're called daughters of Elizabeth. The combination has to relate to her." Sydney hurried to the safe and entered 1-7-0-3, the year of Elizabeth's birth. They waited only a second before hearing the mechanical sound of a lock sliding open.

Deacon grabbed her shoulders from behind and squeezed. "You did it!"

Sydney opened the heavy door and found boxes of various sizes stacked up inside. But it was the envelope sitting in front with her name on it that held her attention.

"It's from my great-grandmother," Sydney told Deacon as she picked up the envelope. The handwriting was shaky so she knew this had to have been written recently. When she unfolded the paper, she saw it had been written just three months before.

My dearest Sydney Elizabeth,

It's a fact of life that there must be death. Since I am writing this, I know death is near. But I am not scared. I am secure in the knowledge that I have lived life to the fullest, loved with all my heart, and lived long enough to see what amazing people my great-grandchildren have become. I am at peace with leaving this world in your hands. But I am not quite ready to leave without giving you one last gift.

I met your great-grandfather at a party and I still remember it as if it were yesterday. He was standing across the room with a friend of his. My friend laughed as a man asked her to dance and Beauford turned to see who had arrived. His eyes sailed past my friend and landed on mine. It was instant. I knew I would love him for the rest of my life. Of course, I couldn't let him know that. I had to play a little hard to get.

Our wedding day was a day I will never forget. Not because of the dress or the party. No, I will never forget the one moment in time when Beauford looked down the aisle and our eyes met. I knew it was the beginning of my grandest adventure yet. We raised a family with joy and sadness. I'll never get over the loss of my daughter. But as I leave you, I know I made up for it with you and Katelyn. I pray that you have always felt the love I have for you, for it runs deeper and longer than even my time on earth. Beauford and I have found our passions with horses, with the farm, and with our friends. We have laughed, cried, and taken adventures around the world and in our own house that brought us closer than I ever thought possible. And our adventures are not over yet. Time is just a number. Our hearts and our souls will live on, for that is true love.

And when I found your father naked in my kitchen, I knew my dear Katelyn had found that same kind of love. Of course, it was clearly written for the whole town to see before that; they just needed a little nudge.

Deacon smothered a laugh. "I'm sorry, does that say

naked?"

Sydney shook her head. "It says it, but Mom never said anything about that. I'll have to ask her about it."

Deacon shook his head. "No, please, I beg you, let me ask your father about it. Preferably as we are all sitting down to dinner at Grandma Davies's house. Go on, what else does it say?"

My last gift to you, my dear Sydney, is the family treasure. For I hope he is standing by your side as you read this, and my last gift has now been fulfilled. For I give to you what all the daughters of Elizabeth have passed on – the treasure of true love.

My love always,
Ruth Elizabeth Wyatt

Post Script – Deacon, treat my great-granddaughter well or Beauford and I will haunt you. Just kidding! Kind of. I knew you were the right man for my Sydney the first time we spoke. Take care of her, love her, treasure her, and be happy with her.

Sydney and Deacon stared at the letter, not saying a word. Sydney shook her head. No, it couldn't name Deacon in it. How? What? No.

"That says my name, doesn't it?" Deacon asked as they looked together at the postscript.

"Yes, but how did she do that?" Sydney wondered.

She finally looked up at Deacon and found him smiling. Then he threw his head back and laughed so hard his whole body shook.

"What?" Sydney asked when he finally stopped

laughing and grinned down at her.

"Don't you see? Mrs. Wyatt set us up."

"How? I can't believe it. She used the treasure to get me to meet you and purposefully didn't tell me you would be in Atlanta or that you even existed. She knew you would find me digging around in the backyard."

"And she knew a detective like me would never be able to walk away from a mysterious lost treasure," Deacon chuckled. "She knew we would be together until we found this safe—a safe she conveniently failed to tell you anything about, even though it was right here in her own house."

Deacon pulled her into his arms and smiled down at her. "And now we got engaged with her here." He looked up at the painting he had proposed in front of.

"She gave me the greatest gift of all. She gave me you. Now, let's go home."

"Don't you want to know what's inside?"

Sydney shook her head. "I have my treasure right here. Everything else can wait."

Chapter Twenty-Eight

Four months later . . .

It was the moment Deacon would never forget. The moment Sydney came around the corner of Wyatt Estate and looked up at him. She was exquisite in her great-grandmother's wedding dress with a veil fluttering behind her. He didn't see Marshall walk her down the aisle. He didn't see his father tearing up. He didn't see Marcy and Jake share a sweet kiss. All he saw was his future, his love, and his life.

And then she was his. And he was hers. He sealed his promise to love her in this life and the next with a kiss. Their friends and family cheered and rose petals rained from the sky.

"I love you, Sydney Elizabeth McKnight," Deacon whispered in her ear before taking her hand and running down the aisle together.

Sydney waited for Deacon to fall asleep. She was exhausted from their wedding, the party, and their own private celebration once they returned to their home. But she had one last thing to do before she could fall asleep in her husband's arms.

Sydney quietly slipped from the bed, tiptoed down the stairs and into the living room. There, on the wall, was the new painting of her and Deacon standing lovingly together in front of Twin Oaks. Sydney pulled the key from her pocket and inserted it into the frame of the picture. The picture swung out and she entered 1-7-0-3 into the safe to open the metal door.

"What are you doing?" Deacon asked from behind her. She wasn't surprised. She felt him even though she didn't see him.

"I'm continuing the treasure for the daughters of Elizabeth." Sydney placed an envelope, a picture of her and Deacon at the wedding, a stack of money, and her first design plate of her number-one-selling dress into the safe before shutting it, possibly forever.

"Not just for the daughters of Elizabeth, but *our* daughters. Now, come on, wife. We still have a lot of celebrating to do." Deacon whisked her up into his arms, and she looked forward to celebrating every day with him.

Two weeks later, the grounds of Twin Oaks were packed. Valets had to drive cars to the neighboring farm to park. Out back, a string ensemble played from their place on the balcony overlooking the people dancing beneath them. The backyard had been transformed into a romantic wonderland. White lights twinkled from the trees. Candles floated in water on every table. And people danced on the dance floor that covered the evidence of all the holes he and Sydney had dug in the backyard.

   Deacon checked with the bartender and the caterer before making his way inside the house. Sydney had decided to keep the house and continue the family history. And tonight was her unveiling of that history. Daughters of Elizabeth, a foundation to help women who had escaped or who were trying to escape from sex trafficking, was holding their first fundraiser tonight.

   He walked into the kitchen and found his wife standing next to Ms. Vander and Bailey as they walked through the living room, now set up as an exhibit. People from all walks of society filled the room as they read the framed letters of the daughters of Elizabeth leaning on easels. They stood behind the red velvet ropes to exclaim over the wedding dresses now on display with the artifacts from each daughter of Elizabeth set out in front of them and the portraits of each happy couple hanging on the wall behind them. Private security was stationed with every dress and at every table, for the treasure of love behind each was immeasurable.

   Sydney stopped in front of the wedding dress and portrait of Evelyn Seeley and her husband that had been in Mrs. Wyatt's safe. Bailey leaned forward to read the letter that Deacon knew held the story of how Evelyn met her husband, a US Marshal who had been searching for an escapee and instead found love.

   "Bailey is looking well," Zain said quietly as he came to Deacon's side.

   "Yes, she is. And so is Lacey." Deacon smiled as Lacey came up beside Bailey.

   The girls had survived, and with Zain, Deacon, and

Sydney championing them, they had become vocal supporters of bringing attention to sex trafficking in the United States and all over the world.

"I heard that Barrett, Victor, and Emily are spending life in prison," Zain said as they watched Bailey and Lacey laugh at something Sydney said. The three had pled guilty and spared the girls from testifying in trial in return for their lives.

"And Sebastian will be spending quite a few years with them as well," Deacon added.

"Who is Sydney talking to?" Zain asked as they watched her step away from the girls and join a group of four couples who looked to range from forty to fifty years old.

"It's the Simpson family. They are big here in Atlanta," Deacon told him.

Zain gave a slight nod in recognition of the name. "I'm going to get a drink. Do you want one?"

"No thanks," Deacon said absently as he watched Sydney head his way with a huge smile on her face.

"Simpson Global just donated $100,000 to the Daughters of Elizabeth."

Deacon leaned down and kissed her smiling lips. "That's wonderful. You did a remarkable job putting this together. Your family is out back dancing, and your mother has finally stopped crying."

Sydney looked a little guilty. "I guess I should have told her about all this before having her walk into the house. I just wanted her to get the whole experience of her family's past, to see her wedding picture hanging between Great-grandma's and ours and witness our family's history."

"Well, I think she was surprised in a good way. She loved how you linked it to strong, independent women. And by the way, Bailey and Lacey are lost in it. I think your message of courage, bravery, and love ties in perfectly with the foundation's message."

Sydney leaned her head against his shoulder as they watched people tour the exhibit and, more importantly, listen when Bailey and Lacey took the microphone outside to tell the people the importance of organizations like Daughters of Elizabeth.

"Look at them. Sydney and Deacon are so in love," Kenna Ashton, Sienna's mother, said to her two friends, Dani Ali Rahman, Zain's mother, and Paige Parker, Ryan's mother. The three ladies of Keeneston raised their glasses and clinked them together before Dani pulled out a notebook. The couple in question danced by under the warm Atlanta night sky.

The entire crew from Keeneston had come down to help launch the foundation. There were cousins, aunts, uncles, grandparents, and friends all there in support of one of their own.

"Can we really claim being matchmakers for them?" Dani asked, as she looked at the notebook the Rose sisters had entrusted to them. The Rose sisters had played matchmaker for a hundred fifty Keeneston couples over several generations but had handed off that responsibility to these three best friends.

"Well, we did say Sydney was going to be next,"

Kenna argued.

"Yeah, but when we asked Sienna, she suggested Matt," Paige complained as Dani crossed out Matt's name and wrote Deacon's in the notebook.

"I'm still counting it as a win," Dani said as she took another sip of her champagne.

"Okay, so who is next?" Kenna asked as they all looked around the dance floor.

"I know," Dani said instantly. "You both have one of your children married. It's time for one of mine. Gabe is too busy embracing his playboy status to settle down, but Zain is ready."

"Are you sure?" Paige asked skeptically.

"A mother knows these things. He's ready. He's not happy, and he doesn't know why. I do. He wants to be loved for who he is, not what he is. I know that look well. It's the same one his father had before we fell in love," Dani explained.

The friends all agreed, and Dani wrote the next name in the notebook.

"Who should go on the other side?" Kenna asked as she stared at the blank page opposite Zain's new spot. They would soon fill it with likes, dislikes, and all of his qualities. They would use that to find a woman who was perfect for him.

Dani tapped the pen on the table. "I don't know, but with the summit coming up we could find someone perfect for him there."

"Operation Grandbabies for Dani starts now," Paige teased as the three friends clinked their glasses and talked about the perfect woman for Zain.

The house was finally empty. All of their guests were back at their homes or hotel, and the exhibit had been secured and taken away by armed guards to the museum in downtown Atlanta where it would be on display for the next three months. Sydney watched the last catering truck roll down the long drive and into the night.

She heard Deacon come out onto the balcony. He slid his arms around her middle, and she leaned back and felt the warmth of his bare chest as she looked up at the stars in the sky. "I'm so proud of you," Deacon said from where he rested his chin on the top of her head.

Sydney smiled and turned in his arms so she could look up at him. "And I couldn't have done it without your support. I know we usually discuss things as a couple, but I've made a decision that will impact our future."

"What's that?" Deacon asked.

"I'm moving my headquarters to Lexington. I want to expand our family in the future, and I want to be home in Keeneston when we do."

Deacon smiled down at her. "I like that decision very much. I think your Grandma Davies will as well. Tonight she told me once again that she couldn't die happy until she had a great-grandbaby in her arms."

Sydney laughed, her heart full, as Deacon pulled her tight against him and placed a trail of kisses down the side of her neck. "Now let me show you exactly how much I like that decision."

Deacon pulled the satin slip up her body and tossed it on the balcony floor. He took his time kissing his way down her body, and Sydney let her head fall back in ecstasy. Her ancestors had been right. True love was the greatest treasure of all.

The End

Other Books by Kathleen Brooks

The Forever Bluegrass Series is off to a great start. This series will continue for many more books. And I'll also start a new series later in 2016, so stay connected with me for more information. If you haven't signed up for new release notification, then now is the time to do it. Click below:

www.kathleen-brooks.com/new-release-notifications

If you are new to the writings of Kathleen Brooks, then you will want to try her Bluegrass Series set in the wonderful fictitious town of Keeneston, KY. Here is a list of links to the Bluegrass and Bluegrass Brothers books in order, as well as the separate New York Times Bestselling Women of Power series:

Bluegrass Series

Bluegrass State of Mind

Risky Shot

Dead Heat

Bluegrass Brothers Series

Bluegrass Undercover

Rising Storm

Secret Santa, A Bluegrass Novella

Acquiring Trouble

Relentless Pursuit

Secrets Collide

Final Vow

Bluegrass Singles

All Hung Up

Bluegrass Dawn

The Perfect Gift

The Keeneston Roses

Forever Bluegrass Series

Forever Entangled

Forever Hidden

Forever Betrayed – coming April/May of 2016

Women of Power Series

Chosen for Power

Built for Power

Fashioned for Power

Destined for Power

About the Author

Kathleen Brooks is a New York Times, Wall Street Journal, and USA Today bestselling author. Kathleen's stories are romantic suspense featuring strong female heroines, humor, and happily-ever-afters. Her Bluegrass Series and follow-up Bluegrass Brothers Series feature small town charm with quirky characters that have captured the hearts of readers around the world.

Kathleen is an animal lover who supports rescue organizations and other non-profit organizations such as Friends and Vets Helping Pets whose goals are to protect and save our four-legged family members.

Email Notice of New Releases:
www.kathleen-brooks.com/new-release-notifications

Kathleen's Website: www.kathleen-brooks.com

Facebook Page:
facebook.com/KathleenBrooksAuthor

Twitter:
twitter.com/BluegrassBrooks

Goodreads:
goodreads.com/author/show/5101707.Kathleen_Brooks

Made in United States
North Haven, CT
22 February 2024

49014863R00200